The Orchard Lover

Christianna McCausland

First printing, 2018

Title ID: 7906618
ISBN-13: 978-0692084038

This is a work of fiction. The characters, places, and incidents in this book are entirely fictional. Any resemblance to actual persons living or dead, events, or locales is entirely coincidental.

Spring Idyll Press
Baltimore, Maryland

Cover design: Nina Tou
Cover illustration: tithes

For more information:
www.TheOrchardLover.com

This book is dedicated to my parents

I

April in the valley had chosen to be cruel. Daffodils that opened in a wild celebration of color now hunched their shoulders against a blistering cold, regretting their frivolity. Golden sprays of forsythia whipped at the forbidding sky and the first tufts of young spring grass lay flat where the wind blew it down into the chilled earth. After a few fleeting days of sunshine and warmth, an aggressive cold snap had settled down in the valley where Alden Forth was trying to get her chickens to lay. For the second time in a day she checked the nesting boxes and they were once again bare.

"Lazy girls—can't handle the cold," she reproached them as she pulled the door closed on the hen house.

She was wearing a thick, brown quilted coat that she pulled closer around her shoulders against the wind. She passed the sheep pasture and casually counted twenty-one small, downy lambs' heads in the dusky light —all accounted for this evening. She'd already lost two to a fox so there would be less for the butcher this season.

At the edge of the pasture she turned into the orchard. There were 103 peach trees in the Forth's orchard and Alden knew them all. The buds were just beginning to open; small garnet capsules each putting forth a pink bloom like the tip of a ballet slipper emerging from a velvet box. She stroked a slim gray stem and examined the bud. The Forth farm was a bit far north for peaches. The fickle weather could ruin the crop faster than in Georgia or Florida or even Virginia. The nighttime temperatures were slipping dangerously low, but so far there had been no frost. The trees seemed to understand that danger was imminent; the buds remained tightly closed, holding the vibrant pink blooms rolled inside, a secret whose time was yet to come. In a few weeks they would be set free and the orchard would be full of pink confetti. And in a few months more, the fruits would arrive and the pickers, too, and Alden's spirit would be free for a short time as well, as fragile and mysterious as the fruit she tended like a mother.

The wind gusted through the orchard and rattled the limbs of the trees like bones in a box. An unexplained chill ran down her neck. "The devil must be dancing on my grave," she said aloud to no one. Pulling her coat even tighter, she ran across the short expanse of grass that needed cutting and into the house.

When she pulled open the front door it creaked loudly, and Alden made a mental note to oil it. Then the wind blew down the orchard and swept her inside, slamming the door behind her with a loud thud.

"Who's that banging down my house?" cried Reginald from the living room.

"Me, Pop," Alden called back. Her grandfather was sitting in the dark again, looking out the window with blank eyes. She walked through the room, turning on lights, then sat down on the well-worn ottoman at his feet.

"Didn't you see me coming across the grass, Pop?" she said, placing a hand on his knee. "The wind chased me from the hen house."

"Did you see Francine in the orchard?"

"No, Pop. Remember, Francine left. Long before I was born."

He looked at her then, a long, hard stare that was almost malevolent and for a moment, she was afraid of him. This happened sometimes, but so far, the moments had always passed. He softened and recognition dawned behind his bright blue irises.

"Of course you don't remember Francine. She left long before your time, Alden. Bad luck with love we have. Bad luck. How are the hens behaving?"

"Badly. Still no eggs."

"Ah, so we have bad luck with chickens, too. Thank goodness there are the peach trees. They've not given up on us, have they?"

"No, they're still having a spring nap."

"That's fine then. Why don't we have breakfast?"

"It's dinner time, Pop. We already had breakfast."

"Of course we did. Oatmeal. So it's dinner then. That's just fine."

He turned back and looked out the window.

Alden sighed and stood up. She couldn't quite remember when Reginald was struck by this strange ailment of the mind, and if she were the kind of woman to ask around in town, no one else could recall either. This was not the first time he had confused her with Francine, the grandmother she never met. When it first began, she simply corrected him and thought no more of it. He wasn't that young anymore after all; he was bound to get things mixed up on occasion. A few months later she had found him standing in the orchard in the rain wearing nothing but his undershorts. He had his eyes closed and his faced turned up to the pouring skies and he looked positively blissful, so much so that Alden had hated to make him come inside. She tapped him gently on the shoulder.

"Pop."

He looked at her with an angelic face, full of pure joy.

"God is here."

Alden wasn't sure she believed in God, but she wanted to see whatever it was Reginald saw that gave him such a beatific face. So they stood there, she in her brown quilted coat growing deep black water stains, her long wet hair falling in fat tendrils down her back, he in his undershorts and his bare feet sinking in the mud, until thunder began to rumble low and slow in the distance.

"I think God wants us to go inside now," she had said.

He took her hand, like a child looking for help crossing a street, and they walked hand in hand into the house, which was slick and shiny from the rain.

Months went by without a similar incident and life returned to normal. So much so that Alden forgot that Reginald ever called her Francine and found God in the orchard. Together they worked the farm and ate their meals, Reginald as talkative as ever and Alden as quiet as usual. Outside of farming life there was nothing to talk about but the past, so Alden was raised on stories. As lucky as the Forths seemed to be in fruit, their luck ran the opposite way in love. Reginald recited the losses like a lesson. It began with his own parents, who left him as an infant in a basket on the doorstep of a preacher in a Georgia backwater. Then his wife Francine who left when Alden's father, Albert, was a toddler. Then came Rebecca, her own mother, dead a year after Alden's birth. Finally Albert, dead when Alden was four-years-old after a calamitous fall down the cellar stairs broke his neck.

Like her father and her grandfather, Alden was very superstitious, a family trait that may have migrated with Francine and Reginald from the South, or may have come from some dark, primordial past that no one could trace due to Reginald's ill-begotten birth. Whatever superstition's provenance, when a dish came out of the cupboard cracked it meant that the devil was sitting cross-legged in the house. If it rained when the sun was still shining, the devil was beating his wife. Rain on Sunday signaled bad luck all week. Ladybugs were good luck, mourning doves singing meant rain was coming. Alden had heard these and other truisms from the time Reginald nursed her as a mother-less infant. When Reginald told Alden as a young girl that the Forths were unlucky in love, she believed it like a curse.

These stories she knew by rote, the small, sad chronology of the Forth family. But she still liked to hear them simply for the tone of her grandfather's voice. He never lost his southern drawl, so different from the consonant-ridden accent of the valley that made sink into "zinc," the languorous "creek" into the curt "crick," and overly rounded the Os in words like "home" so it sounded like the speaker had a mouth full of marbles or was struggling to get its mouth over and around the roundness of O itself.

Even though she could not pinpoint when his illness of the mind began, Reginald started to mistake people more and more often. He called people by the wrong name, confusing them with the long dead or those buried somewhere in his southern past. He put equipment away in strange places and forgot where he left it; many days Alden spent hours playing hide and seek with farm implements before she could begin her work. He wet the bed and then denied it in the morning, like a dog running away from an accident, afraid to be scolded. All these little traumas happened so slowly, so insidiously, that they worked themselves into the fabric of Alden's life and that of the Forth farm, and Reginald's strange behavior became a normal of a new sort. Stories would be told as before Reginald developed the ailment or after, and that was the only nod to the fact that there'd been any other form of normal at all.

But Alden believed that the ailment had begun that chilly afternoon when Reginald found God in the rain in the orchard and she wondered if she'd only brought him in sooner if he might have stayed the old Reginald, the Pop from before the ailment. She cursed herself for coveting bliss, for wanting to feel whatever it was that he felt that brought him such pure joy. In seeking that joy, she'd destroyed something. She remembered that always.

Now, she stood in front of her grandfather watching him with the same attention he had turned to the window. Although she knew she saw him, solid and real before her, she sensed that his mind was not there in the room or even out there in the darkening yard, but somewhere else beyond her, beyond memory. She got up and went to make supper.

Despite the battering wind outside, it was quiet inside the

thick stonewalls, quiet and very dark. Because the house was at the bottom of a hill with trees behind, it was always a little darker, a little cooler, a little mustier than Alden liked.

Reginald and Francine eloped on a train that ended in Maryland where they came to the valley and Reginald bought the farm for the land. The acreage suited Reginald's plan for a peach orchard perfectly. The ground sloped gently so the trees could be planted just so where the air would circulate around the lush green limbs, heavy with the promise of fruit, drawing warm air in and pulling cool air away.

At the base of this verdant slope was the house, looking as if a giant had rolled field stones like dice down the hillside and the jumble of rocks that were left at the bottom of the valley were cobbled together into a house by some industrious, would-be architect. There was the main house, a tiny structure just one room up and down that settled lopsided onto its foundation. But that wasn't all. A kitchen was added that sloped precariously off the back of the house and a library with a room above and a proper living room, also with a room above, were tacked on like awkward bookends to either side of the main house. Inside, the wood floors had warped so that they creaked terribly and sloped at precarious angles. When Alden was a child she liked to drop a coin on the floor at one end of the main hallway and watch it pick up speed until it rolled right out the front door. All over the exterior of the house there were small chinks in the stone where resolute patches of grass would take root each spring and summer, and because the house listed to one side, the front porch was slightly crooked as well. Bright green moss grew on every side of the house but that facing south. As she got older, Alden poisoned the grass sprouts and faithfully whitewashed the house every year, yet despite being structurally very sound, it still had the appearance that at any moment it might topple over.

Alden realized her shoes were tracking mud through the house and she took them off in the hallway, walking in her socks and moving with hardly a sound through the silent house. As she made her way into the kitchen she turned on lights, weak electric bulbs that chased old ghosts into the shadowy corners. It was just she and Reginald in the house, and they never expected visitors, but she kept all the lights on anyway, most days and into the night. When a team of workers pushed through the valley a few years earlier, spinning out electrical lines behind them, Alden found the new surge of light kept her company. The house felt dead in the dark.

She turned on the radio, a tabletop Philco Reginald bought with six months' worth of savings. A solo violinist crackled through the air. The farmhouse was so deep in the valley it never got much in the way of reception. There were only a few stations that ever came in clear, and the programs Alden liked best were classical music: Brahms, Chopin, Bach. They kept her company as well.

Alden lit the stove and put a pot of butter on the burner. She chopped carrots and onions. The hot butter spit when the vegetables hit the pan. She pulled yesterday's roast chicken from the icebox and sat at the table picking the meat from the carcass while the radio snapped and crackled, keeping tune with the wind outside. The lights flickered off and on several times but never committed to a full outage. Alden dumped the chicken in with broth and dollops of dough and set it to simmer. Humming with the music, she set her small table, fork on the left, knife on the right, spoon to the outside of the knife, napkin folded and placed under the fork. When the preacher on whose doorstep Reginald landed could not locate the babe's delinquent parents he had no intention of taking the bastard in himself. Instead, he drove Reginald two counties away –

far enough so as not to taint his own God-fearing flock – and left the child at an orphanage run by the Sisters of Immaculate Mercy. It was here he was raised and learned how to read and how to set a table. And it was he who taught these things first to Albert and then to Alden.

When she opened the pot and let the cloud of steam subside, the dumplings had transformed into puffy clouds surrounded by bubbling broth. She scooped it all into soup bowls and set them at the two places.

Despite his unknown ailment, Reginald still had a strong sense of smell and a big appetite, so it wasn't long before he wordlessly came into the kitchen and sat at one of the place settings. Alden sat down with him, unfolded her napkin into her lap, then did the same for Reginald when she noticed he'd forgotten, and they ate their supper in silence while the windows grew black, the electricity flickered in the wind, and Beethoven struggled to be heard on the radio.

The spring winds continued to blow cold, relentless gusts down into the valley, enticing Alden to seek out indoor chores. It was early yet, but she decided to open the labor house and see what sort of state it was in. Perhaps the wind and the cold could blow out the mouse houses, the dust rabbits, and the shadows of old memories.

Many farmers didn't provide housing for the migratory workers who brought in the cherries, peaches, apples, plums, and pears, and carted them in to town where the co-op representatives would take them away to the large canneries and markets in the city. Most farmers let the workers set up tents in the fields or sent the workers to tent colonies erected on the outskirts of the village cross roads. But Reginald liked to keep a close eye on his workers and he felt you got the best work from a man when you took good care of him. So he and Albert had built a barracks of sorts, a straightforward, small dormitory on a wooden slab. It was barely more than a cabin but the windows were screened and had wooden flaps that could be propped open to let in fresh air or shut against heavy rain. Inside, there were rows of wooden bunks on each side with a long table and rough-hewn benches down the middle where the Forths provided breakfast at six each morning and lunch each afternoon at four-thirty.

At the end of the season, Alden swept the house, scrubbed the bunks and the table, and locked the wooden shutters into place. But each spring it seemed that some bird sneaked in and made a nest in the eaves or a mouse found a hole large enough to sneak in and build a little fortress in a corner of the building.

It was early to be getting the house ready, but soon they would come, the laborers, first in a slow trickle, arriving to thin the fruit and manage the insects. By the end of the summer there would be a steady torrent of men and then, like a summer storm, they would be gone again. They came and went and came again in a cycle that made sense to Alden, a cycle like the sun rising and setting, the animals being born and slaughtered, the seasons turning and bringing change.

Alden may have been unsure of the status of God and she certainly didn't believe in love, but on the topic of seasons she was a believer. The seasons brought her real pleasure. The red and yellow leaves of fall filled her with a sweet nostalgia for a past she never knew but she felt like a missing limb. She reveled in the first snowfall when the air was as crisp as a sheet of glass and the trees behind the house transformed into hulking, white creatures. She was joyful when the flowers began their slow, steady growth, sprouting green cuticles from the black earth. There was a promise in that, she knew, the promise of things to come. Of hot, long days and cooling summer storms with vibrant lightning and the buzzing of June beetles against the window screens in the stillness of a summer night.

Like anyone with a grasp of the cycles of the earth, Alden had an innate understanding that all things ended, and even when the seasons returned in the next year, all would never be quite the same. The hyacinths would smell a little different, the summer sunsets would have a different tint, and there would be more or less snow, droughts in summer or depressing autumns full of constant rain, and always the darkening of days. Like anyone who feels pleasure in its purest form, Alden also had a tremendous capacity for melancholy, which usually arrived at the end of summer shortly after the peaches were harvested and before the foliage turned its brilliant colors to cheer her up.

While she didn't understand love, Alden understood passion. She didn't know it, not to speak of it, but on the unspoken level of the soul, passion spoke to her grasp of the fleeting nature of life, the way that joy becomes sorrow and then becomes something that just lives in you like a scar that you neither like or dislike, you simply own. And knowing that that was a cycle of life made her grasp all the more strongly the briefest and most illusory of joys: passion. While Alden would not have known to call it that, that's what it was, and that's what it was like with Frank.

The day's chill seeped into Alden's bones as she swept the dust out of the corners of the boarding house and thought of Frank. She liked the process of remembering. It was neither painful, nor sad, nor joyful, but a parade of images that she could turn on or off that entertained her and reminded her that she was grounded to this earth. Sometimes she could feel so light, so detached, that the only thing anchoring her to the ground was the stream of images that poured out in her brain and formed a torrent that was her life's blood.

Frank stepped into the torrent in a heat wave in August. It was one of those summer seasons when the temperature never broke, and even at night the air was so thick with humidity you could see it hanging in the air like a murky spirit. Frank arrived in a blue pick-up truck with its bumper held on with baling twine, moving slowly into the orchard as if the heat could be so oppressive it could even slow down the Chevy engine.

Everything about Frank was larger than life. He was nearly six feet, five inches tall and barely needed a ladder to reach even the highest fruits in the orchard. He had enormous hands and an enormous laugh that carried from the orchard to the tumbled down stone house and straight into the kitchen where Alden was boiling hams. At first she thought it was thunder and went outside to see if there was a storm approaching, but there was only vibrant sunlight, so hot it made the light around the house shine white like the inside of a glowing pearl. And in the midst of it all was Frank, massive, laughing Frank, standing shoulders above the other workers who were engrossed in his story, in his size, and in his aura.

Alden sat down on one of the bunks and felt the cool, rough wood under her rear end. Frank never did stay in these bunks. He was far too tall, so he slept in a bedroll on the grass outside. It was late one evening and she was returning from the chicken house. She'd forgotten to bring in the hens for the night— the heat was making her head fuzzy—and a spider had bitten her hand somewhere in the darkness as she locked up the barn. She was rubbing the bite, which was growing hot, itchy, and sore, when she fell over Frank in the darkness. Her feet, so accustomed to every undulation of the ground on the property, met with a large mass that let out a low rumbling groan before she toppled over its dark form, and she found herself entangled with Frank on the grass.

"I've had many things drop in on me during the night, but nothing as nice as this," said Frank as his large body pressed upon her small frame.

Then he laughed his deep, loud, rib-splitting laugh, and it rumbled through him and into Alden and gripped her heart with this thing some know is passion but she only knew was wonderful. Before she understood what her body was doing she was kissing big Frank and he, not a man to throw away an opportunity when it falls on him in the night, kissed her back, and there was very little effort from either of them to get untangled and off the grass. In fact, Alden worked rather quickly and efficiently to enmesh herself further in big Frank's long and massive limbs, hoping he could root her to the ground entirely.

Not having been to church or had female friends, or a mother, or a grandmother, Alden moved through instinct alone, a woman raised to listen to nature and cycles and to follow her intuition like a lantern. She had no reason to believe that what she was doing could be considered wrong.

Not being a stupid man, Frank did not broach the subject. Instead, they both followed that same lantern light deep into the darkness of purest joy, and Alden left in the morning before the sun could be brighter than that lovely lantern and shatter the beauty of the night.

That was how Alden's life began to move from a straight line of waking and working and cooking and sleeping to a life with corners and curves that created a pleasurable circle. Like her monthly cycles and moon cycles and birth and death cycles, her love cycle came and went, and she was pragmatic about them all. Sitting on the bunk thinking of Frank she was neither lonely, nor sad, nor rapturous. Each year when the peaches were ripe, Alden took a lover. In a short time, the men would return and one would reveal himself as her parcel of joy for a short time that she could savor until the cycle curved away and she was alone again.

II

Bruce Powell shaved his face in the same mirror where he learned to do such things under the tutelage of his father, and where he'd shaved every morning for nearly twenty years. His eyes were still the same glacial blue they had been as a boy, but his thick black hair that never sat down in front was becoming flecked with gray, and his face was a dark tan with deep lines forming at the eyes, lines that were white when he wasn't squinting into the sun. He smiled in the mirror and though his was a friendly face, when the smile faded, those lines looked like white whiskers, tattle tales of a man aging faster than his thirty-five years. Though once referred to as a handsome man, Bruce could see he was assuming the sunburned, wind-swept anonymity that consumed most farmers in time.

The night before, he had dreamed again of Alden. He had been a vivid dreamer from the time he was a boy. Sometimes he would dream he was a pebble being tumbled in the slow moving current in the creek behind his house, and he would be startled awake when he rolled from his bed onto the floor. Other nights he would run through the darkness, seeing the world through the eyes of a swift moving deer, bounding through pale moon glow across cut cornfields into leafless winter forests. Last night he had dreamed again that he and

Alden were in the forest together. He felt her hand in his as the wood became darker and darker and she was no longer a woman but a light, a bright white light in the dark wood. And then the light went out and he awoke alone.

Bruce never shared his dreams with anyone. The Powells were practical people concerned with only practical things.

Perhaps it was the fact that he was going today to help Reginald and Alden on the farm that brought back the dream. An early spring dawn was emerging cold, hard, and gray against the kitchen windows when Bruce sat down opposite his father. His mother placed two cups of coffee in the silent place between the men at the table. Bruce looked at his father and realized how he was aging. For a moment, he felt a pang of guilt that he was leaving him alone for the day, but then he dissolved into the dream, almost recalling the warmth of Alden's lightly calloused palm in his own, their faces in a dark wood.

In a small community of distant farms, proximity can breed friendship if for no other reason than necessity. Growing up, when Alden forgot to do her homework, Bruce gave her the answers on the way to school; when she needed help on the farm, Bruce would work extra hard for his father so he could leave early to help Alden; when they had precious free time, they spent it together because Bruce was Alden's only friend and Alden was everything to Bruce.

They were twenty when Bruce proposed. They had left the Forths' tumbled down house to go mushrooming in the woods. The sky was the flat deep blue of late summer and with the green trees of the encroaching forest stretched against its blueness, it was like a set a child makes for a play—plain blue sky and green trees painted on big panels of paper and hung against a wall to make the outside world.

As they got closer, the scene took on three dimensions; a light breeze moved the trees and they became a slow vast tide of undulating green. When they stepped from the bright into the cool deep green of the woods, Bruce felt they had penetrated from one world to another. He walked head first through an unseen spider web, sticky and now broken. His eyes adjusted and it wasn't too dark; gnats swarmed in columns of sunlight and Alden and Bruce moved around them, unnoticed and undisturbed.

Alden moved with ease beside him. It was a pleasure to watch her walk. Farming gave men hands like bloated hams and women deep creases in their faces that aged them decades beyond their years. But Alden's youthful freckles had faded to a deep brown that gave her a permanent glow of good health. It was no wonder that around the valley she had taken on the mythical quality previously reserved for the Forth peaches. She drifted on the outskirts of the other residents' plain lives, beautiful and elusive. But Bruce felt her loneliness and suspected even she did not know it was there. Solitude on a farm is simply accepted, like early mornings, broken equipment, and bad weather.

Although it was more fashionable for women to wear their hair short, Alden's smooth auburn hair rippled down her back. When they were children, she would plait it in a braid that fell to her waist and he would tug it gently as they played in her yard. "Just like Rapunzel," he would say. As they got older, he longed to feel that silky expanse running through his grown man's hands.

They continued through the woods and birds sang from the high treetops, sounding very far away, so that Bruce felt like they were going deep into something, like they were submerged beneath a sea. Bruce held her hand there in the underwater world and Alden did not resist. He felt the warm comfort of it, and a movement like electricity that made his heart beat quickly. He felt important in that moment. How delicate she seemed and how right it was for his rough hand to be folded protectively over her slim fingers.

"I think we should get married," he said, so plainly, so simply, so trustingly. Looking back, he wondered at his audacity. Or was it his stupidity?

"Why?" was all she said.

He looked at her in the pale light and shifting shadows.

Her face was impassive.

"Because I love you," he said. "Because I could help you run the farm and take care of you. Because I love you."

"But I don't love you."

Did she sense his sadness? Or was it simply kindness? Or worse – pity? Whatever she felt, her face remained expressionless, but she squeezed his hand, and he grasped it tighter, like hope.

"We could still get married," he said.

"You know I can't get married, Bruce. It's bad luck."

"That's crazy, Alden. You know that's just a silly old thought stuck in your head by your granddad. No family passes down bad luck in love. Besides, I love you."

"I can't get married."

And just like that, the conversation was finished. They never did pick any mushrooms; they just left the woods holding hands. He felt like he needed it then, needed to hold her hand and have her pull him up and through something, out of the woods and into the reality of the light. After that summer they would sometimes still hold hands when they were alone, because sometimes it just feels good to have someone to hold on to.

The dreams of that day plagued him. Always there was the charge of touching in the half-dark of the forest and then Alden's bleary image being pulled away from him and into the undergrowth.

The smell of bacon grease and hot bread brought his attention back to the table. His mother stood over him, watching him with compassionate eyes, and for a moment he feared she could read his thoughts. Then she pushed a hand through his rough hair and smiled, and his mother sat and the family ate their breakfast in silence.

The Powells lived in a tidy little house not unlike any other farmhouse in the valley, a place where there was always just enough food but never quite enough money, and no room or purpose to dreams and clairvoyance. Bruce pushed eggs in his mouth and occupied his mind with wrestling open the Mason jar of peach preserves.

That morning, Bruce was helping Alden and Reginald move the sheep to a new pasture when Reginald stopped dead in the grass, his gray hair bristling in the cold wind and said, "Spring is coming. You can taste it."

Bruce said he didn't quite know how to taste the spring, but Alden breathed deep and nodded as though she understood what Reginald meant. Certainly there was a new dampness in the air, a taste like mown hay covered in dew lying beneath the chill that had become a constant in each of their days. Two days later the winds broke and the air became warm and sweet and precious, that rarified springtime that only lasts for a short time lest it not be appreciated the next year.

The warmer weather nudged the peach blooms out of their fragile cases and as anticipated, in a few weeks the entire orchard was full of plush pom poms of color ranging from the deepest, most ostentatious pinks to the softest blush, as tenuous and tempting as virginity itself. One night the wind picked up, but unlike the earlier breezes of late winter, this was a wind blowing in warmth and the new summer season. And because it had such a big job to do, that wind blew hard and steady all night so that Bruce could not sleep for all its showy bluster gnawing at his windows like an insistent child wanting attention. The next morning, he walked over the hill to make sure the Forth farm had not sustained any damage. He walked along the peach orchard, the trees now nothing but leaves. The pink petals, knocked down by the wind, lay about the bases of the trees as if a troop of flamboyant showgirls had stepped out of their skirts and left them on a green stage. Bruce felt inexplicably embarrassed, bearing witness to the tree's nakedness and abundance of new leaf. He cast his eyes around the property and seeing that everything was in order and no one was about, he turned and quickly returned home.

Not long after Reginald smelled the coming of spring, Bruce brought the news. He knocked on the door jam at the Forth house.

"I told you, you don't need to knock Bruce," Alden called from the kitchen.

The door creaked open and he pulled his boots off inside the front door. He came into the kitchen where Alden was wiping her hands on a tea towel, leaning against the counter. She was wearing an old pair of Albert's trousers, oft mended. A blue gingham shirt, unbuttoned at the neck, showed a glimpse of creamy freckled skin. Her hair hung in loose waves, rippling over her breasts. Bruce cleared his throat and pulled out a kitchen chair with both hands on either side of the chair. He took off his hat, slapping it against both knees before he set it on the table, then sat deliberately. Bruce was not a man to throw himself carelessly into a chair. He was a man who stood with both feet parallel to the legs of the chair and lowered himself with consideration. He liked to feel grounded. He leaned his forearms on the table and twined his fingers together.

"There's some news in town," he said.

Alden pulled up a chair next to him, sat down, and crossed her arms over her chest.

"What's that?"

"There's a new church person around."

"What sort of church person?"

"Reverend Greene says he thinks he's an evangelical," he said, pronouncing each syllable like a separate, magical word: Eve-van-gelly-cal.

"He's a Christian," he added.

"Well of course he's Christian, Bruce. Isn't everyone a Christian around here?"

He paused for a moment, rubbing his thumbs together.

"Nope, this is different. He just calls himself Christian. Not Methodist. Not Catholic. Just Christian. I think Reverend Greene would like him to identify himself. I get the feeling he's a little awkward, having an unclassified Christian in town."

"Hmmm," was all Alden said, getting up from her chair. She was so quiet, so lithe. Even in life she was as ephemeral as in his dreams.

"Do you want some cake? I made a layer cake last night with the frosting you like."

But Bruce was still rubbing his thumbs together.

"What's gotten into you Bruce?"

"I don't know Alden, but I've got a bad feeling. That Christian asked a lot of questions of me when I saw him. Lots of personal questions. I didn't want to be rude to a stranger, but I didn't like the way he kept asking me about Jesus and whether or not I prayed and did I think I was saved."

"You just avoid him, and if you can't you just say that you appreciate his concern, but that your relationship with Jesus is between you and God."

Alden cut the cake and put a piece in front of Bruce. He looked at it, then back at her.

"It'll be fine, Bruce. He's just a preacher. A Christian. Just like everyone else. Maybe just a little nosier. Eat your cake."

He unfolded his hands. He shook his head, picked up his fork and started to eat in slow, deliberate bites.

III

The Reverend Arnold Beale walked down the main street of the valley's village —the only street, really—and sniffed the air. Small town air. The scent of dust, animal sweat, human toil and gasoline from the few motorcars plying the main street. He knew that smell well, the scent of so many rural backwaters. And beneath it, something more sinister: the fetid musk of a sick animal. The smell of lost souls. He sniffed again and sneezed.

The village was a nameless little place, an inconsequential stopover in a vast expanse of nothing much. There was a general store where the locals no doubt bought groceries on credit, a mechanic with a lone gas pump, a Protestant church with a tidy stone parish house, and a scattering of plain clapboard houses fading into the countryside. Reverend Beale walked along a fence where sweet peas were threatening to bloom. If there was one thing Reverend Beale despised about country folk, it was their abhorrent reverence for verdure. The grain and grasses the Lord provided was not enough; they needed to plant roses and flowering trees and daffodils and lilacs and wisteria arbors that grew in a sensual abundance and filled the world with perfumes and pollen and the hum of bees darting in and out of blooms and bushes.

Most of his peers, God bless them, were hard at work in the city, where the Negroes and the foreigners had flowed in an unfettered stream into the tenements and shantytowns and gutters of urban America for the better half of a century, polluting the streets with a Babel of languages and gods and foods and customs. While he applauded the efforts of other Christian preachers to corral the heathen masses in America's cities, Reverend Beale could practically trace his ancestry back to the Mayflower, and like his Puritan people, he understood that the devil festered in dark rural places, in forests and in fields, as readily as he grew under the thick soot and filth of the city. Reverend Beale knew too well how one misplaced pat of a horse's haunch could land askew on the bottom of another man's wife in the stall, and how easily young maids tantalized youthful boys in hay barns. The springtime was the worst, when nature opened her legs and showed her ostentatious abundance like a whore in the street, putting into the minds of good people the spark of devilish inspiration. All the mating and blossoming, the warm sunshine in the day and the cool moist dews at night made Reverend Beale pray more fervently for the hot summer to squelch these impulses with its humid breath.

"Morning, Reverend."

The greeting stirred Reverend Beale from his musings. He turned to see a lean man with watery brown eyes and, above them, folds of shiny tan skin where his hair had once been. He was an old man but still had the sinewy muscles of a hard worker.

"Good morning, sir. And you are?"

"Name's Ned Pfieff. I've got the farm right outside town on the main street. Just a piece down from where I understand you've set up camp."

Reverend Beale looked at the gaunt face frosted with stubble, the shirt missing a button and fraying softly at the cuffs. Widower, he surmised.

"Ah, lovely. We're neighbors for now then, you, Mrs. Pfieff and I."

"No missus, I'm afraid. Passed away three years ago now."

The Reverend Beale was happy to see that his eye for discernment was still acute but repressed a grin. No sense showing his prideful mirth before a potential congregant.

"So sorry to hear that, but God is with her soul. Perhaps you will come join my Sunday service this week?"

"I'll be in church in town if I go anywhere, sir. Been going to the old church since, well, since I came here. Must be almost thirty years. Hard to believe."

"If you change your mind, the service is at ten o'clock. And I'm just down the road, remember. My church is only an open field, quite humble, but the Lord doesn't require finery."

"I'm sure you're right on that."

Farmer Pfieff continued toward the store and Reverend Beale rubbed his chin, a sure sign that he was thinking. The deeply afflicted never repented easily; they required calculation, patience. Reverend Beale met the devil's mind with his own cunning, beating the bearer of sin with his own tools. Perhaps this good farmer would be the lynchpin around which all the other sinners would fall. Reverend Beale offered a small prayer to God for guidance then continued down the road toward the parish house.

When Reverend Harold Greene was a boy, his father took a boat to a war on an island where the spine of the East Coast of the United States ended and tipped into the deep blue sea. When his father returned he came with only two things: a brown sack for Harold and a wound on his face that refused to heal. Each morning Harold's mother would clean the seeping edges and redress the wound, and each night the bandages would be full again of yellow puss mixed with the pale spittle of thin blood. While his mother wept over the incurable cut that had bisected her husband's previously handsome face, Harold explored the contents of his brown sack to find that it contained a vibrant yellow tuft of fluff that proved to be a small and terrified parakeet.

"They sell them on street corners, Harold," said his father, wincing as his mother dipped a towel into hot water and pressed it against the foul wound. "They're supposed to sing but that one's got no tongue for it."

The bird seemed dumbstruck in the bottom of the dusty satchel, and its fear made Harold brave. He reached in gently and grasped it around the body, surprised at how small and light it was. He held it like that for a long time, looking into the bird's eyes as they darted first this way, then that, its head moving in tiny, swift jerks and its beak opening and closing without ever uttering a sound. When finally it stopped and returned Harold's stare, Harold set it on his finger and opened the palm he'd closed over its wings. The bird fluttered a bit, adjusting itself on his new perch, and then let Harold pet its sleek feathers, smooth as glass. Harold whistled a short tune and the bird cocked its head but did not return the song.

And so Harold tried to teach the parakeet to sing, and his mother tried to will his father to heal, and both their efforts seemed futile. Harold started to pray to God that He would let his new feathery friend find his voice and that He would help his father get well. And on the day that Harold's father hung himself in the bathroom the parakeet did sing a very beautiful and appropriately sad song that helped drown out the sound of Harold's mother wailing. In his small boy's mind, Harold decided that God had heard at least some of his prayer, and therefore, He must be real, and that is how he came to be the parish minister in the valley. Because Harold felt that he and the bird witnessed something of a miracle that day, they were never parted, and when that bird died Harold got another and then another, until he filled his little house with bright yellow and blue parakeets that always made him think of death and joy at the same time. So when Reverend Arnold Beale entered the home of Reverend Harold Greene he sat in a parlor full of birds in elaborate cages like living Chinoiserie wallpaper.

"Reverend Beale is it? I'd heard a rumor that a clergyman was passing through. Word travels quickly in such a small town."

Reverend Greene was not expecting company, was not even in his dress shirt,

much less his collar, on account of the warm spring day. He rolled down his shirtsleeves, having the feeling that this meeting required some formality.

"Yes, I thought it would be so. I've had some experience in small towns myself."

"How nice. Where abouts?"

"Nowhere you would know."

Reverend Beale sat awkwardly on the edge of Reverend Greene's shabby yellow sofa, his stout legs, square body, and coarse, graying hair all a little too stolid for the ladylike furniture in the effeminate room. Three obstreperous blue parakeets in his right ear made him irritable.

"Let me come to the point," said Reverend Beale. "I wanted to visit you so you knew my intentions and so you didn't feel I was usurping your flock with my presence."

Reverend Greene seemed to draw peace from the persistent twittering. He crossed long, slim legs and settled into his chair, lightly running tapered fingertips through fine, sandy hair, a man as lean and delicate as his surroundings.

"That's very kind of you Reverend, but we're open-hearted people here. I would never think that mine is the only pathway to the Lord, and my parishioners have the free will to seek God wherever they please."

Reverend Beale rubbed his chin.

"How very forward thinking of you. Many men would be threatened."

"We're a small parish and a small town. We're close people not accustomed to big change. With all due respect, Reverend Beale, I think you'll find the people of this valley some of the kindest you've ever met in your travels, but not too interested in rocking the boat, spiritually speaking. They are creatures of habit not much taken in by tent revivals and the like."

"Perhaps you are right," said Reverend Beale. "And what of the seasonal workers? No doubt you have laborers who will come through this summer? On the farms?"

"Oh, yes," said Reverend Greene, rising from his chair and opening a small jar full of bird seed and pouring a bit into some of the bird cages. "They'll come and God bless you if you can bring them to a service. It's difficult to get them to church when they work so hard just to make their living. And the harvest doesn't wait, even for God. They're here for a few days or a few weeks, no more. Like you, they usually stay in tents on the outskirts of town, so they won't be hard for you to find. Except those at the Forths."

"The Forths?"

"Alden Forth and her grandfather, Reginald. They have a farm outside town. Fabulous peaches." The reverend chuckled. "But you won't be seeing them under your tent, Reverend. The Forths are funny people. Good people, but funny people."

"How can there be good when there is no God, Reverend Greene?"

Reverend Greene stopped his feeding regimen and studied Reverend Beale. "God is always in our hearts even if our bodies are not in His church."

"Mmm. I suppose I come from a more literal approach to faith, but perhaps there's some truth to your theory as well."

Reverend Beale rose and brushed his lap as if some crumb had fallen from Reverend Greene's home and befouled his suit. He was already thinking that perhaps he would not need good farmer Pfieff after all. A flock under such lax leadership was certain to have many weak lambs waiting to be shepherded back into place.

"It was a pleasure to meet you, Reverend Greene, and I hope we have occasion to discuss matters of faith again in the future."

"And you as well, Reverend Beale." Reverend Greene felt compelled to add: "I hope I don't lose too many souls to you!" But Reverend Beale was already out the front door, making quick time on his stubby legs.

The door shut and all eyes, those of Reverend Greene and those of twelve parakeets the color of the sky and the color of gold, looked in the direction of the door for a few quiet moments. With Reverend Beale gone, Reverend Greene was left to ponder the curious visit. The parakeets were all quiet as well, as if they too were thinking about this small dark man whose gentlemanly words hung heavy in the air with the weight of many meanings. Then one bird began to twitter and then another and another, and Reverend Greene was borne out of his thoughts by the transcendent power of song.

Only a few miles from where Reverend Beale was stomping with determined strides back to his humble and, thus far, uninhabited field church, Jane Scott pointed her chestnut mare around an open field freshly turned and ready for seed. Her horse pounded the earth at a quick trot until she turned towards the woods where a triangular chicken coop provided an opening in the field's fence. The horse stretched into a brief cantering stride then took off strong, jumping the fence a little big. Jane reached her hands toward the animal's head, lifting her seat gently from the saddle then recovered her posting position on the opposite side of the fence inside the lime green enclave of the woods. The spring rains had made the forest thick and lush, the trees heavy with soft green emerging leaves. Clods of dark, pliable mud flew from beneath the mare's hooves.

Jane continued home at a quick pace, the horse knowing as well as she did that they were close and Jane was anxious to be back in the barn. She slowed the animal to a walk when the barn came into view but the mare continued at an aggressive clip, knowing that she would soon be free of her rider and back in her comfortable stall with water and feed. Outside the paddock Jane gently alighted from the horse's back. Pulling the reins over the animal's head, she led her inside the paddock.

"Hulo," called a male voice, not quite questioning but not quite certain he'd heard the mare and Jane's arrival. His voice was soft and warm belying his Irish origin.

"Hello!" called Jane in return, Her voice was throaty with the unwitting affectation of wealth.

Ronan McCallister had been at Avon Ledge Farm for six months. Before that he'd worked on a racetrack where he saw a posting that Jane Scott's father, Robert Scott, was looking for a groom to maintain his stable of pleasure horses. Before that he was on a boat that plied the Atlantic Ocean from Ireland, a surprisingly calm trip given the Atlantic's reputation for storms. The McCallister farm was an insignificant stretch of land that held a few sheep and two ancient horses, where the mud could get ankle deep when the island's perpetual rain held the region in its moist grasp. The rain in Ireland was a living thing. One day it could be a soft rain, a mist that hung in the air without ever seeming to really fall at all; others the rain was so hard and penetrating it would find its way into every crevice of one's being. At night it was a constant drumbeat on the roof. The rain gave Ronan no peace, and therefore, he left Ireland for a place where it was dry and he could finally think.

Avon Ledge Farm had twelve horses and what remained of four sisters: Anna, Elise, Bethany, and Jane. Robert Scott was very lucky with money, even after the Crash, having made quite a bit of it in light industrial manufacturing concerns, subsequent investments, and a socially acceptable amount of discreet corruption. He was not particularly lucky with his wife, with whom he'd tried four times to produce a son and each time produced another daughter. Finally tired of trying to make him happy, or perhaps simply unhappy with the long hours he spent at his club in the city, Mrs. Scott went to Paris and never returned, leaving Robert Scott to raise his troop of daughters alone.

Robert Scott did not want daughters and he told them so.

"You would have been Robert the Third," he told Anna, the eldest.

To Elise he said: "I will call you Charles as that is what you were meant to be called."

For years he called Elise "Charlie" and, with no one there to correct him, the name stuck, and eventually even she thought of herself as Charlie.

As soon as each girl was old enough to go to boarding school she would watch the maid pack her trunks and then she would be shuttled off to the train station without any ceremony. When the girls became older and more enjoyable, Mrs. Scott hosted them for the summers at her apartment in Paris, which Robert Scott magnanimously paid for because he was secretly content to have one less woman in his already overburdened household. Everyone followed this perfect path except Jane.

"You were my last hope, Jane, my last chance at a son and heir," Robert Scott told his youngest daughter. "And even you failed me. You were such a disappointment to us that it was after you that your mother left. That's why I called you Jane. Just Jane. The plainest, least significant name I could imagine."

When Robert Scott derided his other daughters in a similar fashion they each responded in ways that indicated their personality. Anna stuck out her tongue and said something sassy using language she no doubt picked up by eavesdropping on the farm workers in the barn. She was so prone to sticking out her tongue and sassing her father that he took to slapping her with great frequency and little result. When it was time for Anna to make the trip to boarding school she packed her own trunk without any help from the maid and laughed all through the house the day the driver came to take her to the station.

Elise responded to her father's remarks by sulking. She would fall into long, deep bouts of brooding and tuck herself away in the window seat in her bedroom, staring longingly out the window with large, baleful eyes. Bethany went into such fits of tears that Robert Scott was required to call one of the servants to carry her away, but her wails could still be heard throughout the house and he was forced to retreat to the city and the comforts of his club to escape the racket.

When he told Jane at age eight that she was plain and unwanted and an utter disappointment, the servants waited aghast at what might befall them next, and her father stared her down with cold, unwavering eyes. But Jane simply stared back as if she knew something her father did not, something that made her feel sorry for him and happy for herself, and after a while of staring at each other like that she simply said: "I think I'll go upstairs and read a book." And with that she walked out of the living room, quietly shutting the door behind her. From then on the two coexisted in the large house without much in the way of interaction, like tenants in a boarding house who do not share a language and therefore dispense with common pleasantries. Their coexistence was occasionally punctuated by incursions by Robert Scott's other daughters, but as he successfully married them off one by one, they mostly disappeared from his life until only Jane was left. He was right that Jane was the most insignificant of them all to him, because she was so quiet and so willing to live completely unto herself at Avon Ledge Farm that eventually Robert Scott forgot about her, and he would be caught by surprise when she would wander silently into the library or when he saw her walking across the yard to the barn. He wondered to himself how it was that she had never left for school like the other girls. But then she would walk out of the library or disappear into the barn and the thought would pass and she would be gone from his memory once again.

Thus, when Ronan arrived at Avon Ledge he found twelve horses and four siblings, though only one remained, and that one, Jane, now age seventeen, had been quiet for a very long time. For several weeks Jane circled him like a curious dog sniffing a new arrival. He offered her small, insignificant kindnesses: giving her a leg up on her horse or chatting to her about Ireland as she removed her tack. Slowly she circled closer, closer, closer, until in a moment of trust Ronan patted her hand and Jane felt a shock to her system that brought forth a torrent of talking that started that day and never seemed to stop. Ronan could barely ever squeeze a word in between Jane's elaborate tales of her rides and her books and the stray cats she nurtured under a stump in the yard and her thoughts on the weather and on horses and on the color of the sky and everything else she could possibly wrap her tongue around.

Ronan thought that when he left Ireland and its insistent rain, he'd finally jettisoned the one uncontrollable force of nature that could drive a man insane. Then he met Jane. Unlike the persistent foul weather of Ireland, Jane had a few things in her favor, including her sweet and trusting nature and certainly the fact that she was young and rather pretty, a soft, round girl with the red cheeks of an outdoorswoman and curly brown hair that bounced about her shoulders in a coy way that was not like Jane at all, and therefore, made her more endearing. When Ronan thought his good nature was at an end and he could no longer bear the brunt of Jane's chattiness any longer he did the only thing he thought decent and effective: he pressed his lips against her mobile mouth and held it there until the lips became still. Then they began to move, but this time in a completely different fashion that was not saying any words at all, but was certainly sending a very distinct message.

On that day when Jane returned from her ride and stepped into the paddock with her chestnut mare, she talked about the state of the woods and how thick the wildflowers were going to be this year and how the mare had jumped the last fence quite big. As she prattled, Ronan removed the tack from the horse, gave her a good rub down and turned her out into the adjacent field. When he was done, he took Jane by the hand and she knew by now it was time for talking to cease, and she happily followed him into the stall he had recently mucked and strewn with clean, golden straw that smelled of dust and oncoming summertime.

IV

It was before dawn when Alden awoke. A gray light the color of a kitten's underbelly and just as soft filled her bedroom, turning normally colorful objects—the pink glass bedside lamp, the chintz cushions of the reading chair—monochromatic. It was early, too early even for Alden to be awake. Alden rarely dreamed. But she woke this morning gently and slowly with a word rolling in her mouth. *Silky.* She could still feel it there like a tangible thing, this word *silky* rolling about like a jeweler might roll a smooth bead on his tongue. She lay in bed watching color return to her room with the rising of the sun, saying over and over, *silkysilkysilkysilky*, slowly rolling the pearl of the word around in her subconscious. What it meant she didn't know, but when she finally got out of bed, she was smiling.

Alden pulled on her bathrobe, and still saying her morning mantra but thinking of very little else, she stood by the window and watched the progress of the sunrise. She could see the top of the orchard. The sun on the peach tree leaves, wet with dew, caused them to grow shiny like slices of silver, gleaming minnows moving on the wave of the wind until the sun dissolved them into the deep green ocean of the peach trees. Magic lost in an instant to the light.

A sigh escaped her lips, so imperceptible she didn't notice it. She slipped her hand inside her robe and laid it against her warm sternum, feeling for her heart. There was a pang there, a small throb she did not understand. This was the place where her last lover, John Dahlgren, liked to rest his head of spiky red hair, right there on the warm, flat plain above her heart.

John was a man who never used a word he didn't need. A silent lover, he created a cocoon of soundlessness and wrapped him and Alden inside. In their quiet moments she would whisper "*Dahli, Dahli,*" over and over, not a pet abbreviation of his name but because his unruly red hair reminded her of the fiery dahlias she sometimes planted in the summer, and because her whisper was a fragile tether that tied them together in an embrace that would dissipate in the frail light of early dawn. Dahli. Silky. Memory and sound. The tangible and the lost. Alden moved her tongue in her mouth. The light was getting stronger, the sun slanting in hard angles across the yard. She moved her hand from her heart and turned away from the window.

In the hallway outside her door she heard a sudden pounding on the floor. It carried through the warping wood and up through the floorboards and ever so slightly shook Alden's bureau. She walked to the doorway and looked down the hall, still the dark, deep blue of pre-dawn shadow. Thump. Thump. Thumpthump. She walked down the corridor in step to its rhythm, the floorboards alive and growing more agile beneath her bare feet as she approached Reginald's door. Thump. Thump. Thumpthump. She pushed open the door without knocking.

"Pop?"

Unlike Alden, Reginald didn't like the light and slept with the curtains drawn tight. It was nearly as dark in the room as it was in the hallway though the drapes were aglow as light attempted to penetrate. Although Alden could see the form on the ground she was drawn to the light, stepped nimbly across the floor, and pulled back the drapes. Sunshine eviscerated the room and sliced directly across Reginald, who was lying on the floor. He took his hand that had been pounding on the floorboards and threw it across his eyes.

"Franny, my sweetheart, why are you hurting me?" he wailed.

Alden crouched low beside her grandfather, one hand clutching closed the neck of her robe, the other gently pulling his hand from his eyes.

"It's me, Pop, Alden. Francine left long ago, remember?"

He looked at her without understanding, a look of confusion and heartbreak that stirred that little pang in Alden's heart for the second time that morning. She noticed that his eyes had grown rheumy. Tears gathered on his eyelids, now papery and thin with age, and quickly overflowed their meager barriers.

"Why did she leave me? Why have they all left me?" he cried.

Alden soothed him as she would a distressed animal, smoothing her hand across his forehead as if she could wipe the worry away.

"I haven't left you, Pop. I'm here always."

He rolled his head into her lap and released gasping, desperate sobs into the plush fabric of her worn robe. She stroked the back of his head. "Silkysilkysilky," she said, over and over like a mother would say "shoosh" to an upset infant. The weeping ceased and he rolled his head away, angling it awkwardly back toward the bed from which he'd presumably fallen. Alden grasped for normalcy.

"I think it's time to get up, Pop."

Silence.

"Would you like something special for breakfast?"

Silence.

"We need to repair the fence today where that old tree brought it down, remember?"

"I want to stay here by the campfire. I want to wait for my old friends and the old songs. I want to lie here and wait for everyone to come back."

"Pop, it's just you and me. There are no others. There's no

campfire. I don't know any songs."

"I'm calling them through the floor, didn't you hear it? You came. They'll come, too."

He raised a weathered hand and beat out thump. Thump. Thumpthump.

"Can you get up Pop? Can you get up on your own?"

Thump. Thump. Thumpthump. "They'll come sing old songs. I should've taught them to you. Now I forget. But they'll remember."

She stroked his back and when she said, "Okay, Pop, that's just fine. I'll be back soon," she surprised herself that the pang in her heart had crept without warning into her throat and caught itself up there, making her voice a deep croak and bringing stinging tears to her eyes. She got up and walked silently, deliberately, down the steps, barely causing a creak along the hallway to the front door where she slipped on her boots, unlocked the door, and pushed it open.

Outside all was normal.

The sun was warm on the porch, and the birds were offering their enthusiastic song of approval for the fine weather. A vivid hum rose up from the tissue paper blooms of the azaleas where the bees were actively working. She looked across the grassy lawn towards the orchard, the familiar curves of the landscape she could see, and beyond, where she knew the hillside sloped down to the Powells' house. Knowing it was faster, Alden took the road, hiking her robe high above her knees and moving with fleeter feet than one might imagine possible with oversized barn boots slapping against her naked calves.

It was fully morning now, and had Alden been listening she would have heard the purr of an engine approaching. But she was running fast and concentrating hard, curling her bare toes against the soles of the boots to keep them in place, feeling each footfall as it pulled her closer to the Powells' farmhouse.

Reverend Beale was out for a drive, logging some miles in his sedan at dawn when he could creep along at a leisurely pace suitable for examining the tidiness of yards, peeking down long drives, and even glancing through the odd, curtain-less window. He crested the hill, and there before him was a lost soul, a woman in a blue gown sweeping along the road, her auburn hair flowing like a russet current behind her.

For a moment, Reverend Beale couldn't catch his breath. Then the vision became practical as he took in the green boots, the bathrobe and, drawing closer, the start of sweat rolling down the young woman's face, down her neck and into the gaping V where the bathrobe was coming undone.

"What on earth has happened to you, miss?" he shouted through the open window because Alden had neither glanced his way nor broken her stride when he pulled the car even with her.

"Miss! Miss! Are you in some distress?"

Alden slowed to a rapid walk, causing Reverend Beale to lurch ahead of her. He decompressed the gas pedal and resumed a pace at her side. She did not look at him, only stared straight ahead with tearful dark eyes.

"I must get to the Powells. I must get some help. Everything'll be fine as soon as there is someone besides me."

Alden had decided that she and Reginald were perpetuating some sort of spell-like trance in the house, that the normal world outside was not reaching into the confines of the dark little stone cottage at the foot of the hill, and if someone from the outside would just come and break that spell then all would be well again.

"Let me take you there, miss. I don't know that it is wise to be in the street this way."

"What way?"

Alden stopped and turned fully to look at the reverend. He slammed on the brakes. Before her, she saw a dark, square face, a close crop of gray-flecked dark hair and something that could have been a smirk. Before him, the reverend saw a wild abundance of auburn hair billowing around a freckled, heart-shaped face strewn with tears falling from eyes the color of green leaves just turning brown in the autumn, and a slim frame only barely hidden by the light cloth of the blue robe.

The skin above her breasts was bare and pure white, a smooth cloud in a clear sky.

He thrust his eyes forward to the road. "Miss, you are running down the street in a bathrobe. *That* is the way."

Alden looked down over herself, seeing but not seeing. Though not one to cultivate frivolous characteristics like modesty or vanity, she pulled the robe closed.

"I suppose you're right."

With that she hitched up her robe and commenced her jog. Over her shoulder she shouted, "Thank you for the offer, sir, but I can get help just up here."

Reverend Beale compressed the gas, spewing dust as he accelerated to catch up with the disappearing spirit.

"What is your name, miss? Perhaps I can stop by later to see if everything is well?"

She slowed down at the entrance to the Powell's' farm.

"Alden Forth." Her breathing was heavy and it came out like a bit of wind. Then she darted down the driveway and was gone.

Maggie Powell didn't seem taken aback when she came to the door to find a panting, robed Alden on her front step. Then she saw Alden's tears.

"Lord, Alden, I don't think I've seen you cry since I slapped you at your birth," said Maggie, a hint of alarm rising in her voice.

"Can you get Bruce? I need him. Now."

Maggie took off at a run for the barn that was more dangerous than a woman of her years and girth should attempt shouting, "Bruce, get up here Bruce! Bruce! Bruce!" like an angry mother hen.

Maggie Powell had born four boys and then lost them one by one, all but Bruce. The first was cold and blue at birth. One she lost to a war, one she lost to influenza. For one she'd folded the flag. For the others she'd bathed their bodies herself and placed them in the coffins her husband built. She was particularly amazed even in her grief at how light her vibrant boy of nine could become. She was not a woman easily rattled. So there's no doubt that when Bruce heard his mother's distressed shouts coming across the yard, he knew something was wrong. Alden waited on the porch as Bruce ran across the yard, his gait awkward and lumbering, a man not accustomed to hurry.

Bruce and Alden drove back to the Forths' place in silence in the Powells' truck. Alden had stopped crying but she still couldn't shake the pain in her heart. At the front door Alden turned to Bruce.

"It will be okay when you get inside, won't it, Bruce?"

Perhaps Bruce knew what it was like to need reassurance, to need to hear the good word even if it wasn't the accurate word. He, too, had grown so accustomed to Reginald's odd behaviors that a new and terrible development like Alden described would be shocking. But somehow, this just didn't seem the time for wishful words. He said them anyway.

"It'll be alright, Alden. 'Course it'll be all right."

The words tasted like a lie.

Inside they could hear the insistent Thump. Thump. Thumpthump. Alden took the stairs two at a time, uncharacteristically impatient. Bruce took them in stride, measured, thinking of what was to come at the top of the stairs. Reginald was in the same position as Alden left him, adjacent to the bed with his feet under its frame, his face turned away from them at the door and looking under the bed as if he'd made acquaintance with the childhood monsters there. When he lifted his hand to begin his drumbeat anew, Alden noticed that it was growing red and angry-looking.

"Mr. Forth, it's me, Bruce Powell. Whatcha doin' down there, Mr. Forth? Dontcha know it's way beyond breakfast time now?"

Reginald rolled over. He looked sad and tired and very old.

"They never came."

"Well, we came. Me and Alden are here. And we sure

would be happier if you'd let us get you back in bed."

Reginald said nothing but stretched out his sore, red hand. Bruce slung it behind his head and gently lifted Reginald off the floor and laid him down on the bed like a child. Alden spread a blanket over top of him and smoothed the creases methodically. Reginald held her hand.

"Will you leave me, too, Alden? Everyone leaves me."

"I won't leave you, Pop."

In the kitchen, Alden made oatmeal, put it on a tray and, on a whim, broke off a branch of bright pink azalea outside the front door and placed it beside the coffee cup. Reginald was sleeping when she reentered his room, so she left the tray on the bedside table and went downstairs. Alden made two bowls of oatmeal, one for herself and one for Bruce. There were lilacs on the table in a Mason jar and the air was thick and sweet between them, full of scent and the weight of conversation not taking place, the heaviness of unspoken words.

"Should we get a doctor, Alden?"

"No, I don't think so." She paused. "There's no money for one, and I don't think there's much anyone can do anyway."

Alden put down her spoon and stared at the lilacs, so beautiful, so fragrant. And yet they smelled sweetest before dying, their last gasp a rich, velvety puff of perfume before their purple turned to brown and their tiny trumpets pulled tight and crusty. Alden loved lilacs, but today they smelled like loss. She thought of Reginald and how a lifetime of losing can fill you so high that eventually it weighs you down and you can sink, sink deep and away to where even your own mind can't reach you. She thought about the things she'd lost, her mother and father, her grandmother. If you don't know what you've lost, do you still carry the weight? Would she wake one day with the irrepressible need to resurrect long lost loved ones? But then, she thought, you can't miss something you've never known.

"There might be places he could go," continued Bruce, his voice cautious. "There are special places in town for people who are, you know, not quite right."

Alden gave him a hard look. "He's not crazy, he's just old. He needs to be taken care of here. We aren't going anywhere."

Bruce looked down at his bowl, cleared his throat. "Are you doing okay, with money, I mean?"

Alden thought about the bank. It had been close last year, breaking even, but it was close every year. If the peach harvest was good, they would survive again. If the weather was bad she would make the long, humbling drive to town to ask for leniency. A drive that had always been Reginald's responsibility when times got tough.

"We're okay," she said.

"I'm just saying, we're going to have to make plans, Alden. Your grandfather…He's not going to be able to be much help on the farm if things keep going like this. And you should be careful. He could be dangerous, to you or himself. He might not mean it, but it could happen."

She continued to stare deep into the lilacs. Bruce cleared his throat.

"My offer still stands. We could still get married. I can help you. Love you. If you'll let me."

She sighed and dropped her eyes to her oatmeal. Instinctively she reached out and placed her hand over his. They stayed like that a while, she staring into her oatmeal, he staring at her hand, she feeling his dry knuckles against her palm, he feeling the calluses on her hand and the cool reaches of her fingers entwined with his own. She squeezed his hand as lightly as a breeze.

"I must get out of this robe. I'll be fixing the fence alone today."

V

Life on the road of salvation was not as difficult as one might imagine. Reverend Beale made himself a cup of tea, putting the kettle on his small gas camp stove and selected one (and only one) cookie from a box he'd purchased at the village store. He settled into the ample canvas seat of his collapsible camp chair and set his tin cup of tea on the small side table. An oil lantern swung from the center of the spacious canvas tent by which he could read his Bible. He retained a collapsible dining table, two more camp chairs, and a very respectable Oriental rug spread beneath it all. These things Reverend Beale could easily roll up, collapse, and compress into the back of his large, aging Ford Model A, and move on to the next town awaiting the word of God. Though some felt the era of tent revivals was waning, this was the life Reverend Beale had chosen, the only life he knew, and one in which he was quite comfortable.

He sipped his tea and tried to nibble the chocolate fudge cookie to make it last. Though plagued by an insatiable sweet tooth from childhood, Reverend Beale took great pains to restrict his diet and felt that regulating his portion of sweets to one a day was an act of reverent restraint. As he savored the sweetness of fudge melting on his tongue, he reflected on the information he'd garnered during his brief acquaintance with the little farming community he intended to call home for the summer season. Completing the cookie with one last, luscious bite and licking the crumbs from his lower lip, he removed a small notebook from his breast pocket and began to write notes about each person he'd met.

Sarah French: works in the general store, husband drives a dairy delivery truck, two sons, ages/proclivities unknown

John Ashburn: property owner, willing to give a portion of his farm to the church's pursuit, in Europe for the summer, not useful

Ned Pfieff: neighbor, widower, farmer

Rev. Greene: pastor, bird enthusiast, radical?

Forth family: Farmers, esp. peaches. Not church goers.

He let his mind wander over his strange encounter with Alden in the street, the watercolor blur of hair and robe and dawn light. Deep within he felt a surge of memory that he pushed down, down to the quiet and dark place where it belonged.

The reverend sipped his tea and pondered his accrued knowledge of small towns, places where everyone knew each other's business but secrets still remained, deep and tawdry and poisonous, hiding in the furthest corners where even prying neighbor eyes could not find them. Would there be a gossip? Perhaps Mrs. French would let slip some tiny gem of information that would allow Reverend Beale to engender himself into this tiny community. These village shopkeepers always knew more than they let on.

The saving of souls was not easy. You could not show up in a small town and expect to attract more than the curious and the bored with your average evangelical sermon. People simply would not come. Oh they had once, back in the heyday of camp meetings. They would come in the thousands in the post-Civil War religious awakening, back when they wanted to wash the blood from their hands, when they wanted to believe in Heaven, when they wanted there to be a hell.

Not so now. The Great War, the Great Crash, the gin and

the poverty, the wealth and corruption. The innocence of the country was irrevocably broken. Yet it was in this state of lost virginity that Reverend Beale was most needed. He understood that to gain souls now one must exert a powerful force; that such power was in knowledge, and knowledge was to be gained through any means necessary when it was done in the name of God and bringing those who sin, and especially those who've lost the faith, to the humbling hand of the Lord. Reverend Beale knew only too well what could happen if sin was left to fester too long, how quickly and insidiously the embrace of earthly pleasures could choke the good out of a human being. Even now he could feel the terrible power of his own mother's brutality, remember his confusion at her savage yet beautiful violence.

He shook his head, drawing a shroud over those old wounds. What he required was a census, a chance to bring together the whole community and wander among them, taking the temperature of the crowd and feeling each individual for pockets of cold and heat. The tin cup rattled as the reverend put it down and placed his fingers on his temples, massaging out the thread of an idea, a very small bud of a plan to put this town and its people in one place, like puppies in a basket that he could wrap his arms around and extricate the runts from the litter.

There was dust on the shelves again. No matter how hard Sarah worked to keep it under control, there was always dust. It seemed to seep out of the walls of the old village store as if the place were in a constant state of sloughing off its old skin. If this was its act of self renewal, the store never looked much better for it; it was still a little ramshackle, a little worn down, a bit like Sarah herself, who was a little fatter, a little slower, a little grayer than she was when she first married Chester French and moved into the rooms above the store. She had picked up the feather duster like a queen receiving a scepter, gracefully acknowledging her commitment to a lifetime of serving customers.

The bell at the door tinkled, a light joyful noise that was incongruous in the store. Sarah's head popped over the single aisle, emerging between the cereal boxes and the canned corn. Almost immediately she ducked down like a soldier attempting to dodge a bullet, but it was too late; she'd already been spotted. And really, she'd learned long ago that there was nowhere to hide in this small town anyway.

"Good morning, Mrs. French," said Anna Scott, her voice like a silken wave flooding the reaches of the store.

Sarah scuttled back behind the worn wooden counter and watched as Anna fingered the chocolate bars with long creamy fingers, one displaying a brilliant sapphire ring that shone as bright as the blue eyes for which she was practically famous. Ever since Anna had moved back to the valley, men were forever comparing her eyes to the sky and the sea. If they'd not been so mesmerized they might have noticed those eyes had not the gentle tonality of the sky or the varying vibrancy of the sea, but the cool hardness of cobalt.

Anna bent to pick up a loaf of bread and then shook out her blonde bob as she stood up. She wore her vanity like a beautiful accessory, a prized possession.

"Have you heard anything about the tent revivalist in town, Mrs. French?"

Sarah rang the loaf of bread into the register.

"Oh, I've seen him 'round, dear, been in to buy a few odds and ends, you know. Can't say I know much about him."

"Well, I think this town could do with a little dust-up, don't you? It can get so unbearably dull out here."

Anna dropped the exact change past Mrs. French's waiting palm, and it jangled on the counter, a penny rolling to the floor. Sarah bent behind the counter to retrieve it saying, "I'm not one to rock the boat. I like it nice and quiet. I'm no spring chicken like you pretty young girls are."

While Sarah searched for the wayward penny, Anna swiped two chocolate bars off the counter. As Sarah's head emerged from below the counter, Anna turned on her well-clad heel and over her shoulder said: "Please put the candy bars on my account, Mrs. French. I simply cannot show up at home without something for the twins, and I'm positively destitute today. Cheers!"

With that she was gone, and Sarah stood slightly dumbstruck behind the counter holding a penny pinched between her thumb and forefinger. Whenever Anna came and went in the store Sarah was always left with the same feeling—that she had encountered something beautiful yet unpredictable and slightly dangerous, like being hit on the head with a Ming vase. Outside, she heard the slam of a car door, the low growl of an engine idling.

In her car, Anna threw the bread into the sprawling back seat and opened one of the chocolate bars. The convertible Cadillac Roadster was a five-year anniversary gift from David, the first gift he'd ever given her that she hadn't treated with complete disdain and forced him to return for something better. Anna frequently quipped at parties that David had asked her to marry him with such a small diamond that she had been too busy trying to find the stone to hear his proposal. He obediently returned the ring to the store in exchange for the sapphire encircled with diamonds that now weighed heavily on her ring finger. That time, she said yes.

With one hand on the wheel and one wrapped around the candy, she pressed down the accelerator and leapt out of her space in front of the store with the speed and agility of a horse out of the starting gate, nearly running over two pedestrians who jumped back in fear. Her foot firmly on the accelerator, she shouted an apology out the window as gravel spewed from beneath her wheels and the pedestrians simply shook their heads and said, "That Anna, she always was a handful," and smiled.

It had taken Anna exactly seven years on earth to identify, grasp, and feel the power of her beauty. The maid never scolded the young Anna for spilling things in her room or on her dresses though she was notoriously careless; governesses allowed her to slip in her studies and rarely disciplined her despite her merciless torture of her sisters. Then, when she was seven years old and Bethany just four, Anna told her little sibling of a very special wild strawberry patch, knowing full well that the child was wandering into a mass of poison ivy. A day later, Bethany was covered in weeping pustules and sobbing uncontrollably. Anna just smiled and petted her sister's brow. That same year she cut all of Charlie's hair off, saying that if she had a boy's name then she needed a boy's haircut. No one said a word to her in admonishment, and that's when she knew she could spit poison in the eye of the world, and the world would only ask for more.

When Anna outgrew harassing her sisters, she moved on to the next logical targets: men. Men were drawn to Anna and could not escape her even if they tried. Though she could easily have stuck her virulent fangs into them that would have rendered them useless; men were more fun to Anna when they were on the run, when they were so terrified, mesmerized, and energized with pursuit that they were too concerned with winning her to understand how easily she could and would destroy them.

Like all games that Anna enjoyed, this too came to an end only when she declared it over. She was hardly going to become a spinster. No, as much as the thought made her stomach tense, she needed a man, one man, to marry her. With so many to choose from, Anna picked wisely, bypassing the New York lawyers, the aspiring politicians, even the extremely eager and attractive military officers, and settled on a financial broker who survived the Crash, one from an old family with cash reserves and roots in the city, not far from the valley in which she grew up. David Radcliffe was passing attractive, not unlike a balloon just shy of full inflation, destined never to get the last puff of air. His devotion to Anna was a certitude she acknowledged then disregarded with the disdain of one returning an unsatisfactory bottle of wine. Anna required neither love nor devotion, not even fidelity, from David, though he gave her all those things. She wanted a new sport to entertain herself. She wanted a home in the valley – a big one – and David Radcliffe would get her one.

If there was one thing Anna's father Robert Scott wanted from his family it was to be left alone by every one of its members. The child known as Charlie married a banker and moved to New York City. Bethany married a merchant marine and moved to a coastal community up north where the sound of waves crashing against a craggy shoreline could swallow up the sound of her tears each time her husband went to sea. Jane developed such a gift for disappearance it was like she was never born, which suited Robert Scott perfectly well.

Then there was Anna.

David bought her the only thing she loved more than her car: a brick manse that was situated on a hillside and looked deep into the valley. It was a beautiful house that Anna filled with textiles gathered on trips to visit her mother in France. Large doors opened onto gardens maintained by horticulturists David imported from England, long corridors gleamed with polished wood floors, deep bellied fireplaces crackled from October until the last damp days of spring. But Anna loved the house most in winter when the trees were skeletal, when she could look out her bedroom window, stand on the tips of her toes, and barely make out the roofline of her father's home across the road and atop another hill. Her childhood home was lower than that which she now owned. She would look and smile to herself, knowing she would always be a foul odor faintly on her father's doorstep, the dead mouse beneath the floorboards, the nuisance that is so close and yet cannot be eradicated. There was never a day Robert Scott would not look up and see his eldest daughter's home towering over him.

As she sped by her father's driveway she laid on the horn, letting out a blast like a gaggle of startled geese. She whipped past her own driveway, feeling no compulsion to return home to her children. Now that the twins were nearly four they were rambunctious and demanding, Beryl constantly pulling on her hem wanting to be held and petted, and John like a nor'easter constantly blowing through the house, climbing and falling and knocking things over. Even with the nanny, Anna could never break free of them; they were mosquitoes in her ears on a summer night. Just thinking about them made her open the other candy bar. She complained to David about them constantly, but discussions of the children were the only words Anna uttered that fell on deaf ears with David, for, much to her disgust, he doted on them almost as much as he doted on his wife. But while his attentions to Anna sometimes seemed to be almost against his will, like a man under a spell, David wrought true joy from his children. Anna relished the fact that the birth had practically killed her; she could almost always keep David at bay ensuring that there would be no more children, not that he'd ever put physical demands on her, or any demands of any kind. She referred to her children, attractive, blonde, and blue-eyed like their mother, as "scene stealers" to her friends, and they would all laugh. No one ever noticed that Anna didn't laugh at all.

Recalling the state of affairs in her own home made Anna agitated, and she pressed the accelerator practically to the floor, enjoying the sensation of the trees and grasses blurring into a green vortex that might suck the Cadillac into a different time and place if she could just get enough speed. Suddenly, a figure stepped into the vortex and Anna slammed onto the brakes. The figure leapt out of the road as the Cadillac squealed and sputtered to a halt, smoke wisping off the tires. For a moment, Anna sat with her hands clasped tightly to the steering wheel, feeling the beat of her own heart as it tried to escape through her sternum. Then the sensation of her ring cutting into her finger reminded her to unclench her hands. Slipping the car into reverse gear, she back tracked several yards, pulled off the side of the road in front of a Ford with its hood ajar and stepped out.

"Lord above, woman, you could have killed me!"

Anna regarded the small stump of a man in front of her wiping his prodigious forehead with a hankie.

"Perhaps if you do not wish to be run over you shouldn't stand in the middle of a public thoroughfare," she stated. In a tone that withered the blooms of the roadside buttercups she added, "You are not from around here."

Reverend Beale was not a man given to fluster. Ashamed that he'd been frightened enough by the near miss to exclaim like a girl in a schoolyard, he quickly reclaimed his composure.

"You are very rational, ma'am. I suppose I should be more careful on these country roads. Allow me to introduce myself. I'm Reverend Arnold Beale."

He produced a hand, which Anna eagerly took in her own. While the good Lord bestowed great beauty on Anna he didn't forget a few other things as well, namely the innate ability to sense potential mischief. The cat in Anna awoke, stretched, and licked its paws, eager for new games. Her tone went from frost to warm honey.

"Your ears must be positively ringing, Reverend, as I was just asking Mrs. French at the general store if she'd had a chance to meet you. And here I nearly run you right over. What a lovely coincidence. I'm Anna Scott Radcliffe."

The good Lord had given the Reverend Beale the ability to resist temptations of the flesh, and so he was therefore not taken in by Anna's loveliness, but He had also given the reverend an eye for opportunity. Wealth and beauty could be strong allies to a lowly man of the cloth trying to make his way in a small town.

"I must apologize profusely for the setting of this meeting," he continued, as if it was his fault Anna had nearly run him over. "I would have much preferred to call at your home. Or perhaps I would meet you at one of my Sunday services?"

Anna smiled and winked.

"Well, well, aren't you a busy businessman already stumping for parishioners, you shameless thing, you. But we'll see. Maybe we'll stop by sometime. Do you take children at your services, Reverend? I do so love to spend Sundays with my little ones."

"Children are the most innocent lambs of God and are always welcome," he said. Turning to his car he uttered just audibly, "Given they are well-behaved."

Anna stepped next to him and stared into the belly of the Ford.

"Is it broken, Reverend? I'm a complete simpleton when it comes to cars."

"I'm afraid I might need a mechanic. I suppose I will need to forgo my afternoon appointment and beg you for a ride back into the village. It would be a long walk."

Before getting into the Cadillac Anna dropped the convertible top down, remarking that the weather was "just *too* fine," and with Reverend Beale in the passenger seat and she gripping the steering wheel, Anna made a neat u-turn and headed back toward the village, adopting the slower pace she felt a member of the clergy might appreciate. As they drew near town she blared the horn at Ned Pfieff mowing the long grass along a fence line and waved exuberantly. Not accustomed to such outbursts of neighborliness from Anna, he stared at the Cadillac and its occupants as if they were a rare bug he could not identify.

"He's such a sweetheart, that man. He practically mows everyone's fields around here." Anna dropped her voice. "He's a widower, you know." She took her eyes off to the road and stared deeply at Reverend Beale, tapping the area between her breasts with a slim, white index finger. "She had a bad heart. So sad."

"Mrs. Radcliffe!"

Anna whipped her eyes back to the road in time to see that she was drifting into the oncoming lane.

"My goodness, Reverend, you certainly are a jumpy one aren't you? Chocolate?" she thrust the recently opened second candy bar at him.

Reverend Beale's sweet tooth was quelled by the fear for which he held his life while Anna commanded the wheel of the car. He turned away from the candy bar and focused on the words that were spilling from Anna's mouth as quickly as the pavement disappeared beneath the tires. Anna was a better topographer of the valley and its inhabitants than Reverend

Beale could ever have been on his own. As the verdant roadside melted away behind them she pointed out the farms and the tenant houses and explained the stories of each and every person inside.

"Where were you off to before you had that darn car trouble, Reverend?"

"I was hoping to reach the Forths' farm."

Anna guffawed inadvertently then, too late, regained her composure.

"Do you know the Forths? I haven't had a proper introduction so I was going to be intrusive I'm afraid, and simply knock on their door."

"Well, I don't *know* the Forths socially, but of course I know them. That family has this town wrapped around its little finger, but I think they're just odd. Hello Reverend!"

Anna slowed the car to almost a crawl as it slipped through the village, certain to draw attention. As they passed Reverend Greene's house she blared the horn again, causing the man to leap in surprise and send a shower of roses out of a basket into which he'd been placing some of his favorite fragrant hybrids.

"Goodness, all the Lord's men are jumpy today," she said as she pulled in front of the mechanic's garage. Reverend Beale got out, happy to be on solid ground.

"I'm not one to judge, Reverend, so you don't take anything I said about the Forths to heart, you hear? You'll meet them yourself. I'm sure they'll just love the company."

She ground the car into reverse and peeled out of town on screeching tires.

VI

The pickers arrived with the clairvoyance of honeybees, bringing with them the smell of sun and sweat and sugar from other orchards further south. They came as they always did, in a slow stream that would become a torrent as the fruit ripened. For the Forths, the peak would happen in August, but the stream of anonymous male faces would circulate through the valley until late fall when the last of the apples were harvested. They came and went, and to Alden they were like the clouds, entities that blew through her life and out again with no real place of origin and no real destination ahead. Normally, the arrival of the first man looking for work stirred in Alden a flagging ember, but this season her heart was heavy with the weight of bad feelings she did not understand.

Bob Johnson had been picking fruit at the Forth farm and remembered when Alden was just a child. In truth, he was getting too old for the rigors of physical labor, but this was the only steady work he knew. Bob was of a class of country people whose children grew up shoeless and never quite made it to school. With no ability to read, and no training except for his experience working on farms, this was the life that suited him. He had never owned anything, never been married, and never left the east where he migrated like a bird, south to north then south again, following the work. The Forths were some of his favorite people. Reginald was always fair; Alden was capable and a good cook, too, though perhaps a little quiet and a touch strange, but certainly easy on the eyes.

But that is not why Bob would go out of his way to pick peaches for the Forths. While Bob was too poor and too much of a drifter to own anything under his own name, he possessed a sweet and sacred memory rooted in the Forth farm, and that made it a special place for him to which he always returned, a pilgrim to his sacred shrine.

This year he'd hitched a ride with John Gray, a West Virginian he met in a pub near the Charlestown racetrack where they were both drinking to ward off the soreness of a bet gone wrong on the same horse. Bob liked to bet the races now and again, but John followed the track with the same zeal that some men follow the Bible, and Bob had seen his new friend bet most of the money he made on the job on a dark horse at the track. When he won, it was drinks all around. When he lost, Bob made sure to sleep with his own money tucked deep into his sleep sack for fear it wouldn't otherwise be there in the morning—and John Gray gone with it.

The two men entered the Forth bunk house. The migrant workers moved by instinct, pack animals with their own natural hierarchy that required no verbal cues to express. When Bob and John arrived, everyone adhered to a primal sense of order established by Bob Johnson's obvious familiarity with the farm and his even more obvious age. The new arrivals slinked into the corners of the house, away from the bunks close to the windows, and gave Bob a wide radius of comfort. When he settled into his bunk, Bob found a leaflet there, a piece of paper covered in flowery handwriting, but as Bob was unable to read, disinterested in asking one of his fellow men for help, and unlikely to find any of them more adept at reading anyway, he tossed it aside.

The first man, Nikolay Ivanov, could not have understood Bob even had he asked the younger man to stand on his head. Ivanov spoke hardly any English and what he did speak none of the men could understand. Unable to get their tongues around the jagged edges of Nikolay Ivanov, the men simply called him "Nick" and Nick seemed perfectly content with that and to be left alone so he could spend his moments of free time staring at the ceiling of the labor house. The second man, Will Field, had hair on his face that was as fair and soft as the fuzz on a peach. He said he came from Ohio, but Bob thought his accent said otherwise, maybe southern Virginia or even the Carolinas, but it was not Bob Johnson's business to get into other people's business, and if the boy wanted to be from Ohio that was fine by him. Bob spread his sleep sack on his bunk like a lion getting comfortable in his den and looked out the window. Rain was falling on the deep green canopy of peach trees that held ripening fruit, yet he felt a lightness in his heart he had not experienced since he'd been at the Forths' last season.

Rain had become a persistent lover, following Alden wherever she went in the days after Reginald's illness took its turn for the worse, and the workers began landing from their migration north. After the morning of Reginald's terrifying episode, she had dressed, fixed the fence, and eaten dinner alone with only the radio for company. The next day, Reginald came downstairs for breakfast wordless, senseless, like a man in a dream, then returned to his room and slept all day. At night Alden heard him moving downstairs but felt the weight of her own body, fatigued from working alone on the farm, and could not lift herself from the oppressive need for sleep to check on him. Exhaustion overtook her as if by force, shoving her into unconsciousness, and the rain slipped in that night when she was unaware, and stalked her every day since.

On the fifth night of rain, a week after Reginald's serious bout with the unnamed ailment of the mind, Alden awoke near dawn, forcing her eyes open, and saw nothing out the window but a dirty whitewash of sky. Then the overwhelming power of severe fatigue took her away, and when she woke again it was to the sound of knocking. Alden crawled from under the blankets, soporifically donned her robe, and plodded down the stairs.

"I told you not to knock, Bruce."

The front door was swollen from days of damp, and she leaned her shoulder against the jamb to wrench it free. It swung open like a startled animal. Alden knew that she was not one for dreams, but with everything in the house turning slowly upside down, she had to wonder whether the world had become a vision she'd manufactured in her mind, starting with this man on the porch with a familiar face she couldn't place, a stout, dark figure framed by a gray halo of rain.

"Miss Forth?"

Alden nodded.

"Have I come at a bad time? I'm Reverend Arnold Beale," he said. "I thought you would be awake by now. Farming people rise so early."

"What time is it?

"Going on ten."

Alden's eyes grew large in shock.

"I'm so sorry. I can't believe I slept so late. My grandfather's been unwell."

Alden was already walking down the hallway, turning on what lights there were as she went. Reverend Beale hesitated a moment then followed. Inside, he froze, locked in a moment of sensory recognition, of a potent memory born on the breath of a scent. Beneath the furniture polish and musky farm smells, and faint, old cooking smells of the Forth house was the unmistakable scent of fragile deterioration a few steps away from dust: the smell of books.

"Reverend, would you like coffee?"

Alden was at his elbow.

"Do you have a library, Miss Forth?"

"There are books, in the living room. They belonged to my mother."

Alden didn't know what her mother loved or didn't love, just the material things that came with her and made up the only sense of her presence Alden ever knew. There were no photos of Rebecca; her life with Albert was too swift for the slow shutter of a camera. If Alden had the ability to retrieve a memory and put into words the scent of her mother's breast nourishing her infant body, the cool touch of slender fingers soothing her powdery head in the evening, the lyrical soprano of a softly murmured lullaby, then she could say she remembered her mother, Rebecca. But those thoughts were as infantile as Alden was when her mother died, and the passing years erased that faintest wisp of memory.

Alden made coffee and Reverend Beale requested permission to be seated at the kitchen table.

"My mother died the year I was born," said Alden, setting down mugs of coffee and two slices of coffeecake that filled the room with the scent of butter and brown sugar. "My father's dead as well. I only know the books belonged to her. She liked poems, I think."

"My mother loved books about flowers."

"I like flowers, too. Do you take after your mother?"

"No."

The aggression of the single word deadened the air in the room. Alden cleared her throat and sat down, the scuff of the chair on the wood floor the only sound.

"It is unfortunate that you are always in your bathrobe when we meet, Miss Forth."

Alden stared him directly in the eye. "But you came uninvited."

Reginald taught her to always look people in the eye when she spoke and to always speak plainly, and she took all of Reginald's lessons as the only gospel she knew. But Reverend Beale was noticeably disarmed by her directness. It was unapologetic, innocent, yet knowing. Reverend Beale quickly gulped his coffee then sputtered and coughed when he realized it was too hot.

"I suppose it was rude for me to drop in like this."

Alden sipped her coffee and said nothing. Reverend Beale was an anomaly to her, a visitor, but also a stranger. She regarded him as she would a cactus sprung up in the orchard—an oddity, a rarity, a sign.

"Our door is always open to friends and well-meaning strangers. My grandfather taught me that."

Alden had always had a soft, steady voice, so like a breeze caressing one's face that people needed to lean closer to her to properly hear her, giving even the most mundane conversations a false sense of intimacy. Reverend Beale tipped forward on his chair, his face bowing towards hers. A strand of her loose hair, caught in a draft, lifted up gently and brushed across his face. He sneezed and leaned back, frantically brushing his hand across his forehead.

"Are you okay?" asked Alden, still holding him under her unflappable stare.

Reverend Beale took the opportunity to discuss banal family relations to settle himself back in his chair.

"How lucky for you after the loss of your parents to have the comfort of your grandparents to raise you." His voice boomed through the kitchen as he overcompensated for her quiet tone.

"I never knew my grandmother. Only my grandfather. Everyone's gone." Alden sipped her coffee. "We're unlucky."

Reverend Beale was reaching for the coffeecake but his hand snatched back as if Alden had struck it.

"If you believe in God, Miss Forth, you do not believe in luck. Our lives are guided by something bigger than an instrument of chance."

Alden built the foundation of her life on the cornerstone of Reginald telling her that the Forths were unlucky in love, and there was no denying that the Lord, or providence, or destiny, seemed to be telling the Forths something, to be teaching them a lesson about loss over and over again, because they just weren't learning fast enough to pass the test.

"Perhaps we can thank God for our peaches, Reverend. You can come back soon and pick them straight from the tree."

"I'd hoped I might see you sooner, perhaps at my church

service?"

"We don't go to church, thank you."

"Why don't you attend? I conduct a beautiful service in the open air. I'm sure you would enjoy being outside for something other than work."

No one ever directly asked Alden why she didn't attend church; it was widely accepted around the valley that even though everyone knew everyone's business you never pushed too far into it lest someone else pushed back. The fragile ecosystem of a small town was based on the balance of knowledge and secrecy, gossip and discretion. As Alden mulled over the question, beyond the capacity of her hearing was the sound of a boundary splintering.

In that moment, at the kitchen table, Alden thought about the movement of seasons, the rising of the moon, the birth of lambs, and the death of ewes. She thought for the first time in many years about the dusty volumes in the living room, the sepia photo of Albert in Reginald's bedroom. She thought of her grandfather's ailment and the day he found God in the orchard. Her life was a whirlpool of beginnings and endings, a comfortable swirl she had been dropped into at birth, so that she could neither remember the top nor see the bottom.

"I find God all around me, Reverend. Every day. I don't need to go to church."

Reverend Beale recoiled in his chair. For a moment, he looked like he might lunge at her, but her quizzical stare seemed to mollify him.

"Perhaps your grandfather will come then," he said, his hand advancing again on the coffeecake. "Or some of the orchard workers."

"Yes, maybe."

"I'd at least like to invite you to a small, casual gathering this Friday at my humble tent. Perhaps if you come you will change your mind."

He slipped a leaflet onto the table.

She was only half-listening to him now. Something was not right in the house.

"Is your grandfather at home? I would like to introduce myself, properly."

"My grandfather isn't well."

She stood up abruptly, and Reverend Beale stumbled to his feet as well, leaving the coffeecake unmolested.

"I'm afraid I must get to work now. I've gotten a late start," said Alden, walking toward the door.

"Yes, of course. I'll come back then. The presence of a clergyman can be of great solace to the sick."

They paused at the door and Alden noticed a bit of lint on the lapel of his dark suit. Instinctively she reached out her hand and brushed it away, but as her hand fluttered across his chest he leapt away from her as if she passed an electric current through him.

"Don't touch!" he exclaimed, banging his head on the doorjamb.

He looked at her with wild eyes and then, in a moment, a dark cloud moved over them and he was composed again. Without a word he was out the door on steady, quick feet.

Alden didn't jump when the engine backfired once. She was not thinking about Reverend Beale or even the incessant rain she felt on the farm like a bad omen that wouldn't blow away. She was thinking only one thing: why is the house so quiet?

Reginald was not in his bedroom.

When she was dressed in her worn trousers and the old quilted coat she stepped into the foul weather. Alden's eyes moved quickly across the front yard; the peach trees were hidden behind a wall of gray. She thought of calling out for Reginald, but feared what might happen if he was startled in the dense fog. For a moment she remembered Bruce's caution, that Reginald could become a danger to himself, and she suppressed a rising panic. She cut across the lawn and walked along the edge of the orchard until she reached the sheep pasture where gray, sodden humps of fleeces were loosely sketched in the damp. Then she saw her grandfather walking the fence line. She sensed his lucidity by the sureness of his steps.

"I thought you said the fence needed to be mended?"

"I fixed it, Pop. Days ago."

He laid his aging hands on the top rail and looked out across the field. "I'm not well, am I, Alden?"

"I don't know."

"Yes, you do. I know it, too. My mind's playing tricks on me."

He turned to look at his granddaughter, his face slick with rain.

"It's you I worry about. One day you're going to have all this to handle alone." His hand swept over unkempt grass, bent low by rain, and the meandering acres beyond that were screened by mist.

"Let's talk about this another time, Pop. Please. Let's talk about this another time."

"We must be honest with each other, Alden. I didn't raise you to be a liar."

Alden registered the pleading in her grandfather's voice, and the pain that had settled so firmly in her chest in the area above her heart began to press so hard on her that she found it difficult to breathe. For so long Reginald's ailment of the mind had been there with them in the house, never spoken of, never acknowledged. Now Alden knew what she had to do. She had to let the truth out even if saying what she knew to be true would release it into their lives where it would roam free and untamed.

"You're getting old, Pop, and close to dying, and there's something terribly wrong with your mind, and I don't want to talk about because I don't want you to be upset." She gulped a big, wet breath. "But I'm afraid."

Reginald put his hand across his eyes and his shoulders began to shake. Alden knew he was crying but didn't know what to do because she'd rarely seen her grandfather cry, and because she had left one vital thing out of what she had told him, which was that she thought his ailment was her fault, that if she'd only brought him inside sooner that day he found God in the orchard, this all could be different.

Her heart and head swam in the weary gray light of the rainy day until the pain in her chest broke free and flew up through her throat and out of her mouth and she, too, was crying, tears of relief and of sadness, and tears of an unfamiliar feeling: impending loss. Reginald would die and she would be completely alone. Finally, the Forths' bad luck with love would stop with her. But her life would stretch for years more – a lonely plain – before it could all come to an end. Then she would know real sadness. Before, grief and loss were mementos passed down to Alden like family heirlooms. Now, the fear of losing someone, the acknowledgement of the reality of loss, was an unwanted gift being handed to her.

Overwhelmed by the need to touch her grandfather, to feel the rough papery texture of his hand, the warmth of his chest, to know the life within him and hold it close to her as if to cast it in relief against her own frame, Alden put her arms around her grandfather and hugged him tightly. Reginald had not held his granddaughter since she was a girl, and he was a man who'd forgotten the touch of a human body. Alden's figure touching his brought back the remembrance of something warm, and kind, and familiar. After a moment of wonder, he put his arms around her and held her, breathing her smell, so like his own but charged with the vitality of youth.

Reginald ended the embrace, wiped his eyes and looked back over the field, seeing clearly the grass growing too long from the incessant rain. "We'll need to cut hay early this year, won't we?"

She stood beside him, leaning her forearms on the top rail of the fence and looked over the field. "I bet you're right." And that was all that could be said or done about that and all other things.

VII

Reverend Beale sat in his rain-soaked tent. The faint stench of mold seeping out of the canvas tent was growing more pungent, and his Oriental rug – now hanging from the roof of the tent in a failing attempt to keep it dry – was giving off the distinct odor of wet dog. He slumped in his collapsible camp chair and tried to force his mind to drift away from his sopping wet socks and clammy flesh. He rubbed his chin and went over and over his meeting with Alden. He thought of her like a botanist examining a butterfly about to be pinned to a velvet background: beautiful, rare, and ultimately tamed by the hand of man.

He was despondent. He had floundered for conversation with this yet unpinned creature. She had no faith! She was a bohemian! It was said she wore men's trousers! She was the pinnacle of everything he set himself to conquer. How he wanted to argue with her in that musty little kitchen at the back of the tumbled-down stone shack, to present a cohesive theology, to flex his evangelical muscles that had thus far been limpid in this lackadaisical, ecclesiastical town. She was a loose, ungrounded thing, and he preferred all things to be firmly rooted to the ground in the place God allotted.

Worse, everyone in the village seemed to brush aside her

bizarre nature. Like Anna with her money and beauty, Alden was mystical and lovely with a hard, inscrutable center he could not fathom. What was this insidious power in women? That touch. Why had he felt it like a stab to his heart? Yes, this was his most dangerous foe. He and the sensual female – had they not been locked in combat since he was young?

He did not want to go back to these thoughts, but he was pushed –Alden pushed him— with her lack of inhibition, her voluptuous swell of unfashionably long hair, and her bottomless, complicated eyes. This morning those eyes had taken him back, had tumbled him over a chasm into an old memory of sitting by the fireplace watching his mother roll the auburn husks off hazelnuts at Christmastime. He had gulped Alden's coffee to squelch that memory, but now it rose up again.

He turned from thoughts of Alden only to be confronted with himself as a reserved, intense little boy, raised without siblings and neither loved nor unloved by his classmates, but rather completely overlooked, a boy with a square head like a chunk of marble, too big for his slender prepubescent shoulders, a head that harbored a voracious brain that consumed books. Mr. Beale, his father, worked a demanding job as a fruit and vegetable merchant. When he came home from a day in the loud, crowded markets, he sought quiet and order. He fed his son books like a doctor medicating a patient to keep him somnolent.

Arnold was an exceptionally quiet child, able to appear soundlessly and to move around the house with the stealth of a burglar. So perhaps it is unsurprising that his mother was caught unawares when Arnold, mystified by the botanical drawings of flora in the *Encyclopedia of Living Things*, entered her bedroom to show her *Dicentra eximia* and found her standing naked in front of her full-length mirror, her arms raised to her head where she was rearranging her voluminous black hair. For a moment, Arnold was so entranced by the curves of his mother's naked body, so totally foreign to him in its bareness and yet so familiar, too, that he did not notice a man who was not his father lying in his parents' bed.

"You mustn't tell anyone, Arnie," said his mother's reflection in the mirror, using the diminutive of his name she only used when he was ill and needed to be soothed.

"This must be a secret. *Our* secret."

Always an obedient child, Arnold turned and walked out as he felt was best to do. But being an obedient child he had assiduously studied the Ten Commandments and been taught to obey the Golden Rules of please, thank you, and truth telling, and he knew there was something not right about this secret he had with his mother. Every morning he watched his father leave for the market, and many afternoons after lunch he heard the front door open and close and the heavy footsteps of the man walking up the stairs of his father's house. Arnold carried the secret into the library and buried it in the *Encyclopedia of Living Things*, memorizing the names of *Narcissus* "Angel's Tears," Belladonna lily, and *Nigella damascena,* "Love-in-the-mist," like a poem he could tell himself over and over.

Two hours later, the footsteps would walk back down to open and shut the door, the same door· Arnold's father returned through at the end of the workday.

Each Sunday, Arnold sat between his parents in the pew at church, and when the priest said "love thy neighbor" he did not think that meant what his mother was doing with the lunchtime stranger. When he said, "do not covet thy neighbor's wife," he thought the priest might be onto something, and when he said, "do unto others as you would have done unto you," he knew what he needed to do. He must tell his father this secret that was burning a hole in his soul because it was wrong to keep secrets, even when your mother tells you to. She'd fed him that secret like candy, but it lodged in his throat. He could not swallow it down.

But he was an obedient child, and it was hard to cough it up, so hard to defy his mother's wishes, because she was so beautiful, and charming, and distant, and he loved her so much across the great space that separated his childhood from her motherhood. And it was hard to determine how best to speak to his father because he was so large, and commanding, and the space between Arnold's childhood and his father's fatherhood was infinite and seemed unable to be traversed.

So he waited and read, and when he reached *Zinnia peruviana* in the *Encyclopedia of Living Things*, then Arnold did the unheard of and knocked on the door of his father's study and told him exactly what he'd seen with the precision of the botanical artists whose gift for detail young Arnold so respected.

Contrary to the warm embrace of filial approval he expected, Mr. Beale was extremely somber and shut Arnold out of the room. The next day, his father came home in the middle of the afternoon, opening and closing the front door, walking up the stairs where there was a tremendous cry and masculine shouts and the rush of feet stomping down the stairs so fast and hard Arnold thought it could be thunder. The door never opened and closed in the middle of the day again.

The approbation Arnold sought the day he spoke to his father did not come that day or the next. In fact, it was never to be. Instead, his home was caught in the cold grasp that remains behind an infidelity exposed. Unable to regain his trust for his wife but unwilling to let her go, Mr. Beale left each morning and returned each evening, but rarely was his wife ever out of his sight. When he was gone, the weight of his wrath was a like a sentinel in the house. Distrust made Mr. Beale cruel, and he began to eat like it was an act of vengeance, as if his actual body needed to fill every space of the house. Under his surveillance, Mrs. Beale decayed, losing the voluptuous curves and round cheeks of which she'd once been vain. Her body became as hard and slim as a reed and when she drew back to strike at Arnold, as she frequently did, it was like a lash on bare skin.

His father's bulk became its own physical punishment to his mother's slim frame. She, in turn, punished Arnold for his treachery to her, her tongue a bitter whip, her skeletal hands quick to smack, to slap, to spank. To his father, Arnold was forgotten as he relentlessly maintained the watchful vigilance of the cuckolded. His mother's vengeance on him was complete and unchecked.

Only at church did the Beale family retain the appearance of normalcy, and only there was there peace, and quiet, and order in the melodic repetition of old rituals. Even as his bruises stung, straining against his clothing in the pew, young Arnold Beale took solace in the only thing he understood, which was the power of righteousness. If virtue was not honored, if sin was left to fester, the frail thread that sewed up the nature of human order would break. Like the great martyrs, he survived his mother's wrath and his father's indifference because he knew his conscience was pure.

Reverend Beale turned away from his young self, disgusted by these memories. Yet he realized, again, that as sickening as these old wounds were to redress, they were a reminder that what he learned as a child was still the one, true way.

VIII

After the rains moved on and the sun of summer returned to warm the sodden valley, there was little left of the roses to salvage, but Reverend Greene continued to try. When he inherited the parish house from his predecessor, there was a rose bush on either side of the gate entering the yard, both white with faint tips of pink as if God had whispered something to them that caused them to blush. Every day that he walked in and out of his gate when the roses were blooming, he was embraced by their delicate scent, a smell so sweet and subtle that it transported him like prayer to a place of reverence for the natural world. Removing the dead heads and clipping the fresh blooms and arranging them in the house became a meditation. He began to think of them like his birds, emissaries of a higher good manifesting on earth. He started to cull catalogs for new varieties and filled the front yard of the parish house with bushes, so that the two whites with the flushed petals were now joined by crimson reds, delicate peaches, variegated pinks, cascading floribundas, and playful climbers.

Sadly, the rain now rotted his prolific blooms, turning their bright silky plumage into brown globs, like a newspaper left to weather on a deserted porch. With sharpened secateurs,

Reverend Greene decapitated each head and let it drop into his basket. He was so intent on the growing pile of dead blooms that he jumped when he heard his name called from the road just outside his gate.

"I'm so sorry to have frightened you, Reverend."

Reverend Beale stood in the gateway, his frame appearing all the more stalwart against the frivolity of foliage from the rose bushes. For his part, Reverend Greene made a rather unimpressive picture in his garden clothing with his shirtsleeves pushed up and sweat rolling from his temples into the collar of his shirt. Always a casual man and comfortable in his informality, there was something he couldn't quite place about Reverend Beale that made him wish he'd had a moment to wash up before they spoke.

"Not at all, just trying to get my roses back in shape now that the rain seems to have finally ended."

"I hope your parishioners are as cared for as your roses."

Reverend Beale's words floated across the yard and stung Reverend Greene, as surprising as the bite of a deer fly that touches lightly on the skin before it strikes. Not a man prone to confrontation, Reverend Greene faced his barbed visitor with congeniality.

"The roses relax me and remind me of God's grace," he replied. "What brings you to town on this fine, warm day?"

"Souls, Reverend. I'm looking for souls."

Reverend Beale thrust his hand over the gate and Reverend Greene took from it a handwritten flier advertising a tea and open prayer session on Friday evening.

"I do hope you will come. As you said, you are openhearted people here who observe many pathways to God's grace."

Then he was gone, and Reverend Greene was left holding the limp flier in one hand like an old handkerchief, the secateurs in the other, a basket of brown lumps at his feet, and the sun beating on his ruddy face. The rose bushes seemed to slump a bit in the gateway, which Reverend Greene attributed to their late recovery from the incessant downpours.

Reverend Beale papered the small village and surrounding farms with efficiency. Ned Pfieff found the announcement at dusk after he'd put the tractor in the barn. Now that the rain was over, the grass in all the fields was thigh high, and he spent most of his days cutting hay. After hours listening to the constant rattle and hum of the old tractor's engine, the silence in the barnyard when he switched off the machine was stunning. He walked to the house through the slanting rays of sunlight, the gentle light at the end of day that toys with the tips of the trees, and dances on gentle feet across the yard in one last bid for freedom before the sun calls its children home and sets for the day.

This was the hour when the Irish melancholy affected him the most. That's what Mrs. Pfieff always called it, the Irish melancholy—an unknown sadness that would creep up on him in the quiet hours and fill him with a deep and reasonless despair. Lila Pfieff knew of what she spoke; her parents made the journey from that island with nothing but their name, Fitzpatrick, which Lila carried with her until Ned came thirty-eight years ago and gave her Pfieff instead. Thirty-eight years they would have been married had her heart been strong enough to make the journey. Now, Ned wondered if his was strong enough to carry on without her. Yes, this was the hour when the Irish melancholy washed over him, the dusky hours Lila loved so much.

Lila was built of whimsy, and like fairies, and leprechauns, and daydreams, Ned felt that all he'd done was close his eyes and opened them and she was gone. He missed her, too, in the mornings. He'd never stopped rolling over to touch her side of the bed and expecting her to be there, even though three years had passed. And he never stopped feeling the heartache each dawn when her side of the bed was cold and empty. A practical man, Ned never believed in having dogs in the house. But after a while, he started to bring Holly, his border collie, inside to keep him company at night. One night, he let Holly get on the bed, and she kept Lila's side of the bed warm all night, and even though Ned found the sound of her heavy, canine breathing totally unlike Lila's quiet, nocturnal sighs, it was a great comfort to have a warm, living companion with him in the bed. He and Holly would sleep together each night, and in the dawn light he woke to a cold nose that kept his heart from breaking a small fraction each day as it had done before the dog joined him in the nuptial bed.

Ned was always a hardworking man, but after Lila died he took on more and more work, farming the land adjacent to him and picking up leased properties in nearby counties. He hired several farm hands to help him keep up with the work and, ironically, started to make about as much money as a farmer could hope for, which wasn't much at that. He had no idea what to do with what little extra he had because all that working from dawn until the wicked dusk hour he did to distract himself from the spirit of Lila, who was always with him, and in a secret bid to weaken his own heart so that he too could die, and he could finally be joined with his sweetheart.

The house when he went in through the screen door would have felt like a dead thing, a tomb, were it not for the clear thump, thump, thump of Holly's tail on the floorboards as she acknowledged her owner's return. Normally, Ned went straight into the kitchen, gave Holly a good long rub behind both of her ears, and sent her out the back door while he made them something to eat. Tonight, something on the floor caught his eye, a piece of paper askew on the floor that someone must have shoved under the door when he was working. He picked it up.

Looking for salvation, redemption, contemplation? Reverend Arnold Beale invites you for Christian Fellowship, tea, and prayer in the open air. This Friday at 7 o'clock in the evening, the field at Plainair Farm Road. All guests and friends welcome.

Ned was not looking for any of those things, but he was looking for a salve to the terrible loneliness that he carried with him like a sore with no succor. Seven in the evening – the dusk hour in summer. Ned placed the flier in the frame of the hall mirror, the place he kept all important notices he didn't want to forget, then went into the kitchen where Holly was beginning to wonder what was taking her owner so long to come say hello.

Alden tread carefully on her dawn walk to gather eggs from the hens so as not to disturb the webs the ground spiders had busily spun in the night. The architecture glittered silvery white in the slanting morning light, a field of miniature marquees. Alden respected the spiders, their limitless capacity for industry. Now, she wondered how they managed it.

For years, Alden and Reginald managed the farm almost entirely alone. Then, when Alden was thinking of other things, she had slipped over an important milestone and started the unyielding slide toward middle age just as Reginald conceded to infirmity. As a child of ill-begotten birth, it was hard to place just how old Reginald was, but he and Alden figured that he was close to seventy-two. The oldest man Alden knew. The exercise of living, of getting up early, working all day, making ends meet, and keeping on top of the many small catastrophes on the farm, wore on them both.

The hens were enjoying the warmer weather, though they would be languid when summer turned her oven on full blast. For now, they were content, and Alden watched them the way she had when she was a girl, how awkwardly they stretched and ambled to the water bucket, always thrusting their heads forward as if poking a hole in the air before they could walk through it. This sudden inclination to remembrance had seized her recently like a disease, yet her recollections were so few, so deeply buried, each one was like a tiny parcel containing something surprising yet familiar. At that moment, she thought of the swing Reginald erected in the front yard when she was perhaps eight. She couldn't recall why he'd built it (perhaps for her birthday?) or why it came down (perhaps in a storm?), but there in the hen house she remembered the feel of her whole body pump, pump, pumping her higher into the air, her feet framing blue sky and the wind pulling her hair.

The sun was getting warm enough that Alden could feel its heat on her back as she leaned into the coop. Alden, always a lover of summer and its abundant beauty, was happy that the perpetual rains had ceased, and that the cold, damp that gripped the valley far later in the season than was normal, had finally appeared to end. There was something amiss in the weather, though, and Alden felt it like a bad omen, like seeing an owl in the daylight, which Reginald said was a portent of bad things to come.

Everything felt different this year. The chickens, the trees, the soft bleats of lambs in the pasture— these things were all she knew and all she needed to know. Yet it was no longer enough. Her limbs ached as they never had before, and the comfortable seclusion of the farm had begun to frighten her. She walked through the orchard, touching trees and thinking about her options. The simple truth was in Bruce and marriage, but the thought of bringing another man under the roof of the old stone cottage gripped her with a profound fear. Reginald would be well again, or she would find another way. The workers had arrived, but this too was different. There was no stirring in her soul this year, no wellspring opening to be filled. Like something from myth, the well seemed to have disappeared into mist, and Alden could not reach it.

Her nose itching, Alden continued to the house. Reginald always said that when your nose itched, company was coming or you would soon kiss a fool, so Alden was not surprised to see a car in the drive in front of the house. She pushed the front door open and heard something rare in the Forth house—the sound of companionable chatter.

"Is that you Alden? We've got a guest."

Reginald was sitting in his wing-backed chair that faced the window looking out to the yard. As Alden came to pat his shoulder, the guest turned in the chair opposite and she noted the salt and pepper hair, the square face, and the over-large smile of the new minister, though she could not remember his name, having forgotten him the moment he left the house after their last meeting.

"I'm so glad to catch you at a more opportune moment," said Reverend Beale. He sat in the Forth parlor like an oyster on the bottom of the ocean, filtering the brine for a useful morsel. "I did say I would come and check on your grandfather. He seems quite well."

"Alden, you'll have the whole valley worried. You know how quickly word travels in this small town."

"The reverend came a while ago, when you weren't feeling well. As you can see, my grandfather's better today."

"Alden does all the work around here now. I'm getting too old, I guess."

"Don't say that, Pop. You aren't old."

"Not old, maybe, but not what I was. I wish I had the strength I had even five years ago."

"We should all accept age as a gift from God," said Reverend Beale.

Reginald chuckled. "Maybe I could take that gift a little easier if it didn't come in such a tough package, you know what I mean, Albert?"

"Arnold."

"What's that?"

"Arnold, my name is the Reverend Arnold Beale."

"Yes, that's what he said, Arnold," Alden, said. "But I'm sure you prefer to go by Reverend Beale."

Alden looked down on her grandfather, but he was studying his lap. She could not know where his mind had gone. There was nothing to do but be rid of this stranger as quickly as possible. How long had he already been in the house? Her mind was searching scenarios for his removal when Reginald said, "How about some coffee?"

"I'm sorry to be a bad hostess, but we don't get a lot of visitors," Alden attempted.

As she walked down the hall she heard Reginald saying, "She's a great girl, and she turned out okay I think, with no women around the house…"

In the kitchen, Alden turned on the radio. Even though the weather was fine and the skies clear, she could only get static. Without the company of her maestros, or the mindless chatter of a serial story, her mind wandered back to the first time Bruce sat at the kitchen table and told her there was a new church person in town. Until she saw this new reverend in her house chatting so easily with her grandfather as if they were old acquaintances, she'd forgotten how nervous Bruce had seemed. Alden was not a woman to pass judgment or register suspicion, but she unwittingly had the fine-tuned instincts of an animal, and there was something about the sound of a stranger's voice in the house that triggered a sensation of flight she could not explain. A believer in instinct as well as omens, she willed the coffee to perk quickly on the stove and she put together a tray as fast as she could, somehow concerned that Reginald, whose no-name ailment had gone into one of its half-sleeps but had become increasingly unpredictable with its arrival and duration, was in some danger without her.

She filled the coffee things and hustled down the hall with the tray.

"Your grandfather is quite charming, Miss Forth. And he certainly knows this valley very well. He's been so helpful to someone like me who's just trying to get to know everyone."

Alden sat quietly on the ottoman at Reginald's feet, the spot where she always sat whenever he was in his wingchair, the same place she'd sat since she was a child: On an ottoman covered in a fabric chosen by a grandmother she never knew, but who must have liked chintz.

"My grandfather isn't usually a gossip. You must be real persuasive."

"Alden is overprotective of me," said Reginald, laying a gnarled hand on her shoulder. "We don't get a lot of visitors outside of the peach season."

"Yes, the peach season," Reverend Beale became alert in his seat. "I hoped I might offer my ecclesiastical services to the men, if you don't mind."

"The men work hard, and we let them make their own

choices about how they spend their Sundays," Alden said. "That's not for us to say."

"Certainly you can't object, Miss Forth, to my bringing the word of God to those who can't easily bring themselves to a house of worship?"

"Like I said, sir, we leave that up to them."

"I'm sorry, Reverend Beale, but I agree with Alden. We aren't a church-going family, so we let the workers make their own choices on that and all other things 'long as the work gets done."

"If it suits you, I would like to come back and see you again, Mr. Forth. I so enjoyed listening to your stories."

"Call me Reginald. And sure, you can come on by whenever. Door's always open, though if we're not inside, you're out of luck. That'll mean we're working."

Alden saw Reverend Beale out the front door, watched his short, staccato march to his car, and filled with a sense of relief at his going. Then she returned to the living room and took the coffee dishes into the kitchen. Reginald followed, still sipping from his mug.

"Funny man, that one. Really smart, I think, but odd. But he likes my stories."

"I don't know, Pop. Strangers asking a lot of questions seems more than a little odd to me."

"He's harmless, I think. Carpetbagger Christian is what the nuns at the orphanage called his kind. I don't think he'll get far here, so we may as well be nice to him."

"Maybe, but I'd not tell him all your stories, just the same."

Reverend Beale was learning the roads of the valley with each trip he made, and now he expertly maneuvered his car out of the Forth drive and down the lane where the day lilies that filled the ditches were opening their yawning tiger mouths to the sun. But he was not paying attention to their showy display; he was thinking about Reginald Forth. For the first time since dirt from the small valley town had sullied the soles of his shoes, he felt lighthearted, his conscience eased by the wafting scent of sick souls. It was faint now, but come Friday, he imagined everything could change.

He parked outside the general store and small billows of dust floated from his tires.

"Hello, Mrs. French," he called, as the doorbell tinkled his arrival. A head popped up from below the tinned meats.

"Nice to see you, Reverend. If you came looking for more of those fudge cookies, I'm all out. Won't have more 'til Friday."

"And on Friday I will take all that you have. Perhaps you received my flier?"

"I even put it up on the community board." She gestured to the section of wall where Reverend Beale's prayer evening invitation was speared to a sheet of warped cork where it shared space with a notice for a salvage yard, a tractor for sale, and a lost terrier. Reverend Beale suppressed a shudder.

"That's too kind. I hope to see you and Mr. French there as well."

"That's nice of you, but I'm not sure that's Chester's cup of tea. I don't mean any offense, but he's a little conservative in his religion. He likes things to stay the same. You know how it is."

"Hm, yes. And your children, Mrs. French? Are they available for church? I believe you said you had two sons."

"They're both gone now. Randy moved out west and my oldest, Chester Jr., he got work in a mine all the way up in western Pennsylvania. It breaks a mother's heart, but I guess boys need to grow up. And jobs are so hard to find nowadays. They needed to go where there's work."

"Interesting that Randy moved so far away. What made him choose the west coast?"

Reverend Beale could not be sure, but he thought the woman shivered.

"They say there's a lot of opportunity out there. Jobs, I guess."

"And do you keep in touch?"

Sarah replied slowly, as if she was calculating her words. "We get a letter at least once a month from little Chester, but we don't keep up so well with Randy. People say life is different out west. I guess he's busy making his way."

"Where out west?"

"California. The last we heard he was near San Francisco, but it's been a while since Randy wrote. He was never one for writing."

"I've done some traveling myself out west, you know," he stated. "Sadly, I found the whole place a bit lawless. Too many people go there under the guise of starting over when what they really want is to disappear, to get away from poor choices and regrets that dogged them at home. "

"Randy left to make his way in the world, Reverend, there's no more to say."

Sarah's words were firm enough, but Reverend Beale could hear the fear in them. He navigated around the store's one aisle so he squarely boxed Sarah into the far corner. She took a step back, but bumped into the racks of flour, cornmeal, and other baking supplies. A bottle of molasses teetered dangerously, and she steadied it with a shaking hand.

Reverend Beale ran his finger along a shelf, rubbed the bit of lint against his thumb then casually flicked it away.

"I loathe gossip, but for your sake I feel I must be honest and tell you that I have heard a different story about why Randy left town. It involves a farm laborer, a young man, and a – well, I won't be indelicate, but I will say the rumor is very colorful."

The chill that had afflicted Mrs. French became a heat wave that crashed over her cheeks and burned them into two seething red plains. She said nothing.

"Lies of course. That sort of…interaction, is immoral and criminal. Yet in these small towns, rumors do run amok, and if word were to spread that your son Randy went out west because he had something to run away from, a misguided romance perhaps?" He broke off and ruefully shook his head.

"No, I'm sure we can both agree that such a nasty idea should never be allowed to surface."

Sarah's mouth seemed to have lost its mechanics, but her head bobbed furiously even as tears began to stream down her cheeks.

"Of course, it may be that no one will ever spread such a vicious rumor. What do I know?"

Reverend Beale turned on his heel and marched back toward the front door. "Now, I do expect to see you and Mr. French on Friday evening," he said. "Please spread the word to your friends, too, and I will be by Friday morning to relieve you of all the fudge cookies you can spare."

He stopped with the door ajar, the bell jingling pleasantly overhead. "You know, Mrs. French, we have a saying in my vocation it might be wise for you to contemplate: 'Confession is the cure.' You may wish to unburden yourself as the relief of communal expression of sin is liberating. Or perhaps you or know someone else who has something they want to be free of? Secrecy is the devil's tool."

IX

Alden rarely went into the local village. Most of what she and Reginald required was already on the farm. But with the worker cabin almost full and hungry men to provide for, Alden lumbered toward the Frenchs' store in Reginald's pickup to stock up on essentials.

This year was like the last and all the others that preceded it. Like a mirror reflecting a scene from the previous summer, Sarah, in her same cotton dress as the prior year, had only just flipped over the "open" sign and unlocked the door and was wiping down the wooden counter and the gleaming metal of the cash register when Alden entered.

"I knew I'd be seeing you soon, Alden. I've put a few things aside for you, just waiting on you."

"That's kind, Sarah. I'll only be a few minutes then I'll get back on the road."

Sarah stashed the rag beneath the counter and pulled out the crate of goods she'd set aside, the register clanking to life.

"You're no bother to me, Alden. I always like your company. You're always so… calm."

Alden tipped her nose toward the crate.

"Mmm, lavender soap. How did you know I liked lavender soap?"

"You've only bought it every season since you were a teenager, Alden. I pay attention."

But Alden was already wandering down the aisle of the store, piling her arms with dry goods. Watching her shop she looked to Sarah like a displaced wood nymph. There was always something ethereal about Alden, even when she was a little girl. Sarah shook her head and thought to herself how silly she could be. Alden was just an old maid with a slim waist and nice hair.

But as Alden deftly piled her purchases on the counter, her slim fingers moving with the grace and agility of moths and just as silently, Sarah couldn't help but be amused. Sarah, with hands that belied their washing of a thousand dishes and wringing of countless loads of laundry, rang Alden's purchases into the register, its clanks and dings the only sound in the empty store.

"Have you been busy this summer, Sarah?"

Sarah had known Alden her whole life and knew the girl was not one for small talk, so she stood agape for an instant, holding aloft a sack of flour.

"About the same as ever," she finally muttered. "Why do you ask?"

Alden's brown eyes met Sarah's intently over the counter, searched her face and bore deep into her, as if looking for an answer written in Sarah's very skin.

"I thought you might be tired is all. Something about you seems a little different. You know, sometimes when you don't see someone a lot, you see a change in them other people don't see what see them every day. I see a change in you, but I couldn't say what."

"What a funny thing to say, Alden. I'm sure I don't know what you mean."

The look of intense interest faded, and Alden reassumed the faraway look of a dreamer that Sarah knew so well. A moment to be captured slipped away in that instant, and right away Sarah wanted it back. She rang a sack of flour into the register and put it into the crate along with the rest of the groceries and sighed.

"Have you met the new minister, Alden?"

"You know we've never been a family that's big on church."

Sarah shook her head and for a moment Alden felt the weight of Sarah's world in that gesture and had to hold herself back from reaching out to help hold up the woman's heavy head.

"This is no church, Alden. It's like…"

"…a revival? My grandfather used to tell me about those."

"No, I don't think so. That man, Beale's his name, needs to bring people to the Lord like a mother bringing a dirty child to bath water. Like it's his duty, and he'll get you clean no matter how much the child hollers."

"He's come to the house before. He's nosy."

"Alden! Well, I guess you're right, though, and who am I to stand for manners?"

Sarah watched Alden fingering her bills and coins, fastidiously searching for the correct change. She had known Alden's mother, though they had not been friends. Like her daughter, Rebecca was beautiful and quiet, though unlike her daughter, Rebecca lacked Alden's robust health. Rebecca truly was otherworldly, and therefore was too fragile to last long on this harsh earth. But Sarah could still see the young Rebecca's face, flushed and pretty and kind and as unwitting as Alden, which woke in Sarah a dormant mothering need.

"You watch out for yourself, Alden, and your granddad. There's tension in town now. I don't know where it will end."

Alden didn't understand Sarah's meaning, but she knew the day was progressing fast as the temperature in the store was getting warm to the point that it defied the efforts of the electric fan whirring plaintively behind the counter. She put her money in Sarah's hand and gathered her boxes close, pushing open the store's door with her behind.

"Have a good day, Sarah."

"You too. And be good."

The boxes were cumbersome and Alden tripped slightly on the last step leaving the store, but was able to right herself without losing any groceries except a can of condensed milk, which she attempted to push toward the truck with her foot.

"You'll hurt yourself, Miss Forth."

The voice was strange, foreign, thick with accent. When Alden looked up, Nikolay Ivanov was standing in front of her. She looked at him as if butterflies had flown from his mouth, beautiful and strange.

"You speak English."

He shrugged. "Sometimes."

"But I've never heard you speak English before."

He shrugged again, as if he didn't wish for her words to stick to his shirt and linger longer than necessary, drawing attention.

"It's best to be quiet."

"Yes, sometimes, I think you are right."

Like two animals meeting in a wood, they were standing opposite each other in the lot of the grocery, Alden's arms heavy with wares, Nikolay's shoulders bent from the fatigue of his shrugging, each appraising the other while quieting their mutual surprise to find each other there in that clearing. Nikolay breached the space between them, silently taking one of the boxes from Alden's arms, picking up the condensed milk, and putting the two in the bed of the truck.

"How did you get to town?"

Nikolay pointed to the road.

"I walked." He tapped a tin in his shirt pocket. "The American tobacco. I like it."

"I'll give you a ride back."

They drove in silence. At first it was a tense silence, each strangely wary at meeting so unexpectedly. Then the tension rolled away beneath the tires and was replaced by comfortable quiet, the silence usually reserved for old friends or older lovers. Nikolay rolled down his window and the breeze blew in hot and playful, tugging mischievously at Alden's hair and pulling it loose from its bun. Through the tendrils of her roiling hair, Alden looked across the truck to the window and to the man next to it and the silence became thick with her unasked questions.

"You are curious, Miss Forth."

"I guess so."

"This is natural."

It didn't seem he was going to say much more so Alden turned her eyes back to the road and tried to push a few wisps of hair behind her ears. They refused to stay put.

"You are a quiet woman, Miss Forth. And you are alone. No man in your life?"

Many women would have taken this question as an affront, but Alden, unaware of social convention, answered as she did all questions: with honesty.

"I have my grandfather, that's all."

"I thought so. I like that you are quiet. Too many women, they chatter like birds all the time. You are quiet and alone. You are the swan with no mate."

In another place, with another woman, with another man, it could have been romantic. A woman with windswept hair behind the wheel, a tanned man with blonde hair and dark brown eyes following the curve of the road, and yet, there was no beauty in what he said. Nick's English was tainted with despair, a sadness that rubbed the luster off his words and wilted Alden's spirits more than the gathering humidity in the cab of the truck. The air was too heavy, the sorrow too palpable; Alden steered to the side of the road and stopped the truck. The wind stopped. The road was empty. A few day lilies flopped languidly into the road and cows could be heard in the distance. A fly buzzed against the windshield, sensing freedom but unable to attain it.

Nick chuckled a low, sardonic laugh. "Quiet and curious. Perhaps you are a cat, not a swan."

The tense silence caught up to the stopped truck and though tired from its journey where it had been left behind, the silence slipped in between the two people, toying with time to make seconds feel like minutes until Alden was certain the dusk would fall on them at any moment.

"I was born in Russia. Do you know where that is, quiet cat?"

Nick's voice was monotone and foreign, like strange rhythmic music. The truck was hot now and Alden was lulled by the warmth and the metronome of his speaking. She nodded, not knowing the answer to his question.

"I was… What's the word? Spoiled. My brothers and sisters were all grown. I was my mother's baby. She gave me everything. I liked sports, running. And girls. I chased girls." He paused, laughed his cynical, knowing laugh, the laughter that should be reserved for an older man.

"'You're foolish,' said my mother. 'Russians are cautious people, Nikolay, people who know sadness, and here you are such a silly boy.' But she would laugh, too."

"But there were things going on, I had no idea. I was too busy playing and running and too busy with the girls. My father, he was a smart man, an engineer. He worked on trains. He remembered the Tsar and in his heart, he missed the Tsar, but he was no fighter. He was just a man. A man who drank with friends and talked about the world, like men do."

"We lived by a river. When it rained, the river would swell. When I was little, it got so big it came into the house one time. I woke up and my bed was floating, and I screamed because I was afraid."

The truck was still. The silence held its breath and the fly stopped its incessant bid for freedom. Alden thought of the boy Nick would have been and saw a child in a fairy tale floating in slumber until he's awoken by wet, lapping waves.

"It was like that with the troubles. It came slowly, growing while I was not watching. Then the men came in the night and I woke up afraid because there was a banging on the door and the men said, 'Please come with us, Mr. Ivanov,' and the neighbors did a bad job pretending not to watch, but I could see the moonlight shining off their Orthodox crosses as they pressed their faces to the windows."

"The water goes away, but it leaves behind its mark. With

this, it was the same. That night mother said, 'You need to leave now. They'll be back for you.' And I said, 'I don't want to go, I want to stay here and run and chase the girls and be foolish,' and she says no, I must go. And I say, I want you to come with me, and she says no, I belong with your father. They'll bring him back to me or they'll take me to him and we'll be together as it should be. And I said I didn't know what to do, that this was all I know, and she said: "Sadness is a teacher. Now, you'll learn from sadness."

"I left that night. I walked until I found a train and when there was no train I hopped on a cart or I walked or I found more trains. I walked right out of my country. The Germans didn't want me. The French let me work for a while, then I went to England, but it is dark and rainy and cold there and the sadness for me was very bad there. So I took a boat to Florida where people told me it was warm, and I felt a little better and there was work there. When the men started moving north, I moved, too."

"I thought I could walk until there was no more sadness, but the problem with things inside is they go with you no matter where you go. I think many Russians leave that sad place to be joyful. For me it's the other way; I was joyful there and now, only sadness."

The tense silence was gone now, shoved out of the truck but the unbearably large stature of a confided story. The only thing more cumbersome than a secret is the truth, and the magnitude of Nick's reality pressed he and Alden to the seat of the truck, sealed their mouths and froze their limbs. In the heat of summer, Alden felt like a person muffled under snow, unsure of the way to the surface, lacking the strength to dig.
Nick, having grown fit from carrying the burden of his own story for so many miles, was able to break the crust of the snow, reach in and pull Alden back to the surface, back to the valley on the side of the road.

"Now you know why quiet is best," he said and laughed in his peculiar way of laughing without being amused.
A beetle landed on the back of Alden's hand, which, like its

pair, was still clenching the steering wheel. She took one hand and brushed it off the other, surprised that she had the strength, amazed at the warmth of her own skin, at the ceaselessness of life. It might have been best to say that she was sorry for all that he lost, it might have been wise to thank him for choosing her as his confidant, or to ask why he'd shared this with her, but his sadness had reached across the small space between them and touched the fringes of her own, breaching the boundary lands that surrounded her reality.

"Then you are alone, like me. You left the place that brought you joy and I am in the place that brings me joy, but all the people I know, leave."

"Ah, but you still have your grandfather."

She looked at him, confused. But then realized how could he know about the ailment that has no name? He was new here. He knew nothing of the life before and the life now.

"People can leave without going anywhere."

Nick thought about this for a moment. "I think I understand you. That way might be harder."

Alden turned over the engine of the truck.

The fly finally found its way to the rolled down window and disappeared into the late morning heat haze as the truck pulled onto the roadway. Something long dormant stirred within Alden, as imperceptible as the touch of a beetle's antennae exploring skin.

X

Sarah French was a rather congenial person. A bit dull, even, in a mild-mannered, harmless sort of way. But since Reverend Beale confronted her in the store, she had been afflicted with a terrible headache that was causing her temper to flare with surprising alacrity, and giving her a propensity of thinking the worst of just about everyone as she tried to determine who could have let her family secret out. After Reverend Beale's visit, that fearsome anger propelled her down the street to the house of her dearest friend, the equally mild Doris Burns, and her husband, the gregarious though hopelessly drunken Philip.

"Doris, if you didn't tell that awful man about Randy, then who did?"

It is perhaps not surprising that Doris denied any wrong doing, but Sarah made the very valid point she had uttered not a word about Randy to anyone. The shame of it. She could not even tell Chester, it would have killed him to hear such filth about his own son. It was Doris who knew, Doris who held a sobbing Sarah as she divulged the truth that Randy had fallen in love with a farm laborer, Doris who helped her pack Randy's things and make the appropriate excuse for his hasty departure from town, Doris who helped fabricate a canvas of well-place lies and half-truths that repainted Randy's world into one that was completely banal and, after his departure, utterly forgettable. If Doris hadn't told Reverend Beale, she'd told someone else who had.

"Maybe someone knew the boy."

Sarah laughed through a wry smile, so ill-suited to her powdery face with its soft, cow eyes. Doris recoiled a bit at the strangeness of it. "For goodness sake, no one even knows who it was, not even me. Randy never gave me his name and he said the boy'd run off, probably ashamed. Good riddance." While Doris proclaimed she was innocent – it can be so hard to keep track of where one has stored old gossip – she could no doubt feel the opening of her friend's old wound like it was her own. For a child to go astray was a regrettable enough thing, though it probably happened more than most would like to admit. But to fall in love with another man… any whiff of moral dalliance coming from the direction of the general store would be as welcome as rancid milk.

"I feel just awful, but there's nothing I can do," said Doris.

"This 'reverend,' as he calls himself, he wants to make a to-do out of healing the sinners, I know it," said Sarah, tapping her index finger on the table. "I've seen his type come through the store before, revivalists looking to make a big scene. 'Confession is the cure,' he said, though I certainly do not intend to publicly acknowledge anything about Randy and that man knows it."

Doris nodded over her iced tea. "Mmm, yes. I wish I could help."

Sarah looked hard at her friend. Her head throbbed as it tried to come to terms with this new anger pumping through her otherwise placid brain.

"He said I should bring someone who wants to unburden their soul. He wants me to bring an offering, Doris. To get his little ball rolling."

The two women regarded each other, sweating tea glasses creating white rings on Doris's dining table. Sarah watched as understanding illuminated Doris's face, and her eyebrows arched in horror.

"You aren't thinking of Philip?" Doris gasped. "Like some sacrificial lamb?"

"I certainly am. No disrespect, Doris, but Philip's drinking is no big secret. It would be easy grist for the mill. And get me out of the hot seat."

"I don't think he'd do it."

"He will. Or I'll have to mention to Ned Pfieff that I might know a little something about his plow that went missing last year."

Doris gasped. "You know Philip only took that because he'd been drinking! He wasn't in his right mind."

"He certainly could have taken it back when he sobered up, but instead he sold it in Pennsylvania. I know it, and you know it, and we're all going out on Friday night."

Sarah and Chester French pulled into the field off Plainair Farm Road that Friday at dusk. Doris and Philip came with them, and anyone with half an inclination to notice could tell that the climate between the two women friends was frosty. The land was a rough, weedy patch no farmer would ever plant, which is likely why its owner was all too happy to give it over to Reverend Beale to steward for the summer. The reverend had found old, chopped up trees that he'd rolled into neat rows, creating an improvised church setting. His canvas tent faced these pews and at the sound of the car he drew back the canvas flap dramatically.

"Like a huckster at a circus," Sarah said under her breath to no one in particular.

The Frenches and Burnses joined a group gathering at a table full of cookies and iced tea in pitchers. A few tenant farmers milled around, happy for the free food and something mildly new to assuage the boredom of workaday rural life.

"Look, real silver," Doris said to Sarah, fingering the fine beveled edge of a serving tray. "How can he afford it?"

Just then Anna Scott pulled into the field and shimmied out of her car, slim and gorgeous. Her twins tumbled out behind her in sailor suits that complemented their mother's navy dress.

"Looks like our clergyman is making friends in high places," Sarah sniffed. "He certainly was uppity in his hopes for attendees," she added, indicating with a tilt of her head the rustic seating; there were far more logs than there were bottoms to fill them.

The little group finished their cookies and Chester, Sarah, Doris, and Philip took seats, as did Anna Scott, who had given up trying to corral her children and let them wander into a boggy patch of field grass to leap on the spongy earth.

"Would you believe Ned Pfieff is here?" said Philip, as if anyone could have missed the lanky old man striding toward the tent. Sarah gave Doris a hard look and Doris patted her husband's hand. With his bemused smile and unassuming acceptance of their presence at the tent revival, Philip Burns was truly beginning to take on the appearance of a vulnerable sheep.

Reverend Beale stood in front of his tent, sweating profusely in his collar and jacket. He cleared his throat several times and breathed deeply. Onlookers might have taken him for nervous, but he was transforming himself into an instrument of God, which took a little time and a few ministrations. Once he was called to the Lord's work, Reverend Beale had never been an anxious speaker. Had he been more in tune with his spectators, he might have been disappointed there weren't more in attendance, but his mind was not on earthly vanity. He was already ascending to a higher place where plain old preaching transcends into oratory.

"Welcome friends, for we are all friends here, united by our common bond that we are all sinners. We are created through lascivious acts, and we pass our lives telling little and large lies, hurting ourselves, our neighbors and children, stealing, idolizing, and fantasizing the most lurid things. All this amounts to a great debt. I'm here to tell you: if you try to carry that debt into Heaven, it will be too heavy. For Heaven is a place for lightness, whereas weight falls beneath the earth where the sinner toils to be rid of his debt in a pit of endless flame."

Reverend Beale paused to take the pulse of his audience. A few were politely nodding and several were no doubt trying to remember the meaning of the word "lascivious," but most were sipping tea. Anna Scott suppressed a yawn and snapped her fingers at her children, who were wandering off amongst the cars. Undaunted, Reverend Beale switched from grand themes to pragmatic specifics, perhaps more apropos for simple farmers.

"Has not anyone here had a bit too much to drink one night, repented the next day, and then done it again the next week?"

To this, the crowd murmured.

"Of course," said Reverend Beale, with a gentle, understanding smile. "And perhaps you've borrowed a dollar from a friend and never paid it back, even though you know you should have?"

The group was quiet, but he had their attention now.

"We need not say it here, but no doubt you've looked at your neighbor at some point and thought, 'how handsome his cows are. I wish they could be mine.' Or even, 'how beautiful is my neighbor's wife. I wish she were mine.'"

Here's when Reverend Beale shifted his voice from that of a knowing friend to a vengeful preacher.

"These are not small things, my people. These passing thoughts, these simple actions, they grow, and grow, and fester like a mosquito bite you scratch until it is infected. Your lives are infected, full of guilt and puss."

He was shouting now, but a deep, controlled hollering, like a sonorous bellows pumping massive blasts of air beneath flaming embers.

"You are held in the hand of God, over the pit of hell. You are sentenced to fall deep into the flesh-burning void. Only God can save you, but you have provoked His anger, and He waits to tip his palm, to drop you into the gaping maw of the devil's fiery mouth, which is the fate all sinners deserve. Until you clean up your soul and your lives, you will continue to be in the grasp of a wrathful God, you will never be welcome in His house. And the angels will not weep for you. No, as Revelations tells us, they will rejoice that God has executed justice on the damned and shown favor to the saved."

This style of ministering was clearly new to the little group gathered there in the grass; they were more accustomed to the standard liturgy and fusty hymns read and sung by rote on Sunday under the benign direction of Reverend Greene and the succession of reverends that came before him. All this shouting and rancor was quite unusual, especially in the wake of such delicious cookies, and for a time the listeners were mostly dumbfounded. However, after Reverend Beale went on for quite some time with more and more examples of how they each were leading lives marked by terrible sin in even the smallest ways, a few people seemed to get downright nervous, like maybe he was right and they better clean up their act. Most appeared quite browbeaten, and their shoulders bowed under the weight of guilt. When Reverend Beale saw this, what some might have called "being defeated" but Reverend Beale thought of as, "the moment of penitent preparedness," he eased off the sermon's accelerator and asked:

"Would anyone like to stand up this evening and release themselves of sin?"

The small group, perhaps surprised that they were being called to contrition and not simply meant to withstand the great gusts of Reverend Beale's sermon, looked around sheepishly. Reverend Beale assessed his flock of dim-witted ewes and gave them a nudge.

"It's the right thing to do," he said, catching Sarah French's eye. He added encouragingly, "You are welcome here."

Sarah jabbed Doris hard in the ribs, and she in turn jabbed Philip in the ribs. Philip looked just about ready to rest his eyes when he was rudely awakened by his wife's elbow. Doris flicked her head in the direction of Ned Pfieff seated near the back.

"Go on and get it done with," she whispered. Philip gave a resigned shrug and stood up. The Reverend's face broke into a shining smile.

"Brave soul, come, join me here."

Philip walked to the front with his hat in his hands. His wife looked expectant. Behind her was Tom Seager, proprietor of the closest tavern, who'd left his wife in charge at the bar in hopes that he could entice a few customers back after the revival. His expression was curious as his best customer walked forward.

"Make yourself light, friend," said Reverend Beale, clapping his heavy hand on Philip's shoulder, "Light as a feather that can float to Heaven."

Philip cleared his throat. "Well, I'm a drinker, reverend. I drink all the time, even when my wife tells me not to."

"God doesn't approve of drinking. Drinking, dancing – these things muddle the mind and lead to the devil's deeds."

Philip bowed his head. "I know that. But it sure is fun."

A few people muffled laughter. The reverend sighed.

"But it is *wrong*. Drinking hurts you and the ones you love," said Reverend Beale, his voice increasing to a bellow. "You make yourself a slave, man, a slave to a bottle! You let yourself be made weak, half the man you could be. Do you not feel the warm breath of Hell beneath the soles of your feet? Do you not know how you jeopardize yourself and your family with this wickedness?"

Philip cowed. "I guess I don't always pull my weight."

"Pull your weight?" shouted Reverend Beale, throwing up his hands in mock surprise. "Of course you don't pull your weight. How can your body be free to work to the glory of God when you are tethered to the devil's liquid?"

Philip's head was bowed and when he spoke he mumbled, a portrait of public shame. "You might have a point there. And my wife would be happier if I quit."

From her log seat, Doris beamed. While she might not have wished for her husband to be humiliated to help out a friend, she was quite content for her husband to sober up and stop publicly humiliating himself around the valley on Saturday nights just for the heck of it.

"Do you repent for this behavior here, in front of all these witnesses, and swear never to drink again?"

Philip took a good long time to think over the offer until he caught sight of his wife's glacial stare.

"I do. I do apologize for drinking and promise never to do so again."

The little group erupted into applause and Reverend Beale decided one small victory was enough for the evening.

"Quiet, quiet please." It didn't take long for the small gathering to become composed.

"Let's all bow our heads and pray for Philip's salvation. Let us offer him our support here, with God and our neighbors to witness. And let us not forget to search our own souls and think of ways we, too, could become deserving vessels to carry God's love. Let us walk away this evening remembering we must be as vigilant in the purification of our thoughts and actions as God is in watching our minds and deeds. Amen."

There was something in the final prayer that subdued the little group as the meeting broke up. Men tipped their hats to each other over their wives' bent heads, women nodded at their friends without chatter as they caught a child by the hand. It was as if a threat hung in the air. Doris was ebullient toward her husband, but she and Sarah kept a cold and silent distance even as they piled back into Chester's car. Ned Pfieff scratched his balding head, trying to make sense of the whole affair, and Tom Seager went back to his tavern, sullen and irritable, no doubt hopeful that not too many more of his customers would get the idea to be saved.

Anna Scott packed her silver trays into the back of her car.

"I can't thank you enough for lending me these beautiful things," said Reverend Beale as the field emptied and Anna closed her children into the Cadillac. "They leant an atmosphere of refinement to what is otherwise a rather humble proceeding."

"Oh, I found it all utterly entertaining."

Reverend Beale was still feeling quite heated from his sermon, and his tongue, like his mind, was loose and agile, an athlete primed for the race. It was all he could do to hold himself back from a tirade of how the work of God is not meant to be entertainment. But he knew to be careful with her, to give her line and draw her in, like the dance of a fisherman and his prize catch. There were things beyond silver trays he wanted from Anna Scott.

"I hope that means I'll see you next week. I believe I'll keep doing these on Friday evenings. I think it will be so much easier than Sunday morning for people to come after their workday, especially the farm workers."

"I'm sure the good reverend in town will be thrilled not to have competition on Sunday," said Anna.

"Perhaps next week you'll bring some family? Your father, I gather, is quite well regarded in this area. It would be nice to have someone of esteem among us, setting a good example for the others."

"What I wouldn't give to have my father here," said Anna. "What I wouldn't give."

With a wink, she slid into her car and was gone, firing dust and grass into the darkening night.

XI

It was hot in the orchard and the air was thick and slimy with humidity. Crickets and cicadas droned a languid tune around Alden as she inspected the fruit, concerned that the excessive rain and humid temperatures might rot the peaches before they could properly ripen. The rows between the trees were neat and green. Occasionally a man would walk across the path in the distance and she was reminded of the presence of the summer workers around her. She had put them to the monotonous and merciless task of thinning the fruit, sacrificing some peaches so that others could grow.

She worked her way down the rows, one eye on the sky, the other on the trees, trying to calculate the year's potential yield, thinking ahead to harvest. Will Field ducked beneath a tree, slipping in and out of her peripheral vision like a wraith avoiding the sunlight. Alden could feel his eyes watching her as she walked. There was something desperate in the boy, but desperation was common in farming communities, even more so since the Crash, so that it now felt as inevitable as weather. That unpredictable, too, but Alden had no reason to fear Will Field. With Will and those like him she was dispassionate. Her life was benchmarked by summers full of anonymous young men just like him, doing the work that kept them from falling into one of society's large cracks. She herself danced on the edge of that divide.

Nick stepped into the grass a few yards away and motioned for her to come. He was not much taller than Alden. His blonde hair, overdue for a trim, fell over dark eyes, and a long, angular nose -- a strong face with too many angles to be handsome.

"Okay?" he asked, lifting his palms to her like an offering. Cupped in each palm were immature peaches, small and yellow-green. They looked vulnerable against his wide palm and thick, stubbed fingers.

"Okay," she said nodding. "You are doing good work," she said. He stared at her, his face inscrutable, and she suppressed a desire to push the hair off his forehead. They both turned to the sound of a horse's clomping hooves and then voices. She smiled at Nick who only nodded in return and stepped out of her way.

She walked toward the sound and found Reginald talking to Jane Scott, high up on her mare, which was lathered with a thick foam of sweat. Reginald was having one of his good days. He was growing more frail, but when his mind was with him, he was happiest outside working.

"Hello Alden, so sorry to intrude on you," said Jane, little coils of black hair sticking to her pink cheeks. "Isadora was desperate for a slowdown, and when I saw your grandfather I thought I'd stop and say hello."

Alden typically thought little of people. She didn't concern herself with gossip or with liking or disliking people. She had so little interaction with them; they just were, like all living things. But there was something about Jane Scott that always gave Alden a pleasant feeling. Had she had the time or inclination for friends, perhaps they could have been closer. But of course, Jane came from one of the old families, and it was known that an old family and a farming family would never mix.

"Your grandfather was just telling me how he met your grandmother just like this, when she was on a horse and he was in a peach orchard."

"Yes, Pop has been very chatty with his stories lately." Alden surprised herself when she heard the bite in her own words. It wasn't so much that Alden disapproved of all this company and chatter, just that she couldn't shake the feeling of ill will around her, and she read every misstep from the norm of life as yet another sign. Jane Scott in the orchard on a lathered horse speaking of love to Reginald was very out of the ordinary.

"I'd guess you're a bit of a romantic too, aren't you Jane?" said Reginald, who was stroking the horses flank. "I can see it in your eyes."

Reginald made the girl blush a deeper pink, and Alden wondered at the chemistry of that, wondered what it was that burned so inside Jane that it couldn't be contained within her own cheeks.

"I'll leave you all to talk," said Alden, uncomfortable with the idleness of chatter and the coyness of youth.

Alden walked into the depth of the orchard, legs swishing across grass that needed to be trimmed, until even the sound of her footsteps were engulfed by the hot air and thick insect song and the green blanketing of foliage, and Reginald and Jane were folded into the great assumption of privacy that can exist out of doors.

Jane had reason for a long ride. Riding helped her clear her head. Today, she was muddled, and talking to Mr. Forth helped. What was it, she wondered, about the ears of strangers that made it easier to expose your most intimate thoughts? He was going a bit dotty, certainly, but he was still an old sweetheart. So unlike anyone Jane normally interacted with, except for Ronan.

As she and Isadora walked toward home in the thick afternoon air, the brief lightness of heart she'd experienced in the Forths' orchard retracted. The closer she came to home, the heavier felt the plodding of the horse's hooves on the ground. If only Anna would be gone from their father's house when Jane returned, perhaps then it would be better.

As she rode back home, Jane recalled Anna's scheming theatrics of that morning. None of it was ever about Jane, of course, it was about their father, about wanting to torment him. Jane cared little about their father as long as he left her alone. It was a balance they'd fallen into without any contrivance, a parallel life they were both content to live. But Anna was constantly intent on disrupting that fragile peace. Given calm waters, Anna would perpetually choose to do a cannonball into the center of the pond.

Jane's suspicion was piqued the moment she heard Anna was going to the new man's church. Jane had her horses and occupied herself with little else. Until, that is, there was a rumbling of discontent from Anna's portion of the valley. Any slight heave in the foundation of the balance between Robert Scott's home and Anna's was of interest to Jane because the tremors always took more victims than those two alone. When Anna got on about the new church, Jane took interest.

It was, no doubt, a ploy to irritate their father. Anna only went to the church in town because it was seemly. They all did. Robert Scott's great grandfather helped place the foundation stone in the little church and the Scotts had gone every Sunday since. It was a fairly well established rule in the Scott household that one could behave however they wished for six days of the week provided one showed up at church on Sunday. When Anna was not in church last Sunday, her father noticed it immediately. Though it pained him that Anna had returned to the valley, unlike his other two girls, if she chose to stay here beneath his nose he felt it only appropriate that she should act in accordance with tradition. Certainly attending church, where they could pointedly ignore each other, was tradition.

Jane heard them fighting that morning before she even got to the house. She'd risen early to keep Ronan company as he cleaned the stalls and filled the water buckets; in the heat the horses were constantly drinking their buckets dry.

"You should get back to the house, sweet Jane," he said to her. Her heart still warmed to remember the touch of his warm knuckles on her cheek as he brushed her hair off her face and kissed her lips.

But in the yard on her way back to the house she heard raised voices. In the oppressive heat, all the windows and doors were being kept open to try and force any breath of air through the rooms of the house, so there was no containing the pitch of Anna and Robert's argument. Those two could shake the house with their shouting when they really got going. "I simply do not understand why you must constantly disobey me and embarrass me, Anna."

Their father's voice boomed down the sloping yard to where Jane was standing still at her kittens' tree stump. The kitties had grown quickly from mewling balls of fluff into awkward adolescents with pipe cleaner tails and clumsy paws at the tips of their gangly limbs. Jane absentmindedly picked up a calico that rubbed her calf and stroked its soft head until its purr rumbled against her shoulder.

"I am not a stupid man. I know that you want to create a scene. You always were such a one for a scene. And God knows your simple husband can't contain you. But I will not have it. I will not have my daughter at some hootenanny church fest with a bunch of farmers."

"Oh it's just good fun, Daddy. Besides, the children adore it there."

"The children? The children!"

Jane shrunk against the tree trunk to hear her father's voice bellow with such intensity. But his ire only stoked Anna further.

"Oh yes, they run barefoot and everything. They simply love it. You should come and see."

"If it had done you any good as a child I would slap you now, Anna. Taking my grandchildren to some raucous, nameless tent fellowship -- it has no provenance, no foundation. Don't you care about appearances anymore? Have you no shame for your own family name?"

"My family name is Radcliffe now, Daddy. Not that you ever wanted to lay claim to any of us before anyway."

"And David is all the more stupid for taking you on and indulging you like a pet. I may not have been the best father to you, but I think I taught you the importance of our position in this community, and now you flaunt what I gave you. I taught you to at least behave like a lady."

"Did you Daddy? And did you teach Jane to be a lady, too?"

From her position at the tree stump Jane's skin went cold despite the heat of the brightening morning and the warmth of the kitten in her arms. Jane's life might be lonely, but at least it was anonymous. For Anna to take an interest in Jane could mean nothing good. Jane felt the earth move slightly beneath her feet.

"Jane has none of your venom, Anna. Jane is plain and you know it. She's obedient, quiet. Jane is nothing to you or to me."

Jane was too concerned at suddenly being a part of this argument to be hurt by her father's comments.

"I just wonder that you leave her so much to her own devices, what with that handsome stable boy in your employ," said Anna, her angry voice dropped to a honeyed smoothness. "You know what they say about young, moneyed girls and handsome farmhands."

"Oh do try to not be so cliché, Anna. And Jane? For heaven's sake, don't be ridiculous."

"Of course, if you're so certain Jane was raised to be a lady—like I was—why worry?"

Jane didn't wait to hear more. An ocean of sound filled her ears and cold sweat poured down her back. How did she know? How could Anna possibly know? Had Ronan told her? No, he would never betray her like that, what had he to gain? Another servant, maybe? Or was she just bluffing? It was silly to conjecture; Anna always had a way of finding out anything that could be used to her advantage; that Jane knew. She just never thought her life would be significant enough to serve her sister's nefarious purposes. Of course, it was just like Anna to not care about Jane's life—until she had a use to.

Jane covered the yard back to the barn at a sprint, tears of anger and fear and sadness covering her face like a torrent. She was embarrassed for Ronan to see her this way so she spotted him first, in the pasture looking at a fence post. She sneaked in, saddled Isadora hurriedly, and set off at a gallop on a path through the woods that she rarely took, one that quickly took her off the Scott property and across several neighboring fields. That is how she ended up in the Forths' orchard, both she and Isadora wet with sweat, where Reginald was standing with his kind, stranger's ears.

Ronan was waiting in the paddock.

"You've ridden that mare to her end."

"I'm sorry." Jane dropped her head. He was right to be angry. She knew better than to ride Isadora so hard and long in such heat.

"I've a sweat scraper," said Ronan, softening his tone. "I'd a feeling you'd be riding harder than common sense."

He unsaddled the horse while Jane held the reins at the horse's nose. For once, she was quiet. The presence of something foul was there with them in the paddock, and it was Ronan that finally spoke of it.

"Your father's been here."

The presence grew larger.

"I heard him fighting with my sister this morning," said Jane. "I think she said something terrible about me. About you and me. I didn't wait to hear more. I took Isadora, and I left."

Ronan sighed as he rubbed down the horse's sides.

"I thought as much. Your father doesn't come here often just to talk. When I saw Isadora was gone, I'd a mind something was wrong."

He continued to rub the horse. Jane could bear it no longer.

"What did he say? Will he fire you? Will he throw me from the house?"

She would have continued, her tongue having been

gripped by that torrent of language she always found hard to stop. Ronan touched her hand lightly with his own over the horse's reins.

"It's alright, sweet Jane. He came to make sure I know my place."

"But your place is with me." Even as she said the words, Jane thought she sounded like a foolish child.

"Aye, when we're here, in this place, we're to be together. But out there," Ronan cast a hand out over the pastures and woods, the great stone pile of Robert Scott's house, "I'm the help and you're the lady of the house. For sure, we've both known that all along."

"But… will you leave me now?"

Ronan looked at her, the curls of her hair wet and clinging to her distraught face and thought of her alone, wandering the main house like a ghost, keeping company with only the horses. And he thought of himself, cast out of a perfectly good job, to what? Go back to the ramshackle track?

"Nay, I'm not going anywhere. But we must be careful, sweet Jane."

He lifted her hand from the reins and brushed the back of her hand with his lips so quickly Jane thought later she might have imagined it. Then he pulled the bridle off the horse's head and put a halter in its place.

"Get back to the house now, Jane." And, as she was an obedient child, she did as she was told.

Reverend Beale drank a cool glass of iced tea in the Radcliffe's living room. Reverend Beale did not like Anna Scott. He'd known women like her before. Beautiful, bewitching, spoiled. He wasn't a man given to magical beliefs, but she was of the ilk that perpetuated myths about the intangible draw of women, fairy tales that made women bigger and more powerful than they deserved to be. Higher than God. These women always reminded him of his mother, of the years of abuse that followed his revelation of her affair. His mother's beauty made her vulnerable, her vanity made her proud; her refusal to repent made her dangerous.

Yet he was not so proud or so righteous or so stupid to not see the opportunity the Lord had given him in the form of Anna, no matter how repugnant it was to his morality. Anna was playing at her own game, that he knew, but if he was wise, he could hold a stake at the gaming table. She too would fold in the end and be made contrite in the face of God, truly contrite. That he knew.

He allowed himself a moment of vanity when he thought about the successes he had already achieved in his few short weeks in the valley. There were small victories, like the woman Iris who confessed to feeding tramps at the back door and lying to her husband about where the food had gone. Better still was the farmhand who admitted to stealing a chicken from his employer, or, the pinnacle thus far of Reverend Beale's work, the homely housewife Beatrice who confessed to carnal thoughts about her neighbor. Yes, tensions were palpable in the valley now, but Reverend Beale acknowledged this as rightful punishment and a step towards a greater cleansing.

He returned his attention to the enjoyment of his tea. French doors in the room opened onto a flagstone patio and outside the Radcliffe twins, Beryl and John, read books under the shade of a large tree in the front yard in the company of a nanny. Beyond was the grassy glade of the yard, punctuated with sprawling maples and tall oaks that undulated into a pasture that sloped away down a hill and disappeared from view. The setting was perfection.

"I cannot apologize enough for my lateness, Reverend. This heat makes me so slow."

Anna moved into the room, whisker thin in a light blue dress of cotton so fine it was just a moment away from transparent. Her blonde hair was pulled back from her face with a scarf, revealing the cutting edge of her cheekbones and the full red bow of her mouth. So modestly dressed, the sapphire ring seemed even larger than Reverend Beale remembered and appeared to glow from within like a possessed marble.

Witchcraft. The word played at the back of Reverend Beale's mind as it always did when he thought of her until he took the broom of his brain and swept it back into dark corners.

"Your housekeeper brought me some refreshment. It was no trouble to wait."

"You are such a love to be so kind in this weather. I simply cannot abide the summertime here. I've been begging David to take us to Maine in August, but he says the children love it here in the summer."

Her voice dropped low. "He indulges them, I'm afraid."

"I am surprised, Mrs. Radcliffe, that we never see your husband at church these recent Fridays that you've attended with the children."

Her hand swished in the air, dispersing the question.

"Oh, David travels with work and he leaves the matters of the house and children to me. You know what they say, a woman's work is never done and all that."

Anna threw herself languidly along a settee across from Reverend Beale and aimlessly fanned her swan's neck with a magazine she'd discarded earlier on the coffee table. It created a soft flicker of a breeze that toyed like a child's finger at the carelessly fastened neckline of her dress until the little invisible hand pulled back the fabric so gently and fleetingly as to almost be missed. But Reverend Beale captured the unmistakable swell of flesh beneath that flimsy façade, and the curve of his mother's breast returned to his memory and his face flamed with shame.

"I'll get right to the purpose of my visit," said Reverend Beale, repressing the memory. "I wonder why your extended family has not come to worship?"

"Who? Daddy? Reverend if it wasn't so hot, I'd be laughing myself right off this seat. You're a blessed man if my father never darkens your door."

"But you have a sister, do you not?"

"Jane? Well I suppose so, yes, but Jane spends too much time with horses and their little Irish groom to be worried about religious matters." A flash like heat lightening lit up Anna's eyes. "Perhaps I shouldn't have said that. I do have a tendency to say too much."

Reverend Beale sipped his tea.

XII

Alden liked to walk in the evening. It was a warm dusk when she headed toward the Powells' driveway, the sky clotted with humidity so that the sun setting was like light being submerged in dishwater. She wasn't surprised when Bruce emerged in the twilight. It was their way to meet sometimes like this, when the work was finished and there was some precious daylight left. Alden caught up to Bruce and they walked on together past the entrance to the Powells' house with its sparse hedge along the roadside, and out to where the cornfields unfurled in long, uninterrupted currents of green. They talked about farming, and harvesting, and a little about family, and a bit about themselves, but there was no room in their lives for dreams any bigger than their farms, so mostly they talked about work, which was the mainstay of their lives, or were silent. They were happy that way.

"Look at those deer out there," said Bruce, pointing to slow bobbing heads where the corn met the horizon. "Must be two dozen of them."

"Makes me think of venison and winter," said Alden, following his glance. "Summer seems to last forever, but it'll be gone soon."

"Your workers busy?"

"They're thinning fruit." She thought briefly of each of the men residing back at her farm, her mind touching on their faces with a bittersweet hope, but they all faded. "They're pretty busy so we keep out of each other's way."

Bruce nodded and they continued to look at the deer in silhouette against the fading sky until their lines faded into murky humidity. Bruce reached out and held Alden's hand and felt the same lunge in his heart he'd known for so many years, the thrill of partaking in this intimate ritual of touch with her. Alden linked her fingers through his and registered fleeting thoughts of comfort. The closeness ignited an old, protective inclination in Bruce.

"You heard much about the new church?"

"I figured that church had been around for one hundred years."

Alden let Bruce's hand go and they began to walk back toward their homes.

"Not the old church. The new church. The tent church. You really are no good at keeping up with local gossip, Alden."

She laughed a quiet little chuckle that danced gently over Bruce's heart.

"I wouldn't know gossip if you handed it to me."

"Some guy came by the house and talked to mom about some meeting," he continued. "You know my mother. She fed him up real good and brought down the family Bible and told him about losing Wayne to the influenza and Mitchell to the war and that baby in the ground and my father's trouble with his bad leg from when he fell out of the hayloft when he was a kid. She probably talked him right out of the house. Haven't seen him much since."

"He's been to our house, too. I don't know why he makes me so nervous, but he sits and talks to Pop and that seems to keep Pop calm, so I suppose there's no harm in it."

They walked on in silence. Mosquitoes landed on Alden's face and arms with their prickly feet and she waved long fingers over herself, caressing them away. They passed the

Powell drive, but Bruce continued on up the road. It was getting dark now and he would see her home, put her on her porch, watch her go inside, know she remembered to close and lock the door.

"How's your grandfather feeling?"

In the falling dark, her sigh could be felt more than heard.

"Confused. There's good days, but not many. Night is worst. It scares me sometimes."

"It's okay to be afraid of someone who forgets who you are. That's natural."

"I don't mind so much when he doesn't know me. It scares me when he doesn't seem to know himself."

Bruce thought of shaving in the mirror each morning, of the rhythm of it, monotonous but also familiar. He imagined looking in the mirror and watching himself fade away very slowly and understood Alden's terror.

"Are you going to make out okay this year, I mean if he starts having more bad days?" he asked.

"The men are here."

"But what about after?"

They reached the Forths' house. Alden had not thought to put on the porch light and the house was dark and quiet. Bruce stepped on the porch first as if to clear away any monsters in the shadows, and when he did he kicked something.

"What is it?" asked Alden, having heard the slight thud.

Bruce reached down and picked up a small glass bottle. It was wet and he realized it had been full of water. In the half-light he was able to make out a few strands of wildflowers scattered on the porch. He stuffed them in the bottle's neck and handed it to Alden. Her face was blank.

"How strange," she said.

"I think it's a gift," said Bruce, shoving his hands in his pockets. Alden was dismissive.

"Maybe Pop left it for me," she said, even as she remembered that the door was locked from the outside. There was no way he could have gotten onto the porch. Caught in her own confusion, she wanted Bruce gone.

"Have a good night. Tell your parents hello from me."

"Good night, Alden. Be careful."

It was a strange thing to say, and as he lumbered off the porch he wished to start the entire evening over again and end it differently. Then he felt the full weight of the thirty-five years he and Alden shared and was almost comforted by the unlikelihood that either of their lives would ever change all that much. As he headed toward home he noticed the shadow of a man standing off in the darkness. Bruce stopped, hoping his eyes could make out more detail in the dark, but he only caught the movement of something pale retreating – flesh or maybe blonde hair. But he knew it was a man and he knew whoever he was, he too, had been watching to see that Alden got home safely.

After Bruce left, Alden sat at the kitchen table turning over the bottle vase in her hands. There were traces of dirt and faded paper where a label must have been years ago, but the glass was brilliant blue and there was a pattern of flowers in relief above where the medicine label was once adhered. The vase had held Queen Anne's lace, but it did not handle well the trauma of being kicked on the porch. The heads drooped.

She got up, threw the flowers away, and set the bottle back on the table. Suddenly restless and stifled in the warm house, she wandered out and into the orchard. Like the air, thick with humidity, she walked slowly, touching the freckled orb of a ripening peach on occasion, but not feeling the firm, woolly flesh against her fingertips because her mind was elsewhere, beyond the trees that normally grounded her. As the darkness deepened the color of light in the orchard, she walked neither with purpose nor without, lost in a veil of memory that closed around her like the green shroud of the peach trees in the gloaming of evening.

Sleepwalking although awake, Alden walked until she found a place in the orchard where she could sit with her back against a tree trunk and still see the rising moon through the tree branches. It was too hot to wear her hair loose, but now she pulled it down and over one shoulder where it rippled in a russet curve. "Like the mane of a wild horse," was what Charlie Payne had said the summer he was Alden's lover.

"Have you ever seen the mustangs, Alden?" he questioned her one night as he stroked her long hair.

"You can hear them before you see them, because their hoofs are so loud, so loud it's like, well, like thunder. Or heartbeats – really loud heartbeats. And you feel your own heart beating, too, because you're scared to see that much horse flesh moving wild, but you're excited too, you know, because you can feel their wildness and you just want to throw yourself into that crazy, loud herd and get carried away. Do you know that feeling?"

When he looked at her then, she knew he was there with her but not. He was far away on a western plain with an excited glimmer in his eye that she imagined was the same one would see in one of those free roaming horses just living to protect its wildness. She tried to go there with him but the boundaries of her imagination ended just outside the valley in which she lived, and she could not quite see herself standing next to Charlie in a vast grassland being whipped by wild mustangs.

"You'd love it out there Alden," he said, returning them both to the orchard. He buried his head in her hair.

"I'll take you there someday. You'll see. You'll see the ancestors to your pretty mane of hair."

He made himself laugh and to Alden he was like a child, and she stroked his head and he stroked hers and she said, "Yes Charlie," because it was an easy and pleasant thing to say, though she knew she would never go with him. And as they stroked she continued to say, "Yes, Charlie," until he was not at all like a child to her, but a man, and the stroking ceased to be pleasant and became more urgent. When Alden wrapped herself around him her mane of hair fell over them like a cloak.

Now, she stroked her hair alone and tried to follow her thoughts, but they were as bees gathering pollen from many flowers, unwilling to sit down and be obedient. She thought of Bob Johnson and his steady faithfulness to the farm, of the young boy Will, so full of energy and, she believed, secrets, and of John Gray who alerted in her some sense of unruly danger. Her mind lingered for a moment on Nick, before she pushed him away and replaced him with the image of Reginald. She thought about the undeniable stench of age, of his strange new companionship with the evangelical reverend who visited with more frequency than Alden liked, though she could not say why. Then, surprising even herself, she thought of Bruce Powell, her mind wandering above the trees and over the sheep pasture, beyond the property fence and down the adjacent hill to the Powells' clapboard house and the window on the second floor. But when she tried to look inside, it was dark. Alden had never even seen Bruce's bedroom. His life away from her was a darkened pane of glass that reflected her own face back to her.

She turned away from the blackened window, grounded again in the orchard. Her orchard, really, though she could never quite think of it that way, not in her heart. It was Reginald's orchard, her father Albert's orchard even, but never hers. She was merely a steward. But wouldn't it belong to her soon? And what would she do then?

It had gotten dark. She looked at the moon, high in the sky, at how it beamed through the leaf canopy and made shadowy fish on the grass whose schools moved in a breeze so delicate it was imperceptible. And yet, there was heat lightning, too, small explosive bursts of blue and orange light. The world was dynamic and contrary, and she thought, *if only I could catch this little bit of world in my hand and slow it down for a moment, I could see if from every angle and understand it and then I would be free.* But her palms were empty and warm.

Night in the country is not quiet. The cacophony of crickets, cicadas, June bugs, and other creatures can be deafening. Beneath this familiar melee, Alden heard something distinctly human—the shuffling of feet—and waited, quiet and partially hidden, until she saw Reginald shuffle past her tree, the moon bestowing a silver sheen on his white hair. A wood nymph now, she followed behind him, keeping close to the shadowy trees until he walked out of the orchard and into the grassy border of the pasture. She stopped, a deer on the verges, and watched as he laboriously lay down in the grass. Then, his joints moving more freely, he extended his arms and legs so that he was a star beneath the moon.

Alden stayed there in shadow, transported to the day Reginald found God in the orchard, and a little emotion stirred deep in her, something like panic, and she knew she needed to intercede, to pull Reginald up and away from the night and put him in his bed. Yet she felt the space between them was as fragile as glass, and if she broke it to get to him he might crack as well. Instead she sat down at the orchard's edge and waited, and time moved in a seamless ripple without beginning or end, and her thoughts were quieted watching its smooth passage until Reginald got up, first to his knees, then, pushing himself carefully onto one foot then the other, like a colt unsure of its new legs. She followed him back to the house. Inside she stopped him as he mounted the stairs.

"Where have you been, Pop? It's late. We should both be in bed."

"Have you seen the moon? I always said Georgia had the prettiest summer moons."

"This is Maryland, Pop," she said, almost in a whisper for herself to hear. She knew he wasn't listening.

"Most people don't like the summer here. Say it's too hot. But I love a Georgia summer. You get out there and see it," he continued as he walked up the stairs. "I always say there's nothing to compare to a Georgia moon in summer."

XIII

The driveway to Robert Scott's home was the grandest Reverend Beale had ever seen. His aging motorcar turned in at elaborately scrolled wrought iron gates set securely into looming brick pillars. Set into the masonry of each was an ornamental shield with the family crest subtly rendered, an eagle holding an oak branch in its massive talons. Reverend Beale moved slowly over the smooth dirt drive lined with manicured forest and wondered, with a touch of jealousy, at the character of a man who could so ably control the madness of nature. Emerging from the woods, the drive swept away to the right past the meticulous grid work of horse pastures and into an alley of massive boxwood bushes where the reverend stopped the car and looked down onto a sprawling manse of stone.

Like all stately homes, this too gave an intimidating welcome, for only those who truly belonged to its equal class of wealth would ever feel really comfortable there. Reverend Beale knew there would always be tics that would give lesser people away, even those with good upbringing. All but those who truly belonged would be slightly alarmed by the house's size, overwhelmed by its opulence, and lost in its affluent heritage, their bemusement manifesting in small but telling ways: overly formal mannerisms, extraordinary politeness, and a certain fidgetiness that could never quite be masked. Reverend Beale's sensitive nose tested the air. It was early morning and a heavy dew had washed everything clean so that the green notes of cut grass and clipped boxwood mingled pleasantly with the musky undertones of warming horse flesh from the groomed animals in the nearby field. It was the perfectly orchestrated perfume of the rich, one of the reverend's favorite smells, not only because there was a quiet corner of his soul that enjoyed refinement, but because where there was affluence, there was always sin in abundance—the deep, hidden, pure, horrid, sin that could only manifest in the idleness of the very wealthy.

He backed the car up away from the house and took the road where it split to the left, up over a swale that artfully shielded guests on the road from the inner workings of the barns. It was just after sunrise, and the barn was wide awake with activity. Robert Scott's barn was as impressive as his house, a stone structure with stalls made of cedar with wrought iron accents, big, ornate doors facing onto a center aisle. Reverend Beale walked inside with needless caution; there was barely a stray piece of straw to mar the immaculate aisle, much less his shoes. Several horses dropped their heads over their doors to snuffle at him as he passed, the kind ones hopeful he might rub their head or proffer a treat from his flattened palm, the nastier ones wishing to sink their teeth into his gray-tipped hair. He balked at their massive heads and their thick musky smell; he disdained pleasure horses as the playthings of the wealthy, and he feared the rawness of their energy, their unapologetic musculature, and their sheer size.

Ronan came out of the tack room and startled for a moment at a stranger in the barn.

"Can I help you, sir?"

"I think you're just the man I am here to see," said Reverend Beale. The two men shook hands and the feel of rough calloused skin on his own smooth palm made him shudder. Reverend Beale was on eye level with Ronan, but the boy's lithe frame and slight stoop of the shoulder made the reverend think of a taller man. He looked closely at Ronan, rubbing his chin. He was really just a boy, probably no more than twenty, a naughty lost child far from home.

"I do not believe I've had the opportunity to invite you to my Friday evening prayer service," said Reverend Beale. "I'm starting to get quite a little following, and I'd love it if you could join."

The boy sat down on a stack of hay bales releasing a sweet, warm smell that made Reverend Beale sneeze.

"I'm a Catholic, sir, so I'm afraid you won't see me. No offense, of course, but where I come from, church is in a church with a priest. I don't go in for American Protestantism. My Ma would come across the ocean and box my ears."

The boy laughed, but it petered out into a little choking sound when Reverend Beale loomed over him, his face suddenly stern.

"Your mother is the least of your worries. I've heard rumors that you have been dallying where you should not, young man, and I want you to know, I'm not afraid to go to your employer and test whether those rumors are true."

"Now wait a minute, you're way out of line," Ronan tried to get up, but Reverend Beale was so close to him, his big square body would not let Ronan get his footing to stand up. Instead he squirmed on the hay bales. He hated being at that disadvantage, Reverend Beale could tell. He also knew the seed of suspicion Anna had planted was correct. Only liars leapt to righteous indignation. The little triumph made him bolder. He put his hands on the boy's shoulders.

"I am here, dear boy, to help you. I would hate to see good, young people trapped in a public scandal. I'm simply here to offer you deliverance from the evil ways that have obviously overcome you. You are far from home – it is understandable. But now, you need to atone for what you have done. If you do not, I will need to speak with your employer."

Ronan's face was red now with anger. "This is blackmail!"

Reverend Beale let his hands drop away and he stepped

back. "That is a very vile word to use, especially with someone who is giving you a chance to clean your actions and your soul before anyone need know about it."

"I'm a Catholic, didn't you hear me? A Catholic." Ronan finally was on his feet. He kicked the stack of hay then kicked it again, so hard that the top bale tumbled down and split apart in a honey-colored explosion, and the air around them was full of the smell of warm sunshine and harvest. "If there's anything I've done wrong, I'll tell it to a priest. A *real* priest. So you can keep your nose out of my business."

Reverend Beale brushed hay dust off the breast of his jacket with the backs of his hands. This shouting and bluster meant nothing to Reverend Beale. His point was already made, and now he only needed to execute a graceful departure. Reverend Beale shook his head.

"You are a passionate young man, I see that, so all I can say is mine is an open house of God and whenever you are ready to mend your soul, I will welcome you. But I warn you, do not think I am blind to what is going on here."

All the horses in their stalls watched as Reverend Beale strode passed their snuffling, nickering muzzles. He did not look back because he did not need to; he had nothing to fear from a youthful work hand, not to mention a papist. No, his work here was already complete. All one needed to do was put the fox in the chicken house. It was a waste of energy to force the fox to eat. Reverend Beale stepped into the daylight at the end of barn aisle, and it ate him up like a flame.

Jane Scott saw the strange car disappearing down the driveway. Robert Scott was returning that day having spent the week in the city at his club. Few enough visitors came randomly in the day when he was home; a car in the driveway was a real oddity when he was away. Jane walked down to the barn with a strange sense of foreboding.

The horses made nickering sounds of welcome when she came into the barn. She stopped at each stall to scratch the ears of the heavy heads that bowed and she felt the simple joy that can come from giving affection. She did it so rarely, with animals and with Ronan. She was embracing her mare, Isadora, around the neck and the horse was nestling her soft nose into Jane's waist when Ronan touched Jane lightly on her shoulder. She raised her head from the horse and looked at the soft, resigned look in Ronan's eyes, and she started to cry.

"You are so lovely, Jane, really, the sweetest girl I've known." His voice was gentle, and he raised it to be heard over her rising sobs. She thought she could drown out what she knew he was going to say and then it would not be real. Instead, his voice became firmer.

"There are starting to be rumors and if your Dad gets any more suspicious I could lose my job, and I wouldn't want any trouble for you."

"I don't care about me," she wailed. "What could he do to me that he hasn't already done? He hates me, and I hate him."

"Don't say things like that, you're too good. This way, I'll always be here for you, in the barn, like an old friend."

Like her words, once her tears began, they seemed endless and now, the two merged together as she desperately clung to the two things she loved, her horse and Ronan. She heard herself weeping out the silliest things about how much she loved him and how the rumors would fade away and that he was the only joy she had in the world. She hated how young she sounded, how desperate. Ronan kissed her head.

"It's over, sweet Jane."

The words sobered her. She let go of Isadora and wiped her eyes. Ronan stepped away from her, perhaps uncertain what might happen next, but Jane only looked at him with red, baleful eyes.

"How did it all go wrong?" she asked.

"That new priest. He came by today and made a bunch of threats. I guess we weren't careful enough."

Jane sucked in a huge breath and her pretty, round face went hard.

"That bitch."

With that, she turned and ran out of the barn.

Jane Scott was not a gifted driver. She was not, in actuality, a licensed driver. Robert Scott thought driving was a frivolous pastime for women and Jane never saw the need to learn on her own, knowing from an early age that attempts to make her life larger than her father's estate would be futile and lead to disappointment. But on the morning of her break-up with Ronan, when the heat of embarrassment and sadness was still burning at her back, and as she ran away from the barn as if the structure were on fire, she headed directly to the garage and asked the driver to bring around one of Robert Scott's vehicles. Aware of his mistress's lack of driving prowess but hesitant to defy a lady of the house, the driver ventured an offer to drive Miss Jane somewhere.

"Is there no one here who takes me for an adult?" she shouted at the man, who was so stricken by his docile mistress's sudden anger that he actually jumped back slightly before hurrying into the garage to bring out the largest and most durable of Robert Scott's motorcars.

Behind the wheel, Jane's rage was momentarily flummoxed by the reality that she was uncertain how to get the car into gear, and for a moment she thought with humiliation that she might need to call the driver back for assistance. Then she shoved hard on the gearshift so that it made a loud and horrible sound like a bone being ground into powder and she slammed on the gas. The car leaped forward, causing Jane's head to jerk forward and bang against the steering wheel. With stars in her eyes and moving in fits and starts, she motored down her father's long driveway, onto the country turnpike, and to the entrance of her sister's home, where she bravely pressed hard on the gas and chugged uphill, gaining momentum so that she sped up to her sister's front door, where she slammed on the brakes, and the car promptly stalled.

The blaze of anger that fueled Jane's brave journey

between driveways was tempered when Anna opened the front door and stepped into the glare of morning in a white shift with the sun glinting off her like a knife. *No more*, Jane said to tighten her resolve. *No more sweet Jane.*

"Why Jane, I had no idea you knew how to drive. Does Daddy know you've taken the car for a spin? No, I don't think so. You are getting to be a naughty one, aren't you Jane?"

For a terrifying moment Jane was paralyzed in the car, her resolve melting under Anna's acidic charm.

"Are you going to get out of that car and come inside and sit with me, dear Jane, or did you just come to stare at the front door?"

As she got out of the car, Jane regretted having come. Anna was immaculate in the shift dress, her face lightly powdered and her hair perfectly combed into its bob. She was smoking a cigarette, which leant her an air of sophistication despite her casual attire, and when she placed a hand on her hip it only accentuated her tiny frame. Jane felt the mat of her brown curls, already tight and unruly in the humidity, clumping against her round, wet cheeks. Under the scythe of Anna's adult urbanity, Jane felt like a contrite child.

"You are a complete mess, dear," Anna stated, as if knowing her sister's mind. "Is something wrong?"

There was no sense in Jane trying to mimic her sister's cool refinement. Instead, she unleashed a maelstrom of words and tears in hopes that sheer volume could simply knock Anna over and when Jane was finished her sister would be covered in dust, her hair amok and her pale skin bruised from her verbal torrent.

"How could you, Anna? How could you tell on me to that, that meddling priest friend of yours? Ronan told me, he told me you sent Daddy to talk to him, but I never dreamed you'd be so low to enlist that revivalist. I've never done anything to you but stay out of your way and yet here you come and just roll over the one thing that's given me any joy. You always do that, Anna, you always ruin everything. You are selfish and, and spoiled and horrible!"

Jane knew it was not the most erudite oration she'd ever given, but the power of her emotions ran hotter and faster than her tongue. Sadly, when she'd finished, Anna was still standing, smoking her cigarette and showing no signs that Jane's verbal assault had landed a single blow.

"Jane, I have no idea what you are talking about. But clearly you are upset. Would you like to come inside? You always were so fragile."

Anna's patronizing words touched a spark in Jane's resolve. She drew herself up, reaching deep within her breeding to a touchstone of natural haughtiness she'd not realized she possessed.

"You know exactly what I'm talking about and no I will not step inside your horrid house, you nasty bitch. No one else could possibly have uncovered my feelings for Ronan; no one else could possibly have cared -- except for you. And now you're using me to get back at father. Well, I won't have it. I intend to go back to my quiet little life and if you won't let me then, well…"

Anna threw down the cigarette in disdain and crushed it with the tip of her shoe.

"Then what, Jane? Really, these are big girl games you are playing and if you'll forgive me for saying so, my sweet girl, you are completely out of your depth. You have nothing to leverage over me, and now that you've opened your big silly mouth and confirmed what I'd guessed, I have everything to leverage over you. And while I'm sorry that your feelings have been hurt, you really need to stop being such a stupid silly child."

Jane felt the desire to retreat, the sense of panic that comes to those who are so unseasoned in confrontation they feel defeat like a physical blow before a victor has even been named. But she had nowhere left to go but forward. Retreat would not bring relief.

"Well, what if I tell David about all the men you had before him. What then?"

"Please, Jane," said Anna with a little laugh, "You don't

actually think that you are going to hold one ounce of sway over David, do you? You are far sillier than I thought. Besides, David knows there were other men; that's why he wanted me. What's the point in winning a woman no one else is competing for?"

"Well, I could make things up. I could tell father terrible things. I could tell everyone in the valley what a bad mother you really are. I know you don't like your own children. You might put a good face on it, but I know. You're no better than father. You will do away with the children the second they're old enough to go to boarding school."

Anna stepped closer to her sister, so close their faces were practically touching, though Anna had to crane hers slightly to be in line with Jane's. Warm air currents moved between them and Jane felt a stray hair tickle her forehead, smelled the delicate floral essence of Anna's scent.

"Look here, little sister. If you intend to become a liability to me I will have no recourse but to pulverize you. When I'm finished, you will never set foot out of the library at Avon Ledge, much less circulate in society—good, bad, or indifferent society. Now get out of my driveway. If you even know how." She spat out the last words then whisked around and reentered her house, unhurriedly. Jane got in the car and sat for a long time, stewing, trapped with the smell of her own sweat and the lingering sweetness of Anna's perfume.

When Anna pulled up in front of Avon Ledge Farm later that afternoon she'd exchanged the white shift for a formal, deep blue dress and she was wearing her hat and gloves. The Roadster spewed rocks onto the entryway and peppered Robert Scott's urns of geraniums. Jane heard the car approaching and met her sister in the hallway.

"What are you doing here?"

"I came to speak to Daddy. There are important adult matters to discuss. Pardon me, Jane."

Anna pushed past her and headed through the library to Robert Scott's office. Before she shut the door, Anna turned to her sister.

"You gave me no choice. Just remember that. Your behavior brought us to this."

Before Jane could think to protest, the door was closed in her face, and she slinked upstairs to her bedroom, ruminating on what her sister could possibly be saying below. Was it possible that Anna hadn't actually known about her and Ronan until she told her herself this morning? The thought had been lurking at the back of her head all day. Well, certainly she knew everything she needed now.

Jane could not press her ear to the floorboards and hear through the wood and the cobwebs and the abandoned mice nests the reverberations of her sister's lilting, sweet voice as she outlined Jane's barnyard indiscretions, and offered her father the choice to come with her to the new church or have her tell all their social friends that Jane was having an affair with a barn hand.

"Jane, get down here."

Her father's voice boomed up the stairway. It was the first time in recent memory that Jane could remember her father addressing her by name, much less summoning her to him, and hearing the anger in his voice, the suppressed rage she'd heard so often when her mother still lived in the house, and over the many years since Anna had moved to the valley, she was afraid. Jane had only one real talent and that was for disappearing, for being so insignificant and small and meaningless as to be nonexistent, and she called on that power now, the gift of nothingness, which carried her down the back stairway, out the kitchen door where the maid cleaning silver never even raised her head to acknowledge her departure, and out into the yard to hide behind her tree stump where her kittens bounded happily into her lap. Their mother, with her keen sense of survival, tasted danger in the air and slinked away under a bush.

Robert Scott was aging. His hair was the flat gray of worn stone and his shoulders had lost the breadth and bulk of youth, but he was still tall and lean and strong and he covered the space between the house and the stump with straight, determined strides.

"I saw you, Jane, you cowardly girl. Get out here and do not run away from me as if you were a child."

No sooner had she come out from behind the stump and stood before her father then his hand came quick and solid across her face, so hard and shocking it knocked her to the ground where she stayed, on her knees, too shocked to cry.

"I always knew you were a disappointment—a disappointment like all your sisters, but now, now you disgust me."

He spit his words out in quiet, clipped tones, the feel of them in his mouth a sickening aftertaste he couldn't hold on his tongue.

"I don't know how I let you get by me, how I let you slip by when your sisters all went on to respectable, adult lives fitting their upbringing and their heritage, while you got away from me and in my earnestness to look the other way, you've become a vile little harlot who cares nothing but for a filthy Mick and for horses and for, for," as he stuttered the tight hand he held on his anger fell free and he screamed at her.

"And for cats!"

He swiped one of the kittens off the ground by the back of its neck so that the animal, a black cat with a few white wisps on its belly, hung prone in the air with its legs stiff in front of him. Jane tried to say "no" but her jaw was stiff and sore, and she knew he would never listen to her anyway.

"Is this what you care about, Jane? After all I've given you? After I left you alone and didn't force you to school like your sisters?"

He shook the kitten, which tried to meow but found even its mouth was frozen under Robert Scott's grasp.

"You've shamed me with little girl pastimes and silly, childish affairs. Do you care nothing for family? For me? For your own dignity?"

His anger was a storming wave now. He was shouting, completely without composure, and the wave crested and tumbled down, crushing Jane beneath its wrath, rolling her over and over in the rocky ocean bottom. In one swift movement he grabbed the kitten's head and deftly twisted it while he jerked it down and away from its body. The animal let out a shocked cry, abbreviated by a decisive snap, which cured Jane of the pain in her mouth and she cried, "No!" and threw herself at her father's hands, too late.

He dropped the dead kitten at his feet as if the life leaving it would soil his hands. The stormy waters calmed, and he was measured as he said, "We are bound together, Jane. I cannot get rid of you without drawing attention to myself and what you've done. You've put me in an extremely awkward position with your poor judgment. You've allowed this so-called minister to gain a foothold in our private affairs that he or your sister won't hesitate to capitalize upon. You will never see that boy again. You will never defy me again. You will be the picture of obedience and contentment in public. You will go with me to this Godforsaken religious hoe-down in which you have embroiled us with your stupidity, and you will say nothing to anyone. Hopefully, I can convince your mother to take you in Paris this autumn. Until then, and while you are in my home, you will stay out of my sight, out of my hearing. I do not even want to smell the stench of you. Do you understand?"

Jane knelt at his feet, cradling the dead kitten and sobbing, rocking back and forth as she tumbled in the aftermath of Robert Scott's stormy rage. She could not summon words and only nodded her head.

"I addressed you. Stop being a foolish girl and respond to me as a woman. If you will perform a woman's acts, you will speak to me as a woman."

He waited as she laid the kitten aside, pushed herself off her knees and to her feet, wiped her eyes and looked him in the eye.

"Yes, Father."

If Robert Scott were a more perceptible man, he might have noticed that there was a hardness to Jane that was not there a moment before, that the curtness of her reply was due

to more than just the painful swell rising on her cheek, that there was something in her eyes, a spark there that he could easily have recognized had he only cared enough to look for it, for he'd seen it for years when he glowered at Anna. So lost was he in having crushed yet another useless child, having bent her to his will and masterfully regained the balance of power in his home, that he saw no change in his daughter at all.
He indicated the dead kitten with the tip of his foot.

"Bury it."

She gingerly picked up the animal and curled up against the tree with it as Robert Scott returned to the house. The other kittens fumbled out of the hollow of the tree trunk, sensing solemnity but unable to suppress their inherent need to play as well. Smelling death, they stepped away from Jane and frolicked further off in the grass. Jane watched them for a few moments, then stood and with dry eyes, carried the dead kitten toward the garden shed to find a spade.

That Friday evening, Robert Scott left the driver at home and steered his own car to the patch of grass where Reverend Beale had erected his tent so many weeks before. Jane sat by his side in the car. Both stared straight ahead through the windscreen with such intensity one might have wondered how they didn't shatter the glass. Once Robert Scott settled the car in the deep grass, he and his daughter proceeded to the log seating area, speaking to no one, maintaining their gazes forward with the attention of sentinels. When Anna glided toward them with the children, barefoot and tugging at her legs, Robert Scott kissed his daughter on her cheek.

"Lovely to see you, Daddy. You'll find this all too charming, I'm sure."

Reverend Beale did a much better job than the other local residents present at hiding his excitement that he'd gained such an illustrious sinner. Women murmured to each other and men shuffled awkwardly forward, extending weather-beaten hands. Robert Scott ruefully shook hands with Chester French, Ned

Pfieff and a host of other people who only knew him through the services they provided to his estate. There was nothing to say beyond pleasantries. The men shuffled awkwardly back to hover near their wives, the women's ranks closing around the shared pastime of conjecture.

Once again, Jane had become invisible.

Reverend Beale took his position at the front of the group and began his throat clearing, deep breathing ministrations. Little clutches of neighbors broke up and went to take their seats, hesitated, then unknowingly, opened deferentially for Robert Scott, leaving a clear path to the seats at the front. Something in his presence reminded the congregants of an instinctive order. One at a time, each family followed in behind, taking the same seats they would have taken had this been a Sunday in Reverend Greene's church, everyone adhering to a way of being that wasn't necessarily right or wrong but simply the way it was done. Their numbers had grown; there were few free seats to be had, a success that brought Reverend Beale deep satisfaction.

When Reverend Beale stood in front of his congregation and took a moment to reflect before launching into his sermon, he took particular notice of the Scott family, of Robert and Jane sitting side by side in the front seats staring resolutely ahead, Anna sitting a few seats behind with her children in a picturesque heap at her feet, and smiled with satisfaction. Reverend Beale knew his techniques were unorthodox and his allegiances and tactics could be hard to comprehend. He knew that some might even take issue with his approach, but he understood that salvation was the ultimate goal and it was his job to get his followers there even if he dragged them to face their judgment. Robert Scott was a brute, of that Reverend Beale was certain, and the girl, Jane, was wayward and on a path to greater sin. Here, they could find peace as Reverend Beale once found peace from his own shattered home.

The ends justified the means and the means were excruciatingly successful as evidenced by the presence that day of Robert Scott and Jane. Reverend Beale was amassing a gigantic funeral pyre of sin and the stench of its burning left an acrid taste in the mouth of the townspeople, but Reverend Beale knew that when the air cleared everyone would breathe deep the sweet breath of salvation.

XIV

Ned Pfieff was still in disbelief at having seen Robert Scott at the new church. That's what people in the town had started to call it—the "new" church to distinguish it from the "old" church run by Reverend Greene. Of course, some people still went to both since Reverend Beale kindly had his service on Friday night while Reverend Greene continued to own Sunday morning. Going to both was just too much church for Ned, but he did like the company of getting out there under the open sky and watching the little children playing in the grass while they all prayed or really, while Reverend Beale talked, because he sure did talk a lot as far as Ned could tell. But sometimes he'd take his dog Holly with him to the new church and no one said a thing about it, so that seemed to make it just the right place for Ned.

But it sure didn't seem like the right place for Robert Scott. Even now, behind the wheel of his truck as he worked his way back to his own farm, Ned laughed to himself when he thought of that big blowhard sitting in the front of the congregants, with a look on his face like he'd sat on a thorn but had too much pride to tell anyone about it or ask anyone to remove it. He couldn't imagine what had happened to get Robert Scott out there with the common people in the grass, but it sure must have been a good story.

Maybe one of these Fridays he would get up the nerve to talk to Robert about his property line; Ned was pretty sure Robert's crops had pushed further and further onto Ned's field, but he did not yet have the gumption to challenge him about the encroachment. Robert Scott was a bully and Ned was getting too old for confrontation.

Not far from his own home Ned saw a slim young man standing on the roadside with a duffel bag. He slowed the car and hung out the open window.

"You need a ride, friend?"

"Aye, though I'm not sure where."

Ned heard the Irish accent and was carried for a moment back to a memory of the face of his wife, Lila.

"You're that Irish kid that works for Robert Scott, aren't you?"

"You can say *worked* for Robert Scott. I got sacked."

The two men were sitting in Ned's truck now, looking at the road ahead.

"Ah yep, I could see Robert being a taskmaster," said Ned, thinking again about the profits he lost while Robert Scott lined his already padded pockets. "Catch you stealing?"

"No, sir."

"Drinking on the job?"

"No, sir. I like to work. That's what I came here for. Why I came to America."

"Where you going now?"

"Maybe back to West Virginia. I worked there for a while."

Ned tried to touch the memory of his wife's face as he listened to Ronan's voice filling the cab of the truck like music, but when he reached the memory it faded, and he realized he was having a hard time remembering what Lila looked like. A new sadness moved through him. Ned was a man who knew love and lived every day with loss, and there was something in this boy that made him think of both. Though he didn't know Ronan's secrets and didn't want to know them, he felt a need within him to exercise his love on something other than Holly, who was sitting patiently in the bed of the truck. Listening to Ronan speak in the voice of Lila's family made him remember love and how long it had been since he'd dusted that emotion off and brought it into the sunlight. This seemed like a good time to do someone else a fair turn and see how his heart looked in the light.

"There's lots of work to do around here if you know where to find it," said Ned, thinking it might also stick in Robert Scott's craw to have the boy hang around. Whatever the boy had done, Ned felt sure it was more Robert's fault than the young man's. "The Forths' might still need able bodies to help with their peaches. And when the fruit harvests are over, I could use some help, too. It's not horse work, but it's honest money and you won't need to be on the road."

From the passenger side of the pickup truck, Ronan examined his options. He could get out and keep moving down the road where his gaze had settled or he could stay here in this truck and in this valley where things had already gone so wrong. He didn't know if this place could be big enough to hold him and Robert Scott and their secrets, big enough to bury them and start over. What he knew was that he was tired and on the road there was no telling when he might get a decent rest again. His arms were already aching from not working all day and he was restless to be busy again.

"Aye, I'd like to get back to work pretty quick, if you don't mind helping me."

Ned turned over the engine. "No problem. We'll go over and see Alden and Reginald tomorrow, see what can be worked out. You got a place to stay tonight?"

"No, sir."

"Well, you better come on back with me and Holly then. We'll fix you up for the night and start over in the morning."

Ned pulled onto the road and the two men and the dog continued to Ned's farm. He cooked them a supper of fried eggs, bacon and toasted bread, and they thought about the women they'd lost and the places they'd left behind. They spoke about horses and farming and weather and heat and rain, and Holly was happy to have an extra set of hands to pet her and to secretly feed her scraps under the table.

Bob Johnson swung a last crate of peaches into the back of the Forth's truck. Alden got in the driver's seat and turned over the engine. The workers retreated back to the lawn where Alden had left a plate piled with thick-cut ham sandwiches and jugs of lemonade. As he turned to his lunch, Bob patted Nick on the back and indicated the truck with his finger.

"You go with her, ya' understand?"

Nick only nodded and hopped into the passenger seat. As Alden pulled onto the road she snuck a glance at him from the corner of her eye.

"Why don't you tell them you speak English? They could be friends for you. Some of them, anyway."

"Why don't you marry that neighbor man of yours? He could be good company for you."

"It isn't the same. You must be lonely."

"Are you lonely? It isn't the same, alone and lonely."

The cab was hot and dust from the road filtered in through the windows and settled onto Alden's moist skin. Nick was inscrutable with his strange accent and his way of playing with words. She found herself spinning in the pleasant confusion of it all, found herself being drawn to him as the dirt road was drawn under the car, as the landscape outside blurred and melted away.

"The blue bottle on the porch the other night – you left it for me."

"It was something pretty I found in the orchard," said Nick. "It made me think of you."

They sat quietly for a while, bumping along the road. Alden took her time, enjoying being in the cab with Nick, the closeness of him, so close she could smell his body, the combination of sweat and soap. Nick watched the world passing by outside the window seemingly bored with the idea of conversation. Just as suddenly as their conversation ended it began again.

"Why do you always wear trousers, like a man?"

"It's easier to drive a tractor in trousers than a dress," Alden replied.

"Is this why you never marry? You don't want to put on a dress and be in the house?"

"I wear trousers because they are comfortable and because my father left many in good condition when he died. I do not marry because my family has bad luck in love."

Nick harrumphed.

"You don't believe that," he said.

"If you'd lived my life you would understand. Pop's wife left him, his son died having lost his own wife, my mother. Lord knows what happened to Pop's parents, but it must have been bad luck or he would not have ended up in a basket on a stranger's doorstep."

Nick was resolute.

"It's your believing this that makes it true. The world is full of terrible loss, terrible things worse than what you have seen. If everyone gave up on love and marriage over these little losses, humans would end."

His words stung Alden. Her well ordered life was broken into seasons and work. The superstitions and stories that softened the edges of her hard life gave it meaning and shape even as it sucked away its promise. No one had ever challenged her in this way. Without Nick's belief in her she felt bare. Without these truths she was nothing, as transparent as the glass in the windshield in front of her.

"Your grandfather and father – these were great loves they had?"

Alden, never one for a lot of chatter, found a sudden relief in talking.

"Pop talks about Francine like a wild horse: passionate, violent, spirited. And in the end, unbroken. I'm told I look like my mother but that she was very delicate. They say all the boys were wild about her. They piled bouquets of apple blossoms on her doorstep. Not my father. Reginald said he won her with peach ice cream, that he wore out his arm cranking the churn to make her peach ice cream."

It was the first time Alden had ever reiterated these stories. No one asked her about her family and it was always Reginald who told the stories, who carried the family history. Perhaps as he lost the ability to remember the Forth legacy it was Alden's turn to pick it up. Or perhaps, now that it was told, she would simply let it die away.

Nick leaned across the cab.

"I must tell you something important, Alden."

He laid his hand on her thigh and a fierce tremble shot through her. She gripped the wheel tighter.

"I do not like peaches."

Her laughter when it came was a delicate cascade and it was as though a thousand butterflies had been loosed in the cab.

The Forths' driveway was full of cars and trucks when Alden and Nick returned to the farm.

"What's all this?" said Alden, her voice so soft that Nick didn't know whether she was speaking to him or herself.

Ned Pfieff was standing in the yard with a young man Alden had never seen before and the door to the house was open. At the sound of her truck pulling in, the Reverend Greene stepped onto the front porch. Alden recognized Bruce Powell's truck but did not see him in the crowd. A small ball of dread gathered at the base of her neck and began to slide with sickening precision down her spine.

"What's all this?" she repeated to no one in particular as she swung out of the truck.

Ned, Reverend Greene, and the stranger exchanged glances, uncertain who should respond. Alden made the decision for them.

"Reverend, what's going on? Why are you all out here?"

Whether it had always been the case or it was evidence of

his constantly keeping company with his birds no one could know, but Reverend Greene's voice had a twittering quality to it that could make his sermons lively to listen to but also gave him the sound of a slightly hysterical woman when he was agitated.

"Everything's fine now, Alden," he squawked. "There was some confusion in town, but everything's okay now."

"But I was just drove through town."

"We've been here near an hour now," it was Ned speaking now.

The pitch of his voice descending, Reverend Greene gestured for Alden to come near. "Perhaps we should discuss this inside."

She turned back to look at the yard. Ned and the stranger were looking intently at their hands. Nick was standing by the truck. On the fringe of the orchard she saw Bob Johnson shooing the men back into the greenery. Had this not been her house, had her yard not been full of green grass and the flowers of deep summer, had she stumbled upon this scene somewhere that wasn't so obviously her home, she would have expected there to be a bloody body lying somewhere nearby given everyone's actions. She was overwhelmed with the need to disperse them all.

"Ned, what can I do for you?"

She noticed when she was closer that the stranger had a scarlet mark on his face headed to purple, like a blazing birthmark.

"Oh, I was hoping you could take on this boy for some work. He's not skilled with peaches, but I think he's a hard worker—"

Alden cut him short, turning to the orchard and lifting her voice ever so slightly so it carried like a breeze. "Bob, get out here, please."

Bob Johnson emerged from the foliage of the orchard.

"Take this man and find him a place in the cabin then get him to work."

She strode over to Nick and addressed him beyond

earshot of the others.

"Please keep the others away."

Before the action made sense to her, she reached out and laid her hand on his shoulder, felt for an instant the tensing of his muscles, the movement of flesh in her palm. "Thank you."

She returned on agile feet to the tumbled down house, nimbly dodged the reverend's out-stretched hand and walked into her home. Instinctively she went up the stairs into Reginald's bedroom where the curtains were half drawn. Bruce was standing in the window looking at the yard below. Alden stood beside him and followed his gaze to the driveway, to her truck. Unconsciously recalling an old custom he reached up to take her hand. Reverend Greene stepped into the room, but seeing their clasped hands, ducked back into the hallway. Reginald was lying on the bed, staring with unblinking eyes at the ceiling, but Alden saw with relief that his chest was heaving.

"He walked all the way into town," said Bruce in a monotone. "Walked straight into Reverend Greene's garden yelling that you'd left him, that everyone leaves him, that you'd been taken, and he wanted you back.

"Ned was driving by and heard the shouting. He helped get Reginald into the Reverend's car then he came to my place and told me there was trouble. By the time I got here the Reverend had calmed him down, but Ned said he was the dickens to get control of in town. Hit that poor Irish boy in the face I hear. Been like this since I got here," he said, indicating the comatose figure prone on the bed.

Alden sat on the edge of the bed and touched Reginald's hand. He did not move his gaze from the ceiling.

"I'm home, Pop. I'm sorry I left you."

He turned to look at her.

"Who are you? Why are you keeping me here? Where has everyone gone?"

"I am your granddaughter, Pop. I'm home now to take care of you."

Reginald looked back to the ceiling. "They all leave

sooner or later. In their time."

It was more than she could bear. She kissed his hand then got up and walked out of the room. Bruce came quickly behind her and the two almost collided with Reverend Greene in the hallway. There were too many people in Alden's house, too many men with their big feet and scruffy faces and heavy musky smells. She wanted to sweep them out like dust. She walked straight out of the house and breathed deeply, but there was no reprieve. It was midday and the sun was cooking the air to a thick custard that choked her until she coughed.

Bruce was behind her now, his hand resting on her back.

"It will be okay, Alden. We'll figure something out. Together."

But his touch, normally so calming, repelled her. She leaped off the porch. She turned her attention to Reverend Greene, now standing beside Bruce.

"I'm so sorry for the trouble, Reverend. I think it's under control now. I'll be sure to bring you some peaches real soon."

"Alden, I can stay. I'm happy to help —"

"No thank you, Reverend. I'll be fine."

"Of course. I'll come check on you in a few days, Alden. If you need anything…"

"Yes, thank you, Reverend."

He patted her shoulder and walked to his car. Ned was standing alone in the yard. Alden walked to him. He'd grown older since she'd seen him last, or perhaps she was simply sensing everything more clearly on that day, but his face seemed more wrinkled, the skin collapsing into perfect, round folds on his forehead. A large bead of sweat slipped from his balding head and navigated the contours of his skin and Alden was distracted for a moment thinking of hot wax dripping down the side of an old candle.

"I understand I'm obliged to you, Ned."

"Nah, Alden. You've done a good turn taking that kid in. We're even."

He started to walk to his truck then stopped.

"Good luck, girl," he added, though the years of Alden's

girlhood were long behind her. "If you need something, you holler."

Nick was nowhere to be seen. Only Bruce remained.

He was sitting on the edge of the front porch, he legs dangling into the daisies someone had planted in the front of the house, to cheer it up or to make it look less like it was falling down perhaps. Was it Francine? Rebecca? Certainly neither Albert nor Reginald ever turned their green thumbs to frivolous things like flowers. Like so many other remnants in the house, the daisies, too, were a legacy from someone long gone.

Bruce had a daisy in his hand, was plucking the petals and dropping them into the bed. Alden came and sat beside him.

"Does she love you or does she love you not?"

He dropped the flower. "I believe we all know the answer to that."

Alden sighed. She'd often heard people say "I have a heavy heart," but now she knew exactly what they meant. There was a weight in her chest like the organ within its walls that beat with vigor without her conscious vigilance had turned to stone when she was not paying attention. She laid her head on Bruce's shoulder. Had she seen the look in his eyes, had she known how much pain her touch brought him, had she known that like a heavy heart, a broken heart was not just a turn of phrase but a real thing, perhaps she would have thought to pick her head up. But unaware of how her hair brushed the thick skin of his cheek like a kiss, not knowing how her smell tempted his nostrils and filled his body with unrequited longing, not knowing how he had to hold his hands to keep from touching her face, she only rested there in silence aware of nothing but the weight in her heart and a terrible tiredness.

"It cannot continue like this, can it Bruce?"

Her voice, always so soft, was practically a whisper. The touch of her voice was so intimate he closed his eyes to relish the tones until they died away in his ear.

"But what will I do Bruce? We've always been unlucky in so many ways, but always lucky in farming. What am I to do?

Take a husband I can't love? Hire more men I can't afford? Pray?"

Even in the heat of summer she shivered, recalling Reginald in the orchard. "God is here," he had said. Perhaps now was the time for her to look for Him there again.

Bruce seized her quaking as an opportunity to put his arm around her. The feel of her warm, small body was like embracing a bird, a broken bird he had no power to fix. The only cure he offered her was love and it was a medicine she refused to take.

"Why can't you come stay with me, Bruce? I like you. I don't want anyone else. I couldn't bear having another man in the house, sitting in my grandfather's chair, filling his seat at the table. Why is it so wrong for me to want you here, not as my husband but as my friend?"

His arm dropped and he laid his hand behind Alden flat onto the rough wood of the porch. He felt its warmth, its rough texture, so like the word "friend" itself, kind and chastening. His hand moved on the board only to feel the pinch of a splinter lodge itself in his heavily calloused hand.

"Who is that light-haired fellow you came home with?"

Alden was surprised by this change in the conversation.

"Nick? He's a worker."

"I saw you touch him. Today, in the driveway. And he looks at you. Like a man shouldn't look at a woman he's not going with."

"Let's not talk about this, Bruce, please," Alden felt the loose ends of the conversation flying away from her like the strands of many balloons lifting uncontrollably into the air. "Let's change all the rules, and you can stay with me, and we'll care for my grandfather and the farm together. We can be happy that way, can't we?"

He lifted her head from his shoulder, examined the splinter in his hand.

"Do you see this, Alden?"

She looked at his palm, touched it with her long fingertips. "I can get that out for you."

"No, leave it," he said, stepping off the porch. "It's a good reminder. It will remind me of you."

With that he turned around and walked to his truck. Alden followed him.

"Where are you going? Can't you stay? Can't we fix this together?"

"I love you Alden, so I can't be your friend. You will always be this," he held his palm in the air as if making an oath. "You will always be pain to me, and I can't live with this anymore."

He got in his truck and was gone. Alden stood in the yard for a long time, the content of her day filling her just as the lawn filled with lengthening shadows until she realized that when she'd said to Nick, so many eons ago it seemed, that the two were alike in being alone, she hadn't really know the meaning of that word until now.

XV

And so Reginald descended like a whirlybird maple seed, spinning and falling with final, graceful speed. His moods became erratic, his moments of lucidity fleeting, his appetite non-existent. He developed new abilities, like speaking sentences with the words out of order. The worst were the moments when he was himself, when Alden latched onto the hope that the ailment was loosening its grip on his mind and he could return to her, whole. But always the illness returned, and with each effort Reginald made to surface himself in the great sea of his mind, it exhausted his spirit so that his descent back under water was more prolonged and more damaging than the last.

After his breakdown in the village, Alden began locking Reginald's bedroom door. She took breaks from working outside to check on him, afraid he might hurt himself. She hid sharp objects and flammable liquids, unsure whether this new incarnation of his illness might jump free of Reginald and threaten her or the house as well.

Where before there was the specter of the ailment of which no one spoke looming in the house, there was now a functional, breathing entity that lived like one possessed at one turn and like one whose soul had completely escaped this realm in the next moment. Shamed by her own thoughts, Alden found herself hoping for the latter, the days when Reginald seemed to slip the bounds of the earth and disappear into another world. Though his body breathed, his mind was elsewhere and Alden could get through her day without incident.

Like all men accustomed to farmer's hours, Reginald always woke early. But this new, possessed spirit preferred to keep to a mindless clock. Alden often heard him pacing his room at night or speaking to nonexistent visitors. He slept soundly in the warm mornings. Alden woke earlier than ever before and began her day sitting in a chair watching Reginald sleep. Somewhere along the years, fate tripped on its chronological timeline and reversed her role with that of Reginald so that she was now the guardian and he the child.

The peaches were ripening now. Alden would leave her grandfather's bedside early in the morning. In the blue glow of dawn she walked the rows of the orchard in bare feet leaving tracks across the dewy yard like footprints in sand. Inside the orchard she touched the trees, smelled the fruit, examined its skin for blemishes and stroked its silky fuzzed surface. Her stroking stirred old memories: her body bending into the trees as she reached her hand to touch a peach dripping downward from a high branch, her mind recalling the touches of men, one man, each year -- but not this year. Without her knowing it, Alden tapped into a well the night she fell on Frank in the orchard so many years ago. He touched her with intimacy, a touch that filled her and sustained her throughout the year until, like a nomad growing low on provisions, another picking season arrived, another man, and she stumbled into the oasis to gorge her deprived soul on food and drink before the autumn swept her back into the desert for months to come.

Now she wandered the oasis in a dream. She grew parched and brittle as her cycle of autumn to winter to spring to summer became a straight line again, reaching, unrelenting, to the horizon where the sun rose in the morning, tinting the air from blue to pink, reminding her another day was beginning—

another day to make the coffee and cook the bacon and fry the eggs to feed the men who left her full of peaches and bereft of all else.

The men were milling around the labor house when Alden exited the orchard, stretching and scratching and smoking or spitting streams of brown saliva into the tall grass. Alden walked past them all, directly into the house, her life tethered once more to the longitudinal line of routine that had guided it for so many years before Reginald suffered from the disease of the mind and she fell on Frank on a summer night.

In the kitchen, she put the coffee on the back burner to percolate and dropped slices of bacon in a cast iron skillet. Out of habit, she turned on the radio and Tchaikovsky rasped out of the small speaker, too small to hold the voluminous orchestra. Alden wished that the music could grow so large that it would crack open the radio and fill the room and cradle her on a flowing cushion of notes because sometimes making breakfast alone in the early morning for men you don't love can be the most lonely exercise. The music rasped in the background, and she began cracking eggs into a large bowl.

"He's Russian."

Having lived a protected life, a plain life, Alden had no reason to startle easily, and so she did not jump when Nick surprised her in the kitchen.

"The man whose music is on your radio. He's Russian."

"I don't know anything about the composers, not even most of their names. I just like the sounds."

Nick laughed the sad laugh that was becoming familiar to Alden. "I think that's the most important thing, liking the music."

Without a word he picked up a knife and started to slice the loaf of bread that Alden had placed on the counter and she cooked the eggs and flipped the bacon while he sliced and Tchaikovsky kept them company. When Nick was finished slicing, he stood next to her for a few minutes, pretending to watch her stir the scrambled eggs, then reached out his hand and laid its palm against the small of her back, just touching her there without moving, the warmth of his hand radiating through her cotton blouse. With his other hand he placed two delicate wooden hair combs on the counter. Alden picked one up and ran her fingers over the smooth teeth of the comb and the delicately carved flowers that adorned it.

"You made this?"

"Your grandmother's furniture, your grandfather's peaches, your mother's books, even your father's pants. Nothing here is your own. You deserve something that is yours. Something beautiful."

So softly it could have been a moth alighting she felt his lips graze her hair and the press of his palm on her back became more urgent. She leaned into its warmth and he slipped his arm around her waist, his palm firm on her belly, holding her against him so tightly she could feel the contours of his body and the moistness of his breath as he buried his head in her hair. Then there was the sound of men laughing just outside on the porch and Nick stepped away, picked up the coffee pot from the burner, grabbed a handful of old ceramic mugs by their handles and walked outside. In the desert of her mundane world Alden felt the comfortable cushion of grass beneath her feet and hope opened a small wellspring.

After Bruce walked out of Alden's life, there were no more evening strolls. She spent the twilight hours on the porch watching the sunlight disappear. She could feel Bruce's presence. He was so close, just over the hill, and yet he was gone from her. They were a country split in two, equals separated by a fence. She watched the darkness rise up like a curtain drawn out of the ground on the wings of lightning bugs that glimmered and flashed low in the grass and worked their way into the trees; and then it was so dark she could look at the stars, murky behind summer's humid veil, until tiredness overtook her and she checked on Reginald and collapsed into bed.

It was a very hot humid night that she was sitting on the

porch, waiting for Bruce, though not waiting as she knew he would not come, so perhaps creating a new routine for her evening, one of rest and not one of walking. She was sitting on the porch watching night arrive and the faint eruption of occasional heat lightning and wondering if the humidity was building enough that it might thunderstorm in the next few days, when Nick parted the darkness and asked if she would like to go for a walk. She looked inside where Reginald was asleep in his chair in the living room and slipped the new bolt she'd installed on the screen door, and then stepped into the damp grass where Nick waited, his back turned to the house and his hands clasped behind his back.

They walked out the driveway and turned onto the road, headed away from the Powells' and toward nothing in particular. Nick pointed to the daylilies, their bright orange dragon mouths, so garish in the daytime, now closed tight as old-fashioned bonnets in the evening. Alden pointed to the moon on the horizon, which rose from a thick haze and was stained a deep orange.

"It will be hotter tomorrow," said Alden. "And it will storm soon."

"How do you know?" asked Nick.

"You just do. You live in a place long enough, you know everything about it. There are no surprises."

They kept walking. Nick swatted a mosquito on his arm. Alden pulled the tip off a long blade of grass growing out of the rut on the roadside and played with it aimlessly.

"I used to think surprises were important," said Nick. "Now, I'm not so sure. I think about my old home and my life now. You are lucky with your routine, Alden."

"I know."

"Do you like poetry? Or books?"

"I don't really have the time. My grandfather used to read me Walt Whitman's poems, but I can't say either of us always understood them. I like that poems are short, so I have time for those."

"I don't read much either. My father – he always wanted

me to read, but I was better at play. But there's a Russian I like, Chekhov. I'll read you something from him one evening. I think you'd like it." He paused. "And he writes short stories, so they're very fast."

They laughed, Alden her delicate, soft laugh and Nick a true laugh, the first Alden had ever heard that didn't seem bittersweet. Alden wished they could walk on but it was quite dark and Nick suggested they turn back home. They did and Nick reached out and held Alden's hand, and a feeling that was familiar to her from other men rose up in her stomach and into her chest. Yet this was different and she couldn't place how but didn't quite care because it was lovely. When they reached the porch, Nick pulled her hand to lead her into the shadow of the house, placed his heavy palms on her shoulders and drew her into a soft kiss. Alden felt her world drop away beneath her feet.

He pulled back and the earth came up to meet her, but she knew then what was different. Her previous lovers brought her comfort. When her tongue touched her lower lip as she went into the house, she tasted liberation.

XVI

Each summer there are mushrooms that grow obtrusively in the yards of the valley, and when they are kicked and ripped apart, another inevitably emerges in another place, more rotund and unwelcome than the last. Similarly, Reverend Beale continued to arrive unannounced at homes throughout the valley. He was walking up to the Powell house just after dawn when the screen door swung open and Bruce came out. Bruce abruptly stopped on the front porch steps. Reverend Beale faltered for only an instant, then stepped forward, hand outstretched.

"So glad I caught you before you got to work."

Bruce stepped off the porch and shook the clergyman's hand.

"You're the tent minister," he said cautiously. "My mother already talked to you."

"I did speak with your mother, lovely woman. But I have yet to speak with *you*. Shall we walk?"

Reverend Beale turned and cast his arm into the yard, as if ushering Bruce on a tour of his own property. Bruce walked ahead, toward the barn and the animals that needed to be fed and watered, but Reverend Beale knew he had the man's attention, could feel the strain of suspicion pulsating off his skin. Where there is suspicion, there would be secrets.

"If you're here to recruit me to your service, I'm not going. We go to church on Sunday with Reverend Greene and that's that."

Reverend Beale chuckled and patted Bruce's back in an overly friendly gesture that failed sincerity. Bruce's back tightened, and Reverend Beale let his hand drop.

"Of course I would enjoy having your company, but I only came today to get to know you better."

"From what I hear, you've gotten far enough into people's business as it is."

Bruce let himself into the barnyard and hopped onto a wagon. He began pitchforking clumps of golden straw into the barnyard with determination.

"To minister well I believe I must know the people well. I have such limited time, I need to make the most of it. Now, tell me about you."

"You're lookin' at it."

The sun broke the horizon and lit up flying straw like gold dust. Reverend Beale recognized this was busy work, that Bruce could not handle idle hands, could not trust himself without some task in which to release a deep frustration boiling deep within.

"So close in proximity to the Forth farm and so close in age to Miss Forth, surely you are friends. In fact, I've heard you are her only friend."

"We're neighbors. That's all."

Bruce raked the last of the straw with a vengeful sweep of the pitchfork, and a great gust of straw showered onto Reverend Beale. For a moment he was busy with the task of both brushing off his suit and stemming a fit of sneezing. When he recovered himself, he was pleased. By trying to hide from his own bitterness, Bruce had given Reverend Beale all he needed to know. The wound was open; he need only explore its depth.

"Surely as neighbors then, you could come to my service together? Perhaps it would help create a friendship where there is now only neighborly courtesy? And I do worry for Miss Forth, all alone with her grandfather so unwell."

Bruce leaped off the wagon and got very close to Reverend Beale, who was suddenly very aware of the proximity of the pitchfork.

"Listen up. I don't want anything to do with you, and I don't want you on this farm again. And if you want what's good for you, you'll leave Alden alone, too. I don't care if you are clergy, she's bad luck that woman."

Bruce was taller than Reverend Beale and he dropped his shoulders to look the man right in the eye. There, Reverend Beale saw anger, but more importantly there was sadness. Bruce was not mad at Reverend Beale, he was mad at himself, at Alden.

Bruce turned and threw the pitchfork into the wagon, kicking up clouds of straw as he stomped through the barnyard and disappeared into a stall. Reverend Beale brushed the last strands of straw from his suit and suppressed a smile.

At the Forth farm, Reverend Beale found the house quiet. He walked across the yard, pausing on the precipice of the orchard, which at this stage of the summer season was voluptuous with greenery and fruit. The grasses full of wildflowers and bees, the air heavy with sugar as if the atmosphere were leeching it out of the ripening peaches. He heard the murmur of voices inside and plunged himself into that deeper level of daylight.

For a moment everything shone a brilliant emerald as his eyes adjusted to the dappled sunlight. "One of the tricks of the rural world: the constant movement of light," he thought. "Yet another one of the coy games of Mother Nature."

Yet even when his eyesight cleared he was in a fairytale landscape, for the trees were growing not peaches but legs, pairs and pairs of them hanging from the foliage canopy. Irritated now with his own nonsense, he shook his head and walked deeper into the orchard until the legs were grounded by spindly ladders and the soft murmur of voices heard at a distance took on the hard edges of men's words.

Words fell from the trees, disembodied from their owners. They were harsh words, close to an argument. "You're full of crap, Johnson, that horse was favored to win and you know it. I would have pulled in a bundle, but I think they were doping the damn beasts."

"They ain't dopin' the horses, John, you just can't hold onto your money."

Reverend Beale cleared his throat loudly and three men came down from the ladders. Bob Johnson dropped peaches into a waiting crate and Reverend Beale was impressed by the gentleness of the motion, the care the big man took not to bruise the fruit. Bob wiped his hands on his overalls as John Gray chewed a fingernail. Reverend Beale looked closely at the third man, Will Field. Just a boy, in fact. He looked at him hard, trying to place his face. Uncomfortable under his stare, the boy shrugged and climbed back onto his ladder.

None of the workers was wearing a shirt and the hairy barrel of Bob Johnson's chest was hardly contained by the suspenders of his overalls. John Gray was so slight that his pants hung dangerously low on his thin, narrow hips, held up by baling twine. Their skin glimmered with a wet sheen. Never one to appreciate bare flesh, Reverend Beale coughed again as if in defense against inhaling the carnality of the other men.

As strange as the men were to Reverend Beale in the stripped down worker's clothes, Reverend Beale in his dark suit and button down shirt, his stout frame standing almost knee deep in grass, was just as odd to Bob Johnson and John Gray. Bob broke the silence.

"Can we help you with somethin', sir?"

"Ah yes, gentleman, I'm sorry to disturb you, especially in the midst of your heated debate, but I wanted to seize this opportunity to invite you to my Friday evening service. It's very informal," he added. "You can come as you are. With a shirt on, of course."

John Gray withered under the reproach, jamming his hands into his pockets, which only made his pants plunge lower and gave Reverend Beale's heart a quickened step as he feared they'd come down all together. Bob, though, patted the front of his overalls almost proudly.

"We sure appreciate the invite, Reverend. Maybe we'll come by. As you can see, we have a lot of work here."

Bob's hand swept behind him to take in the fullness of the orchard, which Reverend Beale noticed was dotted with crates.

"I also was hoping to speak to Miss Forth. Is she available?"

Bob laughed a big, unapologetic laugh, and John Gray chuckled a bit as well, though it's doubtful he would have laughed without Bob there to say he could.

"This ain't no parlor, Reverend. I'm sure she's here somewhere but darned if I could point her out to you right this minute. And I sure ain't going to holler for her."

"No, no, of course not. I'm not keen on hollering myself," said Reverend Beale. "I'm sure I can find her if I look for a moment."

"Be our guest, mister," said John Gray, recovered from being chastised and feeling braver in Bob's shadow. "Just watch out for the bees."

Reverend Beale wandered down the ordered rows of peach trees waving his arms with a pinwheel's precision against the landing of bees, and Bob and John watched him and shared a good, full laugh before climbing their ladders again.

By the time he found Alden, he had to admit to himself that he'd lost his way. Despite the neatness of the orchard rows, his senses were overwhelmed by greenery, by the heavy summer heat, by the blank canvas of the bleached blue sky visible in ribbons overhead. When he stumbled upon her, Alden had on a wide-brimmed straw hat and was speaking so closely to a young man that Reverend Beale was horrified at first that they were kissing; but as he came closer, he realized the man was leaning in to her, intently listening and looking into her hands. They were so engrossed in their conversation they didn't hear the whisper of Reverend Beale's pants legs against the grass. He cleared his throat and the two people looked up at him.

Reverend Beale was surprised to recognize the young man was the Irishman he'd met at Robert Scott's farm. The boy looked him up and down and, disliking what he saw, said something out of the Reverend's hearing and wandered away into the orchard.

Alden didn't move toward Reverend Beale and Reverend Beale did not move toward her. They stood watching each other, she like a quizzical deer assessing a human in her natural environment, he a hunter determining his approach to his prey. Unable to fathom what could bring this man into her orchard —her sanctuary—Alden did what she always did: the most natural impulse that came into her mind at the time. So she stretched forth her hand in offering. Inside the cup of her palm was the perfect orb of a peach, its slightly freckled skin a creamy yellow with a blush of scarlet. Reverend Beale stepped forward and took the peach from her hand and held it up in the tips of his stubby fingers, rotating it like a gemologist holding a stone to light seeking imperfections.

"A very nice piece of fruit, Miss Forth," he finally commented, handing it back to her.

"You don't know that, Reverend. You need to smell it."

Reverend Beale hesitated then held the peach near his nose and sniffed.

"Not like that. Like this."

She took the peach from his hand and tipped her head back. The straw hat slipped off her head and she closed her eyes to better concentrate her senses. She brought the peach close to her nose and inhaled it deeply, her pale nostrils flaring and opening to allow the peach's essence full entry into her nose. Reverend Beale was suddenly embarrassed and cleared his throat yet again.

Alden opened her eyes and handed the peach back to him.

"I was just explaining to Ronan that you can tell the peaches that are ready to be picked by their color, but the best way to know when they are perfect is to smell them. Now you try it."

Reverend Beale was finished with farmer's games.

"No thank you, Miss Forth. I do not intend to keep you long from your work as I see now that you've begun picking and are probably quite busy. I only wondered if I could inquire after your grandfather's health. I hear he took a bad turn. When I went to the house to pay my respects, the door was locked."

Alden dropped the peach into a nearby crate and reset her hat on her head.

"I'd rather keep my family business private."

Reverend Beale did not have a strongly tuned olfactory sense for peaches, or for flowers, or for many of the finer things that touch the heart of most ordinary souls. But his nose was highly tuned to the human condition, particularly after his rich morning of research, and his nostrils flared at the smell of a weak spirit.

"Perhaps I could assist you in finding a doctor?"

"There's no doctor for miles, and even if there was we couldn't afford it." She hesitated a moment. "I don't think a doctor can help him. The sickness is in his head."

There in the orchard Reverend Beale saw a door of opportunity open just a crack and he reached forward to push it open.

"Often sickness of the mind is a manifestation of a sickness in the soul. Perhaps you could come to my service and pray for your grandfather."

Alden was a creature of habit, and raised without the regularity of church on Sunday, it held no novelty or solace for her now.

"I don't think so, but thanks."

She turned and absently examined a peach on a nearby tree. Reverend Beale watched as the door began to close shut on him. He stuck out his foot to force it ajar.

"Sometimes God is kind and sometimes He is wrathful. He is not afraid to punish those He feels are in need of lessons. Sometimes He will even punish those close to the sinner to bring the sinner to the light."

Alden still faced the tree but her hands fell to her sides.

"Perhaps you should examine your own soul for faults. Perhaps *you* have angered God, Miss Forth."

The door was open. He could feel her vulnerability as certainly as he felt the sweat rolling down his own back. Content with his progress, he turned and walked in the direction he came from, confident that he could find his way out of that ebullient jungle and back to civilization.

When Nick came that evening, Alden did not want to walk.

"Come inside," she said.

"Are you sure?"

But she was already in the house, the screen door banging closed behind her. He followed her retreating back into the kitchen.

"Sit down," she pointed to a kitchen chair.

She fumbled in a drawer and came back to the table with a pair of scissors. She ran her freehand through his pale hair.

"This needs to be cut."

"Yes," he murmured, arching his head into her palm like a cat being stroked.

The scissors commenced their metallic clipping.

"Did you see that minister in the orchard today? I think he knows something about us," said Alden.

"There's nothing to know. Is it wrong that we walk together and you cut my hair? That I kiss you?"

"No, it's feelings. I think he knows about my feelings."

Nick reached up to still her hands, pulled her forward so he could look at her.

"What feelings do you have?"

She pulled her hands away.

"It's nothing. I guess he just makes me nervous."

"The only thing to be afraid of is that you will cut my ear."

She laughed a nervous laugh that was unfamiliar to her. Nick made her feel reckless, made her want to throw her superstitions away and hurl herself into the dangerous void of love. But the void was bottomless, whereas this, what they had now, was comfortably bordered by the parameters of the Forth farm and bookended by the spring that was gone and the autumn yet to come, their time together made richer by its preciousness, and they were happy that way. It was a happiness unlike any Alden had ever experienced before, and she reveled in it like the bees do the sweetness of the bruised peaches that fall in the orchard. Reverend Beale's words to her in the orchard that afternoon followed her happiness like a shadow. The brighter her affection for Nick grew, the deeper a shadow it cast.

She clipped a few more strands then put down the scissors and ruffled his short hair.

"Much better."

Nick put his hands on her waist, rested his forehead against her stomach.

"Yes, better."

Across the valley, Reverend Beale sat out in the evening eating a sandwich of cold meat and cheese with canned beans heated on his small camp stove. Even with the sides pulled up on his tent, the canvas did not breathe and it was stifling hot inside. He pulled his camp chair out into the grass and ate his meal as the sun set. It wasn't more pleasant outside; although he brought his oil lamp out with the chair he didn't dare to light it, afraid he would attract the wrath of every mosquito in the valley. It was bad enough that they got into his ears and squealed their incessant whining. He'd inadvertently boxed his own ears several times in frustrated attempts to swat them.

He'd finally taken off his jacket and sat in the falling light in stocking feet (the mosquitoes in the grass would otherwise devour his bare toes) with his shirt open at the neck. A bit of black chest hair peaked from beneath the shirt, though the reverend couldn't help but notice that like the hair on his head that turned gray so many years ago, his chest hair, too, was now stippled with white. When he finished his meager meal he wiped his hands on his handkerchief and ran his fingers through his hair. This life on the road was aging him quickly. The hard work of routing out sinners and returning them to the path of good was thankless and tiring and never-ending. Soon, he would leave this valley and perhaps head south or west, somewhere where the weather was warm. Or as far as the old Ford could carry him.

Eight years had fallen beneath the wheels of his sedan. Before that, in the beginning, he'd gone on a horse or on foot, sometimes a train, attaching himself when he was starting to other revivalists groups where he honed his gift for oration. But he grew weary of their diluted delivery of the word of God. Worse, the followers did as well. Eventually they stopped coming to the summer revivals, their fervor satiated in conventional new churches that sprang up throughout the countryside. Or their time was occupied by other things with the quickening pace of life as the new century trudged forward.

He was just over fifty now and knew there were less years ahead of him than those behind. He remained relentless in his pursuit of purity for the people, his fervor rising all the more as people fell away from their churches or became lazy in their practice of religion and weak in their grasp on morality. There might come a time when he was too old to continue, and for that he had the money his father left him when he died. It wasn't left to Reverend Beale out of any filial affection, but rather out of necessity because there was no one else to will the money to. His mother, or at least the brittle husk of a woman that remained of her in the end, had long been in her grave. He thought of his father's money moldering in the bank back in Pittsburgh and shuddered at the thought.

It had grown very dark. He fumbled around in his tent to find the tin where he kept his sweets. He'd grown partial to the vanilla cookies Mrs. French carried in the general store, the ones covered in a thick glop of chocolate fudge. He took one out of the box, careful not to get the fudge topping, tacky in the heat, on his fingers. Outside he ate the cookie very slowly and thought about memories, but he did not seek out remembrances of his past in Pittsburgh; in fact, he shoved those memories aside like street urchins. The firm fudge softened in his mouth and he rolled over imagines in his mind, faces from the many places he'd been.

That boy at the Forth farm today—he knew he'd seen the boy somewhere before. And there was something in the way the boy shrugged him off and returned to his work that made Reverend Beale think that the boy *knew* Reverend Beale recognized him. Many people have niggling thoughts that sit on the sideline of their consciousness raising a half-hearted alert at random, and most people simply ignore those thoughts as an annoyance, but Reverend Beale knew that all thoughts, particularly the trivial ones, often proved the most important.

The orderly process of pigeonholing people was extremely satisfying to Reverend Beale. Here are he had the Frenchs who raised a son without scruples or a moral compass; there was Anna Scott with her sexualized manipulation; over here was Robert Scott, a brute like his own father; and on to the Powells, a plain lot with no ambition or education to speak of and mostly harmless. There was the young man Bruce – no, not so young anymore yet so obviously in love with Alden Forth. It made him weak, that unrequired love, but his sadness was its own contrition. Reverend Greene was weak as well, engrossed in his own eccentricity, and Ned Pfeiff was simply lonely and lost. These people made sense to him and he'd tucked them neatly into envelopes and filed them away in his brain where he could pull them out and shuffle them around as necessary like a host placing seating cards at a dinner party.

The entire Forth farm still withstood his orderly hand. A pale moon cast some light on his campsite and he got up and paced.

But he'd made a dent with Alden. He didn't understand it entirely yet, but he knew it was there. And he intended to push it.

XVII

Across the valley, a June beetle was trapped in Jane Scott's room at Avon Ledge Farm. Jane lay awake listening to it struggle against the screen, its wings, like heavy armor, tapping on the window jam and rattling the metal mesh. She could hear its metallic wings click open and closed. Even as darkness sucks away the light, it deepens the canvas of noise; eventually the click clack of the beetle's microscopic feet grew to such a cacophony that Jane covered her head with a pillow. But the heat was oppressive. She threw the pillow off the bed, she tossed and turned on the bed several times, trying to find one cool place where the sheets wouldn't stick to her damp body, but when she did, all was silent and the click clack clatter rose up and the cool spot became hot and finally she tore back the sheet, turned on the light, and stomped to the window where she picked up a shoe. When she'd spotted the June beetle she was enthralled by its clumsy movement, how the weight of its heavy body made it stumble to one side or fall backward off the screen to bobble for a moment on its back only to try again, trying to be free and failing, flailing while Jane watched what she knew was its death dance. Whether she squashed it with her shoe or left it there to exhaust itself working for freedom, it would die.

The inevitably of death moved over her and she put down the shoe to instead watch the fruitless maneuverings of the insect.

"You got yourself in here, can't you get yourself out?" she said to it.

It only continued to climb up the screen, to open and close its mechanical wings, to butt its head or lose its footing, to fall down and start again. She got up and switched off the light, came back to the window and looked across the lawn outside. The barns were dark. In the pale light of the moon she could see the figures of familiar things—the kitten's tree stump, the boxwood hedges, the fence line—but they were mercurial in the half light, as if they were shadow shifting there in front of her eyes, menacing and yet mystical, too. The stars stretched bright toward the horizon and Jane followed them, hopping from one tinseled orb to the next, imagining how the weight of her foot would intensify each star's glow for an instant, so that the sky danced with lights as she tiptoed across and down the sky to the Forth farm where Ronan was, probably sleeping in the workhouse. Or would he be looking at the ceiling and thinking of her? Or of his home across the ocean? Or of the horses he'd left behind and how his hands that grew rough from handling rope and leather were growing soft as ripe fruit?

The June beetle was on her hand now, his feet like barbs gripping her skin. When she clasped its body and plucked it off it pulled the skin, taking a miniscule piece of her with it. She opened the screen and tossed it free. Was it so shocked to find itself in midair that it plummeted to the ground? Had she damaged its wing when she plucked it from her hand so that even as it felt the possibility of flight the hope died? Had it opened its clumsy wings and flapped and flopped to some nearby tree? Or landed and been eaten by a mockingbird? Although her heart was hardening on its edges, it remained soft within, especially to vulnerable creatures. Jane couldn't help but hope it was enjoying its freedom.

Darkness draws up specters and dreams, creating a nightscape where the veil between what is real and what it otherworldly blows in a soft breeze. The touch of a mouse's paw inside a wall becomes the scraping finger of a ghost, the shift of a shadow on the wall is the movement of an intruder, and the mating call of fox is the hoarse cough from the underworld. It was these things that made Jane afraid of the dark, picturing horrible monsters in the gloaming, even when she was old enough to know better. Tonight, however, the darkness made her brave. Imagining the june beetle in its courageous, armored flight, she drew the night's depth around her like a carapace; she pulled on her clothes, slipped down the stairs, got into her boots and covered the distance across the yard to the barn. She removed Isadora from her stall. Isadora, who was awake and waiting, waiting as she had every night for her mistress to come.

In the dark with no tack, Jane and Isadora moved carefully. Even as Jane's eyes grew more accustomed to the dark, the stars seemed more distant on the ground than they did from her bedroom window. Isadora knew where they were to go, could already smell sweat and hay on the air, but she needed her mistress to guide her so she would know she was following her own heart and not the heart of the animal. They picked their way around fields where the corn was high, blank and black in the night; across a stream where Isadora's hoof clipped a stone and made a deep hollow clomp that carried downstream; around the sheep pasture and into the Forths' orchard where the thick leaves brushed Jane's hair and face.

She dismounted and loosely tied Isadora to a nearby tree. In the darkness, Jane was unsure of what direction to head. The sky above still shimmered with starlight, but dark floodwaters filled up the spaces between the trees, making the orderly rows disorienting. Jane recalled a nanny, many years ago, admonishing the girls not to wander in the high cornfields where they would be lost and never found. The landscape around her expanded so that it felt too vast for her to navigate, then retracted until she thought she would be squeezed to death between the depth of the dark and the tightness of the trees. Her disorientation took on the taste of panic in her mouth.

Then she heard a sound, a familiar daylight sound. The sound of a woman's voice. Normally, when one is afraid in the dark in a strange place, something so familiar is as joyful as a light switching on, but the sound moved with a rippling languor over the grass and cascaded around Jane's ankles. Even as it enveloped her in its sensuality, it was making it quite clear she was an intruder. Heedless, she moved through the deepening tide, feeling the soft watery voice pushing-pulling her on a wave, at once wanting to pull her close and trying to push her away. When she was close, she heard a man as well, murmuring somewhere in the trees. Just when she thought she might stumble on them in the dark, she felt pushed in another direction and their voices grew distant.

Her imagination moved faster than her feet. *Alden is the only woman on this farm,* she thought. *Who else could be out here at this time of night?* She thought of her own reasons for being in the orchard at that hour, of the way Ronan's slim body moved with ease and confidence around the horses and how his one broken tooth made his smile more charming, of how he kissed her so easily the first time and the many times afterward, and she thought now, *it was like he'd done it many times before.* A great sickness started deep in her belly and rose into her chest pulling her ribs tight until she had trouble catching her breath, and she knew that she did not want to find those voices in the dark. When the murmurs came close again, she bowed into the sound and then pulled away, her stomach retching.

With some difficulty she found Isadora, whose nostrils flared in surprise as she sucked her mistress's sadness and anger into her huge equine lungs. Jane laid her face against the animal's flank and cried the choking, jerked tears of the betrayed; the sobs that have no cathartic power but instead are the precursor to a swelling bitter rage, just as a flooded river can release another, larger wall of water.

Sleeplessness is a contagion that slips from house to house, infecting residents who feel they bear the burden alone, not knowing that their neighbors are awake in their beds, too, their eyes following shadows on the ceiling or staring out a dark window. If sorrow is where the contagion arose, perhaps it was Jane who spread it on her ride home, recalling her memories of Ronan and mingling them with her visions of him holding Alden in his arms until she could hold the images no longer and she cried them out and dropped them at her neighbors' doorsteps like unwanted children that slipped beneath the door and pattered about the house on ghostly feet.

Sarah French awoke missing her sons with the sorrow of a mother who knows her children will never live close to home again. Chester, awake on the other side of the bed, felt his wife's trembling, and the shameful impotence of his inability to console her.

Ned Pfeiff lay on his back listening to the sound of Holly's wheezing breath trying to recall how the weight of his wife's body used to change the contours of the bed.

Reverend Greene sat in his living room, surrounded by the covered cages of his many birds. He felt their peaceful, sleeping presence and it quieted his mind, which was full of the prescience of something to come that he could not place.

All across the valley, dreamers woke and rubbed their eyes in the night and lay awake thinking waking dreams of making love in the middle of the day when they were young, of walking to the edge of town but turning back at the milepost, of a mother's distant voice, of blood, and warm lips, and fishing in a cold stream or walking in deep snowfalls and all the other visions that flash through the mind on sleepless nights.

Of course, not everyone in the valley was awake under duress. Deep in the orchard on a rough wool blanket spread on high grass looking up at piece of starlit sky framed by the dark leaves of peach trees, Alden and Nick lay on their backs anticipating shooting stars. Alden, in her way of being deaf to the commandments of the civilized world and its mundane requirements and rituals, would not have looked at this, this moment in time in the orchard, as courtship. Theirs was a courtship mostly of silence.

Lying on the blanket with eyes fixed on the sky, two souls

bent toward each other from two bodies separated by only a few inches. These souls did not speak the same language or come from the same place, yet when they saw each other's body there on the blanket in a moment of shared rapture at the surprise of the night sky, they knew this was a special bond. And when a shooting star did cascade from the firmament as, really, they quite often do in very dark, out-of-the-way places, the two bodies twitched with delight at the brilliant spark from inside the universe, and their hands instinctively found each other, clutched each other, in an embrace.

"I don't know that I ever did this at home," said Nick, rolling onto his side to better look at the contours of Alden's face in profile, her cheeks smooth and shadowed, like cemetery stone. He touched her face with the back of his fingers and was surprised at its warmth, at the realization of her realness.

"Bruce and I did just this when we were little," said Alden, still looking at the sky. "Bruce would always want to go back inside after we saw at least one, but I always wanted to stay."

"You like the shooting stars that much?"

"No, the shooting stars still shock me. It's the calm before that I liked. There's so much quiet at night. It's peaceful. Everything can be beautiful in starlight."

"In another life, you could be a poet. You have a poet's soul."

"In another life I would want to come back here. I would want to farm and raise the peaches and sheep and have my quiet moments with the stars. I would want it all to be the same. I wish it was all still the same."

"You thinking about your grandfather? Or your friend Bruce who never comes anymore?"

Alden rolled to her side, too, and in this way, their faces were so close as to lose their shape and form. A darkness fell between them.

"All of that. And none of it. Do you know that the more you try not to think about something, the more you do?"

"These people are the most important to you. It is right for you to think about them."

"I only think about the past, though. I only think of how they used to be. I never did that before. It was only just this, this day. I guess I have that in common with Pop, now, this always thinking of the past."

Silence.

"Do you love Bruce? I believe he loves you."

"I never loved Bruce, not in a special way. I love him like family. But it was never enough. Love is so destructive. My grandfather tried to teach me that, but you can't avoid love. No matter what you do, no matter how careful, it finds you and ruins everything."

"Don't say that, Alden. Love is a good thing. It is a safe place with the right person. I could fall in love with you."

Alden got up on the blanket and sat with her legs crossed.

"Don't say it Nick. It's bad luck."

"I won't believe that. And I won't believe your grandfather wants you to live without love. I won't believe you aren't falling in love with me."

"Don't say anymore."

Alden felt herself faltering. As if touched by a piece of Reginald's ailment she suddenly found herself unable to recall the exact wording of her grandfather's warning. Or was it a statement? It was so long ago. *The Forths are unlucky in love.* The words finally came to her across decades, called out by the voices of those Forths that were long gone, so many of them, starting with Reginald's parents, anonymous lovers so doomed they gave up a child their child on a doorstep and set in motion lifetimes of loss. Or perhaps perpetuated a cycle; as a bastard child of ill begotten birth, there was no way to know if this pattern of love and loss began with Reginald or was given to him, his only inheritance from a family he never knew.

Alden tapped this reserve of knowledge, this deep well of evidence, and felt the strength of her conviction returning. Oddly, she thought back to the visit from the fat little churchman and his warning that God could punish Reginald for her own sins. What was religion but another form of superstition? And thus, wasn't Alden a true believer?

"The picking will be done in a few days," said Alden. "We need to hurry. Rain is coming; you can feel it in the heat. Then you'll leave and I'll stay. It is the way it's always been."

"You know things are different, Alden. You will be alone. More alone than before. It won't be as it's always been, no matter how much you want it that way. Let me stay."

Alden was not a stupid woman, or silly, or even particularly stubborn. Like all creatures of nature, she was in tune with the movement of time and the progression of life toward death. As animals know those in their pack who are sick and dying, Alden felt Reginald's slow decline more than she saw it with her rational mind. And she felt in herself the warmth of new emotion when she encountered Nick. But she also feared that this bad omen that had followed her all summer, that she sensed but never saw, was rooted in the new feelings she had for Nick, feelings that were not only physical, but that were tethering her heart to his presence. Fear drove her to what she knew, to the lessons of childhood, to fundamental truths her grandfather shared, to the realization that people in her life must come and go with the seasons and that coveting, desiring, loving, would only derail everything she knew. Life had proven that you let people go or they left when you were least expecting it.

Yet she remained a creature of nature that lives by instinct, so Alden kissed Nick in the orchard and placed her hands on his bare skin and guided his hands onto her for there was a physical need within her, which was something she could feed and control, the well of human touch that needed to be filled. This, she could say, was nothing like the niggling tug of love that is a more deep and dangerous need. This physical need was safe.

Alden would see these two things—passion and love—intertwining had she but known how to see it. Instead, all conversation and thought faded into kisses and the delicious indulgence of pleasure erased the rational and the past and the future, and tied two people and their kindred souls to the earth, while stars continued their brilliant dance above as they often do in dark, out-of-the-way places when someone bothers to watch.

XVIII

It is hard to describe the fragile bond between discretion and gossip, knowledge and secrecy, intervening and ignoring that balances a small town. In the city, people live crammed together, so close they can hear one another's footsteps through the walls, the crying children, the fights of adults, the lovemaking. They can smell their neighbor's food, see the quality of the washing strung out the window to dry, and know if times are good or bad. There are no secrets, and yet most people in cities do not know their neighbors by name, may even avoid their eyes in the street if they happen to exit the apartment at the same time, as if knowing with such intimacy makes the crowded masses shy of each other.

In the country it is different. Homes are spread across many miles. People live on farms where the trees and grass and fences are high enough to hide happy secrets, dark secrets, illness, birth, death, love, joy, and sorrow. And yet, in the country, everyone knows the drunkard, the wife beater, the adulterer, the gossip, the lonely heart. Whether it is right to speak of these things to someone across a carefully tended fence or leave well enough alone is an instinct bred into the fiber of country beings.

The morning after Jane's evening ride of tears, the

residents of the valley woke bleary eyed and raw nerved, the air thick with the unspoken secrets of the disgruntled and lonely. In his kitchen, Ned Pfieff scolded his dog Holly and slapped her across her ears when she stole a piece of bacon off the table, then found himself weeping on the floor beside her, cradling her head; Sarah French sent an exhausted Chester French off on his dairy route wordlessly. Though most of their lives had been spent in congenial quiet, the silence that lived in the apartment over the store was now suffocating, and Sarah took to heaving deep sighs to breathe her way through the day. Harold Greene uncovered his birds only to notice that they refused to sing. And deep in the valley, down a long manicured drive, up a dark, mahogany staircase in a well-appointed but nondescript bedroom, Jane Scott woke up with rage in her heart, the hurt and disappointment from the night before having set like the stars, to be replaced in the morning with the bright dawn of vengefulness.

As she lay on her bed, she tracked the path of her misery back to its source one more time, making sure she had every detail correct. How could she have been so stupid? All this time, she was so worried about Anna that she had completely forgotten that she had spoken to Reginald about Ronan. Reginald Forth, that decrepit old fool. And now she had pushed Ronan right in front of Alden, the most beautiful girl in town, except for Anna of course. She had been a complete idiot.

Her memory coursed over the murmured voices in the night, the weight of her dead kitten when she placed it in the ground, the feel of her father's hand across her face, the smoke of her sister's cigarette curling around her head like a wraith, and always, always the arrogant sneering face of Reverend Beale staring down over the proceedings like a righteous voyeur. The taste of the secrets of others was bitter in her mouth. She would spit them all over everyone.

Unlike the many weary and despondent residents of the

valley, Reverend Beale woke in the early glow of dawn well rested despite the heat that attempted to smother him all night long. He also awoke with a moment of clarity, rising with an image of the young man from the Forth farm clearly emblazoned in his brain. Before it was even fully light he'd shaved, donned his drab suit and driven his car through the crossroads of the valley as the sun was breaking like a blazing fire over its hillsides. Molten heat and the white gold of sweltering sunlight poured down into the valley, and Reverend Beale disappeared into the liquid light in the direction of town.

Most residents of the valley did not go to town unless they had plenty of good reason. One went to town for special occasions only, namely court dates. For all else, the valley village had a provision. Sarah French distributed the mail from the store. Reverend Greene managed the baptizing, marrying, and dying. Sometimes the wealthy residents might go to town to visit the hospital, but there wasn't much to do there but die, and most people would just as soon do that at home. Robert Scott, of course, spent quite a bit of time in the city at his gentlemen's club or attending to business affairs, but the city was an entirely different affair than town. Town was the way station between the city and the great rolling hills of countryside; it stood for the county seat, the location of the courthouse, the hospital, the train station, and the central post office.

It took Reverend Beale almost an hour to get to town. As he bounced over hard-packed dirt roads onto vaguely paved rural routes that seemed to be one crumbling piece of concrete away from reverting back to dirt, he contemplated the backward nature of agrarian societies. Even as the public works administration was building bigger roadways and connecting up hamlets across the country, the rural masses still clung to their old ways, preferring to have their mail doled out by nosy neighbors who no doubt steamed open their private letters, preferred to give birth on their dining room tables and to be laid out on them as well, to teach their children to read at home or simply not to bother. All this rather than patronize institutions of higher education or medical knowledge. Or funeral homes.

And the roads! How country people loved their roads with their twists and turns and bottomless potholes, and their death trap ditches overflowing with honeysuckle and wild rose and Black-eyed Susan and poison ivy. A dog ran in front of Reverend Beale's car and it was only instinct that caused him to slam on his brakes; had he been thinking more clearly, he would have run the stupid cur over. Twice he had to stop to allow a lumbering piece of farm equipment to saunter from one field to another. Given the time, effort, and patience it required to get to town, it was no wonder people from the valley rarely chose to go.

Eventually, the roads improved. Orderly houses heralded the start of civilization. After his summer spent in pastoral oblivion, Reverend Beale felt his senses so dulled that the sight of manicured lawns, orderly driveways, the plain brick façade of the teachers' college (closed and quiet for the summer), fire trucks slumbering in their berths at the firehouse, and the shingles proclaiming "Barber," "Groceries," and "Shoes," bespoke the highest sophistication. Then his car jolted over the trolley tracks that ran to the city and he was reminded of larger, finer places, of the noise and grime and grandeur of the urban world. And he saw the town for what it was: a place to stop on the way to better things.

Reverend Beale got to the county post office early. There was still an hour at least before it would open its doors. The sun was up and in full blaze; even at that early hour, anyone could tell it was going to be a scorcher. Most of the stores were still closed, but Reverend Beale was able to buy a newspaper from a boy on the corner near the court house, and took it inside the pharmacy that was open and operating a diner counter as well.

"Morning Reverend, sir, what can I bring you?"

Reverend Beale looked at the man opposite him behind the counter and tried to place his country of origin. Polish? German? He was of that short, fat build that Reverend Beale thought ubiquitous among men of Germanic and Slavic descent, say nothing of the guttural accent. No doubt a Catholic or some bizarre incarnation of Eastern Orthodoxy. But Reverend Beale laid aside his prejudices and was cheerful this morning, the excitement of his errand in town making him magnanimous to even these shore invaders. He ordered pancakes that came with a little ceramic pitcher of warm maple syrup that he drained indulgently onto his plate. A fan whizzed on the counter near the register and another on the counter at the pharmacy toward the back of the shop, but it was still hot and the heaviness of the food and the warmth of his coffee made Reverend Beale sweat.

"Here's water for you, sir, with ice fresh from our own ice house here in town," said the fat Pole, for Reverend Beale had decided he was Polish.

"Thank you," said the reverend before snapping his newspaper open in front of his face. While he might be feeling magnanimous, that did not mean he was interested in chattering with the local population. And what the rebuffed owner could not know, the owner who was, in fact, German, was that Reverend Beale was embarrassed by visible signs of his own body's functioning, such as sweating, thereby making him quite cross when others hinted at this unfortunate weakness of his flesh.

The pharmacy soon gained a few regulars, mostly men carrying their suit jackets over their arms and complaining of the heat, come to jabber about the news before heading into the city on the streetcar. Others were banal civil servants who worked in the court house. Reverend Beale welcomed their commotion and sank further behind his newspaper, occasionally lapping up leftover syrup from his plate with a surreptitious finger.

At nine o'clock, Reverend Beale left exact change for his breakfast on the counter, folded his paper neatly and left it on his seat, straightened his moist clothing and walked in the direction of the post office. Behind him the other patrons watched as he waddled out on stout legs, resolute in his suit jacket despite the heat and its being stained with sweat from the collar down through the shoulder blades.

The town was awake now and full of more noise and commotion than Reverend Beale had experienced in weeks: a mother in a hurry to get down the street pulled the hand of a disgruntled child; a distracted lawyer bumped into her in his haste to make it to the court house; a horn blared as a derelict, just coming off an evening bender, blundered out of the way of a rumbling trolley car and into the street. Excitement at his errand made Reverend Beale deaf to the small triumphs, tragedies, and foibles of the workaday world. And it all fell away when his hands touched the smoothness of the post office's stalwart metal door.

Inside it was inexplicably cooler. It was over a month since Reverend Beale collected the mail he had forwarded to this location, yet the stack of letters—legal notifications related to his father's estate, communications from Christian brother organizations, a few unsettled debt notifications, all minor—was so insignificant the reverend could fit them into his jacket pocket.

Carrying the light burdens of his life, Reverend Beale stepped to the community bulletin board and began perusing the many faces of the "Wanted" posters. It was a delicious, slow, studious task, like eating the fudgy vanilla cookies from Sarah French's market. He almost wished he could prolong it, but no, there it was. He pulled the poster off the wall, folded it quickly, and slipped it in his pocket before leaving the coolness of the post office for the blistering reality outdoors.

Reverend Beale departed town with uncharacteristic joy. He navigated the rutted roads without grimacing, did not curse the discomfort of the car's leather seat in the heat, and he paid little heed to the dust in his mouth that was funneled up from the tires off the heat-cracked road and into his vehicle. The only thing that could excite this intrepid clergyman was information, information for salvation. For perhaps the first time since he first crossed into the valley, he saw a path of communication opening before him, a way to civilize the last of the valley's untamed populace and bring them down a difficult but necessary path to publicly acknowledge their sin and submit to the will of God.

So monumental was his enthusiasm, he drove directly to the Forth farm. After the long, rattling drive in and out of town, and the sounds of a real society moving through the course of modern living, the quiet that assaulted Reverend Beale when he shut off his engine was shocking. Getting out of the car, the sound of his door slamming closed seemed an affront in that still place. A breeze, a blessed, wonderful breeze, was just beginning to stir. The wind moving through the leaves of a magnolia tree near the drive sounded like rain. Reverend Beale cleared his throat and liked the way it broke the stillness, liked how his robust voice carried human authority into a place he felt was constantly on the verge of slipping to nature's whim. He cleared his throat again as he strutted over the yard and plunged into the orchard.

Unlike his previous visit, he moved now with confidence through the peach trees. Although he would never be so base as to call it this, he had assumed a role, taken on the character of the bearer of salvation, the bringer of confrontation but also of a means to salvation. Wearing this role made him feel length in his short legs, made him feel the power of God filling him with new ability and consciousness, a physical and spiritual vitality. An overwhelming sense of belonging and of ownership guided his strides. In this role, Reverend Beale was master of the earth and held dominion over its creatures. When Bob Johnson stepped from a line of trees carrying a full crate of peaches, he did not startle Reverend Beale. In this moment, Reverend Beale owned this orchard and all that moved within it.

"Hey there Reverend, back so soon? We'll put you to work if you keep showing up like this."

Reverend Beale was dismissive. "Will Field, please. And do feel free to holler for him if necessary. I'll be waiting right here."

Bob Johnson wanted to reiterate his earlier admonishment

that the orchard was not a parlor, but his curiosity was piqued by the reverend's overbearing confidence. Bob hefted the crate onto a wagon that was already brimming with full boxes. Alden was certain heavy rains were coming and she wanted to finish harvesting as quickly as possible. Bob Johnson wouldn't be surprised if they worked well after dusk in the next few days. He hoped whatever had the reverend so excited wouldn't interfere with the last of the picking. In a few days, they would all be gone.

"I might be a minute. Why don't you take a squat there?" Bob gestured to an upturned peach crate under a nearby tree.

Reverend Beale was too enamored of his own reverie to balk at the notion of squatting in a field; he took off his jacket, which was wet with sweat, laid it over the rough wood slates of the crate and sat down with care. The breeze picked up and blew more steadily and on it danced the sweetness of the peaches piled high on the wagon. The sugared perfume whetted Reverend Beale's longing for something sweet, and he took out the slip of paper from the post office and unfolded it and refolded it to maintain his focus.

He was startled when Will Field came out of the trees directly behind him and he leaped to his feet.

"What are you doing back there?" he asked a bit too loud.

Will Field's blue work shirt fell open at the chest and he scratched a bare patch of skin. "Where else was I supposed to come out but from where I was?"

"I only meant you should not come up on people from behind..." Reverend Beale felt his confident grasp on the situation fading. Oh how he did hate that orchard. Taking a moment to compose himself, he put on his suit jacket.

"Aren't you real hot in that jacket, Reverend?"

"What? No, I'm fine thank you. Will, sit down please."

"Don't mind if I do."

With Will seated on the crate and Reverend Beale able to tower above him, he regained his composure and began pacing theatrically.

"Will, there is something of great importance I must discuss with you."

Like an actor on stage Reverend Beale stopped and turned to face his audience. He dropped his big square head so he could look at Will through his heavy brows.

"Do you believe in God, Will Field?"

"Of course, I do, sir."

"Then perhaps you can explain this."

Here Reverend Beale thrust forward the "Wanted" poster so it was directly in Will's face.

Imagine for a moment being Will Field. Young. Far from home. Working so hard in the heat that any weight is being sweat off. Keeping company with tough men who live off the road. Old enough to be concerned with the basics of getting by in life and young enough to easily forget the secret he's supposed to be keeping. So when that secret comes back and shouts in your face as Reverend Beale's piece of paper did in that moment, you have to take a moment to recall the mistake you made and remember that it was, in fact, yours.

Will ran a hand over his jaw. He had lost weight this summer and his jaw was more pronounced than in the picture. He'd gained more sinewy muscle, not that it made any matter to the likeness. His hair was longer, too. The other men cut their own hair, but he was no good at it, so he was going to let it go until he could go to a barber the next time they went through a town. They'd be leaving here soon, he knew.

"Where did you get that?"

Reverend Beale was a little disappointed at this lackluster response.

"From the central post office, of course. I knew I recognized you the moment I saw you. I saw your picture on the Wanted wall in the post office when I established my mail services."

"It's not what you think it is."

"It's assault, Will Field. Attempted murder. A truly horrendous sin."

"Is your daddy still alive, Reverend?"

"No, he died several years ago."

"Well, you're luckier than me. My daddy wouldn't die no matter what. Do you know that mean son-of-a-bitch got hit by a tractor and still didn't die? It's the meanness that kept him going. The mean ones always live too long."

Reverend Beale felt his grip on the moment loosening. He was on the precipice of memory, looking down, down where his own father's face glowered up from the deep and spoke to him: "You did the right thing to tell me, Arnold, but for the rest of my life I'll wish you hadn't."

Will was talking again even as darkness rimmed Reverend Beale's sight.

"His meanness was so strong he couldn't hold it in. First he beat mamma. Then me. When he started on the girls, man, I couldn't take it. They were so little and he was so big. It wasn't right."

Reverend Beale slipped deeper into the tunnel of memory, watching images from his past move by at such speed they were just snapshots with no sound: his father's red-rimmed eyes scowling at him as he slammed the library door in his son's face; his mother's pinched face, white as stone. He felt across the distance of years the heat of his father's unfettered rage and the cold sting of his mother's bony hand. It brought him back to the moment.

"… so like I said, when the tractor didn't kill him I thought God must have lost His mind, thinkin' my daddy deserved a second chance on earth. I set out to make it right. But damn if I didn't fail, too, and get busted to boot. I hit that man over the head with a log when we was cuttin' wood. I thought sure he's dead. He bled like a pig at the butcher and went white as death itself. But then we was having dinner and he came back in the house. Kicked his own door in while his kin were happy eatin', thinking he was dead by the woodpile. Scared us all to death."

Reverend Beale was strangely rapt in Will's story, comforted by how his rustic accent and straightforward storytelling pulled him up from the edge of his own memory's dangerous gorge.

"He got down the shotgun and sure enough he was gonna kill me. So I ran. He got me, too, got me with some shot here in the back of my leg, but I was runnin' so fast and it was dark and he was off his aim from being whacked so hard in the head. I just popped that shot out myself later. And wouldn't you know, that son-of-a-bitch turned me in, put a price on my head. Like him beatin' the life out of me for years and tryin' to shoot me with his gun wasn't enough to make us square."

The orchard went quiet. The wind held its breath. The trees with limp leaves waited in mute witness.

"Attempted patricide is a terrible sin, Will Field."

"Didn't you hear me, Reverend? The man was crazy."

The wind blew. The leaves rustled. Peach sweetness washed over them both, but it sickened Reverend Beale. The lush green, the tempting breezes, the sensation that nature was there with them, like a living being – it irritated Reverend Beale and the bile taste in his mouth engaged his fire.

"Patricide, even attempted and even in dire situations, is still a terrible sin. You must confess your sins to be free of them."

"I thought I just did."

Reverend Beale dropped his head again and gave Will the seething brow look.

"Look here, Will Field, this is no game. The living and the dead will all be judged, not in the quiet of a confessional box, but together in front of the Lord. Contrition is beneficial for the soul of the individual and the soul of the community. You must come to my service this evening and you must confess your sins."

"You crazy? They'll send me to jail."

Now was the moment Reverend Beale had waited for. With all his excitement reignited, he entered the final act of his performance.

"There is another way."

Will waited.

"Alden Forth."

Will scratched his chest again. "She ain't killed anybody I

know of. Why you wanna talk about her?"

"She's lonely here on this farm. I sense that she's sad. Do you know why she's sad?"

Will was a country boy with little formal education, but he was not stupid in the ways of the world. He understood that Alden was to be his life raft, that Reverend Beale, like all others, put the soul of Will Field pretty low on the pecking order of life. Reverend Beale wanted something bigger. For whatever reason, that thing he wanted was Alden. As no one had ever gone too far out of their way to do much for Will, he wasn't too accustomed to going too far out of his way to help another, so any arrangement that got him our of the way of the law looked fine with him.

"Well, her grandaddy's sick in the head."

"Yes, yes, everyone knows that. What else?"

"Well, this is all just rumor, but I heard from John that if I played my cards right, I could have a bit of fun with her while I was here."

Reverend Beale was stupefied, needing more. "What do you mean, 'a bit of fun?'"

Will smiled a little wickedly. "You know, Reverend, a little roll in the haystack, that sort of thing. No one else will breathe a word of it and Bob Johnson nearly knocked John's head off his shoulders when he mentioned it, but there it is. And she spends an awful lot of time with a couple of the guys workin' here this summer."

Reverend Beale recalled his first meeting with Alden, the open robe, the creamy flesh and ribbon of auburn hair, the unfettered sensuality of it all. He thought back to Bruce's bitter sadness, considered Alden's shrouded life on the farm, and all the pieces that had circulated in his head for so long finally clicked into shape. He was anxious for more. "Well, are *you* one of them?"

Will look around, uncomfortable. It was a big orchard that could hide many ears. If Bob Johnson heard him talking like this he had a feeling it wouldn't end well for him. Satisfied that he and Reverend Beale were alone, he continued.

"Ha! No sir. Like I said, it's all rumor. This place, it's funny. This place just seems to hold up secrets real well. I don't know how, but you know things are going on around here but you can never quite see or hear it, so you start to think you made it all up."

"Yes, I know what you mean." Reverend Beale resumed his pacing.

"Look, Reverend, I need to get back to work. Alden thinks for sure there's big storms comin' and she wants us done. We'll be moving on then. Are we square?"

"Oh no, Will Field, we are not square. Tonight, you will be at my evening service and you will participate in the community confessional. I've been trying to loosen the sinning lips of this town for too long. You are going to help me do it."

"I ain't tellin' no one nothing that's gonna send me to prison."

"No, we will keep that between ourselves." Reverend Beale dropped his voice. He too looked around at the trees, wondered how alone they were in the leafy confessional.

"I want you to share what you know about Alden. I want this town to know the imposters from the truly saved, to stop glorifying idols. And try to bring some of the other men with you. That John person at least."

"And you won't say nothin' about my problems?"

Reverend Beale looked at Will over his brows one last time.

"Not for now, Will Field, but don't think you can put one over on me. Unlike your father, when I shoot, I do not miss, even metaphorically."

Will Field had no idea what "metaphorically" meant, but he knew enough to think that the reverend was just enough touched in the head that he was capable of anything, and he knew he'd be moving on soon enough with cash in his hand if they finished the picking soon, so he might just as well play along and then get himself long gone.

"Alright, Reverend. I'll be there."

XIX

The residents of the valley made their way toward Reverend Beale's open-air meeting on that Friday evening in late summer, a moment in the climatology timeline of the mid-Atlantic when the atmosphere is so heavy with heat and humidity that eventually it cracks and explodes into the violence of thunderstorms. Everyone felt the charge in the air. Chester and Sarah French were the first to arrive, followed by Ned Pfieff. Ned and Chester stood incongruous and sweating in their suits, and speculated to each other about when the heat would break. That is how it was always discussed, the heat like a prison wall that needed to be brought down or driven through for fresher air to flow in, like nature needed to be pushed so far until she couldn't take anymore and finally cracked under the strain.

Anna Scott rolled onto the field in her Cadillac and her children toppled out of the door and ran off into the tall grass.

"This weather!" she exclaimed, joining the Frenchs and Ned Pfieff.

"We were just wondering when it's going to break," said Ned. "I have hay to cut and can't decide when to bring it down."

Truth be told, Anna was growing weary of these Friday

evening socials. At first, it was good fun. Certainly nothing was more pleasant than the first time her father sat in the front row of Reverend Beale's makeshift little congregation with a contrite Jane at his side. She'd smiled to herself for days thereafter. But now there was too much talk of farming and the weather and God, and the game with her father had played out and she was bored. When they were first married and certainly after the birth of the twins, Anna enjoyed that David worked so much and traveled often. She'd hardly seen him at all that summer, though he sent gifts and cards from Philadelphia and New York and Chicago. Now, if she were to be honest, she missed him. Well, no, perhaps it was more accurate to say that she missed the companionship of like-minded people that he gave her. She missed how he would fawn over her when he was home, she missed their evenings in the city having lovely dinners by candlelight and he always with a sparkling present for her when the dessert arrived. She liked being in the company of his work colleagues and their wives, other people with enough means that they didn't need to talk about it, but the commonality was always there, keeping them company and drawing them together in a delicious conspiracy.

Many women in her station would simply take a lover, but that just seemed trite and dull and likely to become messy and require too much attention. In theory, lovers wanted to please, but Anna knew that in reality, they wanted more to know that she was pleased by their attentions, a far more high maintenance arrangement. She had no interest in stroking the egos of young lads only so they could paw her flesh in the dark. It didn't seem worth it. Sex had never held much interest for her except as a means to move a pawn forward.

No, it was time to go away, to get out of the valley for a little while. Perhaps she would take the governess and the children—oh, how David would love her if she brought the children—and meet him in New York. The children could be shunted off to the nursery and she could shop during the day and be lavished by David's attention in the evening. She could once again circulate with a smart set where the women would be openly envious of her good taste in clothes and the men would invigorate her with their lascivious glances. Yes, it had been an amusing summer and she'd certainly gotten one over on dear old father, but now it was time to entertain herself in the manner of her society, time to be reminded that she was still beautiful and vital and special.

"Anna? Anna? I believe that Beryl is eating grass, just over there."

Sarah French gently laid a hand on Anna's arm and Anna flinched at her touch. Sarah snapped away her hand.

"Oh Beryl," called Anna, deftly moving over the grass like a dancer even in her high-heeled shoes. "Do not do that. You are a little lady now."

More residents arrived and some traveling laborers, some from the outer reaches of the valley who came, like Ned Pfieff, mostly for companionship, others from boredom or curiosity or both, until there was a small group of about twenty people all milling around on the grass. Jane and Robert Scott arrived, and although Robert made perfunctory greetings all around—"Yes, it is terribly warm and humid. We can only hope this breaks soon"—Jane went quietly and obediently to the first line of logs and sat down, staring ahead past the patch of grass where Reverend Beale typically sermonized.

Reverend Beale had yet to emerge from his tent. It was a small town and a small group and most people recognized each other and socialized quietly, mildly expectant. A pickup truck pulled up on the grass and the group turned to see who had arrived. Will Field and Bob Johnson got out of John Gray's truck with John following behind. Bob Johnson was not one for tent religion fervor. He was not one for religion much in general. But when Will Field asked for a ride to town to enjoy the sermonizing of Reverend Beale, Bob Johnson took some notice. His nose, made sensitive to mischief from years of living on the road, sensed something awry in the workhouse. John Gray was willing to go anywhere Bob Johnson went, and getting off the farm on a Friday night might mean a game of cards with some of the other farmers later in the evening. So the three men had piled into the truck.

As if drawn from his seclusion by the sound of this last motor dying, Reverend Beale came out of his tent, walked across the grass with hands clasped behind his back, nodding to the gathered company without stopping for pleasantries, and walked directly to the new arrivals to extend his hand to Bob Johnson. The two men squared. Reverend Beale knew that Bob Johnson was the leader of this pack and the others would fall in behind him; Bob Johnson knew a man like Reverend Beale only chose to extend his hand when it suited him and that he was doing so here, for the first time, in front of all these people, meant that he needed to make a show of it. Bob didn't know why, but he was willing to play the role of the dumb laborer to find out. They shook hands and Reverend Beale indicated the rows of tree trunk seats. The rest of the group chose seats, but turned again at the sound of a slamming car door.

Aside from the incident earlier that summer at Reverend Greene's house, Reginald Forth had hardly been seen off his farm since the ailment about which no one spoke struck him. For those that had not seen him in many months, the transformation was terrifying. He was stooped and gray and thin. He shuffled his feet over the ground. Reverend Beale, elated at this unexpected arrival disgorging itself from John's truck, practically tripped over the grass to help Reginald to a seat, but the older man shoved him away.

"Where are the nuns?" he said, looking confusedly at the faces staring back at him with so much familiarity. "I thought the nuns would be here. I guess they're gone, too." He shuffled off into the tall grass where Anna's twins where playing with a one-winged cicada.

Reverend Beale's meetings had taken on the structured calm of a class in session for wayward pupils. Reginald's appearance disturbed the fragile discipline.

"Poor man, he's half the size he was."

"How many years has it been? He looks like death warmed up."

"Well, he must be over seventy now, what can you expect, old as that?"

"I don't think he remembers me."

"I wonder if he remembers us?"

"Do you think his granddaughter neglects him?"

"I wonder how his Alden manages him."

Bob Johnson stepped in among the group, his eyes on Reverend Beale. Around him, the crowd quieted. The men sat.

Energized by the larger crowd and pleased that his ingenuity had brought so many people together—so many souls just waiting to be saved from their flesh's vices—Reverend Beale was more adamant in his pacing, more emphatic with his gesturing, more fervent in his calls for morality, his condemnation of human nature and its tendency to sloth, to greed, to pleasure for pleasure's own sake. He felt an old fear propelling his words, the fear that had motivated him to this work, the fear that in waiting too long to tell his father his mother's dire secret, he had angered God and the years of restrained violence that followed in the Beale household were penance.

Forming his sermon he plunged headlong into his own memories, endangering himself as he treaded water in the deep end of recollection where he confronted his mother's naked body, her ease and frivolity in the affair that caused a lifetime of rancor. Time wound away from him, meaningless, until he finished speaking, physically spent and unaware of how long his sermon had lasted.

He took a moment to wipe his brow and catch his breath. His congregants stared back at him, confounded by his violent intensity.

"And now, I ask of this congregation: who among you would like to be free of sin, would like to be free of the weight of secrecy, and confess your sinful knowledge here in this open field under God's eyes and in the company of your neighbors?"

Silence.

Reverend Beale dropped his gaze pointedly around the

congregants. Jane Scott met his eye and he thought for a moment she wanted to say something but he had no time for her right now. He passed by her and settled his look on Will Field, whose head was bent down staring at the grass between his boots.

Reverend Beale cleared his throat.

"Confession of sin means freedom. Freedom is a gift that can be taken away. Do not, dear people, lose your freedom to sin because you are afraid of earthly consequences. Your contrition on earth will be redoubled in Heaven."

Will was trying to put off the inevitable as long as he could because he knew how angry Bob Johnson was going to be at what he was going to do, but he didn't have any choice and he knew those words about freedom were meant for him, and so he got to his feet and said, "I've got something to say."

"Good, young man. Turn and face your neighbors, Tell us your story. We all share in the healing power of confession."

If there was one thing Will Field knew about dealing with church people it was to keep it quick. He shuffled his feet a little and kept his eyes low and he reminded himself again that pretty soon those peaches were going to be picked and if Bob Johnson wasn't too mad he and John would give Will a ride further up the coast to the next job and he might never see this little town again.

"It's a little embarrassing to talk about, especially with the ladies present," he began, indicating vaguely the direction of Sarah French, sitting nearby, with a shrug.

"Is it a carnal sin then, boy?" Reverend Beale thought some encouragement might be in order.

"Um, maybe. It's like this. I had sinful thoughts about my employer, but it ain't my fault because she asked me to sin with her first."

He sat down quickly. The congregants looked at him, bewildered, then looked at Reverend Beale, who sighed. Several people turned in their seats straining to see what Reginald's reaction would be to what seemed to be an implication being made against his granddaughter. The old man was still standing over the crippled cicada with Anna's twins. John Gray looked at Reginald, at Bob Johnson, looked up at Will Field and back at Bob. Bob seemed suddenly made of stone, every muscle in his body taut and unflinching, which only made John squirm the more.

"Young man, can you please try to be more clear?"

He drew out the words "try" and "clear" and Will was reminded of a school teacher long ago when he was still allowed to attend school, an old maid who was always saying, "Will Field can you please *try* to be more *clear* with your handwriting?" Then she'd drop the ruler on his hands.

Will winced and got back to his feet. He could feel Bob Johnson glowering at him, his eyes burning into his forehead as Will kept his head bent to the ground.

"My employer, Alden Forth, asked me to sin with her in the, the carnal way, like you said. She asks all the workers, all the time. Everyone knows it; it's gone on for years. I said no, but I still had those sinning thoughts and now I'm afraid for her because I think she's sinning with somebody else."

That last part he thought up on his own. If Reverend Beale didn't think that was good enough, well then he, Will Field, was just going to have to run away in the night and not get his pay from Alden and that was gonna be that. But he'd still be a free man, he knew that now for sure. While he was standing, the silence of the people was so loud it terrified the crickets and the cicadas into silence, too, and even halted the high pitched wheeze of the mosquitoes. For a moment, the entire valley felt stricken, waiting for this moment to break more than the heat.

Will sat down and Bob Johnson got immediately to his feet.

"You're a no good liar, you stupid boy."

The people gasped, like for the last minutes no one had breathed and only when Bob broke down that wall of silence could the air get in. The congregants filled their lungs with air and with the wispy trails that remained of Will's confession against the most mythical of all the valley's living creatures. Several started to nod in approval of Bob's defense. That's when Jane Scott got to her feet, wheeled on her heel to face the congregation and wouldn't you know that the stop-gap in her mouth flew out and the quiet, obedient girl was once more caught on a torrent of words that was also filled with her tears.

"It's true! She's a whore, a whore I tell you!"

"Jane, please…" Robert Scott pulled on his daughter's sleeve, horrified.

But he hesitated to stand up, to embroil himself in the scene already unfolding. She shrugged off his hand.

"You're a beast of a man and you," she indicated the grass full of people, "you all know it, too, but no one cares."

Reverend Beale, who had been a little dumbstruck by this outburst, quickly recovered and raised a hand to try and regain order, to channel this new shift in course toward his own ends. The hand was like a tiny distress flag trying to signal a very large and very distant ship. Jane and her fury sailed by.

"You know Alden whores around to her own rules. Look at her grandfather. The man's lost his mind and should be locked up. Yet no one cares! Like no one cares that my sister Anna is an evil, selfish bitch who short-changes you," Jane thrust a pointed finger at Sarah French, "on everything from milk to candy, and you," the finger swung to Ned Pfeiff, "on buying hay for her stupid ornamental horses she doesn't even ride. You let them do it because they're pretty. No one cares what Alden does because it doesn't hurt you and she's "pretty" and "special." You don't give a damn! You are so blind and stupid, but I know! I heard it. I heard her in her orchard with a man. And you all eat those peaches as if they weren't disgusting, covered in lust."

Right then the vehemence of those words exhausted the speaker. Flushed and wet with sweat, she started sobbing. It seemed that everyone was talking at once and Bob Johnson grabbed Will Field by the scruff of his neck like a kitten and dragged him to the truck with John Gray not far behind, and Will was just as happy to get out of there one way or another, even if it met being dragged out by Bob's paw. John Gray was sad that there was definitely not going to be anyone in the mood to play cards that night.

Bob Johnson was in such a hurry that he almost forgot Reginald. The twins had wandered closer to their mother when the shouting started. Anna paid little attention to their clawing little hands; she watched the back of her father's erect head, the threat of a smile twitching at the corners of her mouth. Reginald was staring at his feet in the grassy causeway where the row of cars faded into the rows of seats. Bob just about picked up the frail old man he was in such a hurry to get out of that field, but Reginald flung him off with astounding strength.

"Don't touch me you awful revivalist! I know your kind, the kind that left me at the orphanage. If it wasn't for the nuns I'd be dead now. Dead!"

Reginald's shouting silenced everyone in the field for a moment, their bickering suppressed by this new development.

Bob Johnson had seen this a few times before, these moments when Reginald's mind fought so hard against being lost that the rage in his head spilled out of his body and he was uncharacteristic in his anger.

"I'm no revivalist, Mr. Forth. I'm a farmer. Just like you. And we need to be getting back to the farm. Those peaches won't wait."

From far away, the sound of familiar words resonated in Reginald's distressed mind.

"My peaches. Where are they, my peaches?"

"Back home, Mr. Forth. You come with me back in that pickup right there and we'll go get them."

With the departure of the rage, Reginald deflated. He left the field as he arrived, stooped and shuffling and already forgetting he was ever there. John's truck rattled to a start and the sound of grinding gears broke the suspension of silence that had momentarily held everyone aloft, everyone but Jane Scott who was sobbing inconsolably on the ground yet still invisible. The moment passed and everyone erupted into angry little skirmishes yet again.

For many years, the people in the valley had lived with their farms abutting each other, their little triumphs and failures and private miseries mostly kept well-tended like their fences. Though people might know other's business and even chat about it in a moment of gossipy weakness, folks were mostly embroiled in the business of surviving, of raising crops and children, and dealing with sore muscles and broken tractors and lame horses. They lived in a distracted peacefulness that was both a reality and a suspension of disbelief. Will Field tore the thread that sewed up the little community and Jane Scott poured tears through the opening like rain, and Reginald's madness swept through and all the well-tended fences came down.

It only took a matter of minutes. The grievances and grief of generations threw open their dusty doors and spilled forth; the valley filled with the fetid scent of decay unleashed.

Chester French, never one to speak much at all, much less in anger, took to his wife about the accounting of the books in the shop and she turned on Anna over her constant pilfering from her shelves; men who worked happily for years under Ned Pfeiff turned their backs on him, accusing him of having held back on their wages while he grew wealthier off the land, and he accused Robert Scott of constantly encroaching on the property lines of the fields he, Ned Pfieff, had lawfully purchased over the years.

This is not, of course, what Reverend Beale had in mind. Instead of the great mass of souls he wanted to release through the exercise of shared confession, he'd brought the devil into his midst. He watched from the outside, dismayed at the skirmishes between the townspeople, watched as some people slunk away to their cars or bicycles and slowly pulled away, the dust from their wheels laying a fine coating of finality in the grass. They would not come again. He watched as Robert Scott dragged his youngest daughter away, practically throwing the girl into his car, his red face set in a determined grimace as he stammered through clenched teeth, "I've had enough of you, girl. If you want to act like a whoring actress, you can do it in Paris with your Mother. You won't do it in sight of my doorstep."

If before she was missing her husband, Anna Scott was surely wanting him here now. Anna excelled at controlling a situation and disliked chaos beyond her manipulation. Sarah French broke down into tears and her husband, finally humbled and humiliated back into silence, glared at Anna and put his arm around his distraught wife to lead her back to his truck. Ned, in a threatening manner Anna never thought him capable of, pushed by her with a quick, "I'll be reviewing my account with you, Anna, to make sure everything's in order. You can tell David I'll be calling him."

Anna realized that this game was in fact no more fun, and it was time to talk to David, time to take a vacation—Manhattan in autumn!—time to resume the game of happy housewife for a while until something new came along. It was not in Anna's nature to break down in an undignified fashion in front of anyone and she certainly wasn't going to allow a little village infighting to break her now. Tapping a reserve of haughtiness that was endlessly deep, Anna gathered up her children, who had begun crying because it seemed the thing to do with so many upset adults around, and calmly placed them in her car.

When she met Reverend Beale's eye, he was seething with unveiled hatred and disgust for her. No matter to Anna Scott, of course, who was accustomed to the glowering of jilted men of all persuasions. Her pearly face, so pretty even when so hard, reflected his hatred back with such forcefulness that Reverend Beale felt it like a blow. He spun his head around, watching as the congregants disappeared one by one. He wasn't thinking of them anymore. Their souls, their tainted souls, they weren't worthy of his efforts. Selfishness! Pettiness! In the end they couldn't sever their attachment to worldly needs, to flesh, romance, love, money, property! They were unable to see God's hand in their lives, how it hovered above them and would one day sweep them from the earth for their blindness like a cleansing wind. They defied his efforts to save them, and their stubbornness, whether it was his fault or not, spelled failure.

No. He would not fail. He would make someone penitent.

Alden Forth. From practically the first moment he came to town her name was whispered like a prayer, like something beyond touch and rule and earth. She was the idol this godforsaken peasantry worshipped. She was a spirit running amok in the ordered house of God. A church with cracks that let in the wind will be forever struggling to keep the candles lit, those that make the light that draws in the sinners seeking salvation. Alden was that wind, a distraction, a whisper of sensuality and vice that could be heard, just beyond the ears of those who would live with more rectitude were they not so tempted by the vague utterance of something beautiful and special just beyond their hearing.

No more. Reverend Beale was not a stupid man and he knew he had lost the greater war for the individual souls of this town. He could smell already the viscous oil of the damned seeping up from the very ground beneath his feet as the last cars left and the sounds of summer insects filled the void where human voices were just minutes before. But what the sinner couldn't do for himself, Reverend Beale would do on his behalf, one last act of mercy. He would free the valley from the vice of idol worship. He would destroy the idol.

XX

Ned Pfieff was disgusted, with himself and with his friends and with his neighbors. As he guided his truck back to his farm, he kept shaking his head as if the movement from side to side would dislodge something bad and send it spinning out of his ears or shake some piece into place so that all that accusing and shouting and dredging up of old business might make sense. It was unseemly, that's what it was. Unseemly to put private things in the light like that and he was ashamed that he'd let the fervor of the group get so under his skin that he got into it, too. He knew that Reverend Beale was a strange man with strange ways, but he'd created a real trap tonight, a real spectacle. Well, if he thought that kind of play acting was going to get people to believe in God, then Ned was finished with that and he was willing to hope a whole lot of other people felt the same way, that keeping themselves to themselves was the way to go, and maybe the old ways and church in a building and only on Sunday and everyone shaking hands nicely and going home to their own lives wasn't such a bad way to do things.

Poor Alden, he thought, his head still moving back and forth. Poor Alden. There sure would be some fallout for the girl. But for the most part, Ned couldn't help but think that most people would probably leave well enough alone. Jane, Alden, the whole lot of them. *Lonely souls,* he thought. Lonely souls not much different than him. If someone was going to judge another person for what they did in a fit of loneliness, it sure was not going to be Ned Pfeiff. In fact, all he could think about as he shook his head from side to side was what Lila would think of the mess that had been made. But then, he knew, if she was alive, he would never have gone to that first Friday evening prayer social. If Lila was alive he would have come home late in the evening and she would have dinner made and they would have sat on the porch. He would scratch Holly's ears and they would all watch lightning bugs drift in the yard and Lila would tell him stories about the night insects and they'd hold hands. Just thinking about the old memory made Ned Pfeiff realize he couldn't remember exactly what Lila's skin felt like when they held hands and he knew he was losing her, the clear memories of her, every day. He'd already lost the smell of her hair, the sound of her laugh, the gait of her walk. Someday soon he would only remember the remembrance of her; the little details would all be gone.

It was dark now. The summer apex was past and as the season bled into the next, the days were shortening. In the heat of August no one would be thinking about autumn just around the corner, but as the day shed the whimsical drift into night it had in early summer and took on the efficient formality of setting earlier each evening, it was a harbinger of the end of one season and the start of another to anyone who might be looking for a sign. As a farmer, Ned couldn't help but pay attention to the changing light and thoughts of harvests helped push away thoughts of Lila. Then, up from the gloom in the road, he saw something strange that took him out of his thoughts altogether and focused his eyes on the street ahead near his driveway.

He switched on his headlamps to see more clearly in the growing darkness. There was a humped mass in the road. Ned slowed his truck to a crawl, a feeling of knowing the truth even before he could see it overtaking him. He thought for a second of Lila, of coming home one evening, of her slumped on the floor of the kitchen, of the awkward shape she made in death, like a bundle of blankets. And here too in the road, a dark mass familiar to him in a way that he couldn't place but that put dread in his stomach. The headlights were weak, the truck rolling slowly, the vision clouded by old age and memories, but then the outreach of the beams caught up to the bundle and it took shape like a sunrise breaking over a field and in a matter of seconds Ned had stopped the car and thrown open the door and was cradling Holly's limp head in his arms.

It just so happens that Reverend Harold Greene, whom no one had really thought much about in general and certainly not much that summer what with all the commotion of a strange preacher in their midst, had taken up the pursuit of riding his bicycle in the evening. It made sense: there were almost no cars on the road at dusk and the temperature was generally cooler. Reverend Greene could enjoy the quiet communion of himself and God through nature, which was always his favorite way to connect with the great Creator, and get some exercise, too. So it was fortuitous that he was peddling home when he saw a truck stopped in the middle of the road after dark on a Friday night, which in a small rural community is a strange sight indeed.

Reverend Greene peddled to the side of the road and stepped into the truck's headlights and felt how much darker the darkness suddenly became so that he and Ned were encased in a column of light floating in a black universe. Ned addressed Reverend Greene as if he had expected him.

"She must have been chasing a squirrel or a raccoon. It's in her blood to keep other animals in line. Somebody wasn't watching their driving. They weren't watching what was in the road. They were careless."

Ned paused. Holly whimpered and her tongue lolled out from the corner of her mouth.

"There's not much life in her, Reverend. I'd just like to stay here with her until the end."

If there was anything that Reverend Greene knew a little

more about than the average man it was death and loss, and how animals could be a great consolation, and how losing an animal could be one of the greatest losses to a certain person at a certain juncture in his life. This was that time and place and animal for Ned Pfeiff, and both men knew it so no one needed to say it. Reverend Greene just stood behind Ned with his hand on his old, strong shoulder and Ned sat in the road with his dog's head in his lap, and even though her back end was busted to bits she didn't bite at him like some animals do, even to their devoted owners, when they see death coming for them and they are hurt and afraid. She rolled her head in his lap and let him scratch her ears like she was grateful that the last thing she would feel on earth was her owner's touch and not the lightning impact of metal on fur. But her eyes were sad, too, because she knew she was leaving him, that her owner would be even more alone than before, and she felt bad letting him down. But the scratching of the ears felt so good, so nice, and she slipped into the pleasure of it and was gone.

"I think she might have passed, Ned. I think we might need to put her in the truck now. If you put my bicycle in the back, I'd sure be willing to help you take her home. No man needs to bury a friend alone."

That word "bury" bit down into Ned's heart as if Holly herself had woken up and decided to be angry and afraid after all, and she'd bitten deep into the flesh of his arm, deep enough to make the bone sing.

"She's all I had!" He hollered it loud enough that it startled Reverend Greene, and he twittered in his birdlike imitation the way he always does when he's startled or emotional or at a loss, and then he was all three. He was especially at a loss to know whether Ned was talking about the dog or about Lila or about both.

"Who would do this? Who would leave her here like this? They should've stayed with her. Everyone here, they all know she's all I had. What will I do without her? What will I do?"

The man was wailing now and Reverend Greene could only think of the terrible howl his mother sent up the day she found his father hanging in the bathroom, the day the bird finally sang, and Reverend Greene stayed there with that bird because he was afraid of his mother and afraid that even if he tried, he could never console her. Over many years of attending death, he learned that he really was powerless to console, that nothing consoles but time and God if someone had enough faith. But he also knew there were words to say, right words that helped, and he said them: that he was so sorry, that people can be careless, that animals are special and only here for a short time and we're lucky to have them, that he was sorry, he was sorry, so very sorry.

Ned knew in his heart that Reverend Greene was telling him the right things, and that these were the words that you say to someone who is sad, but it wasn't enough. He'd been carrying grief too long. His body was tired from work, and from working to stave off grief. He just couldn't put more hurt inside, and so he heaped it on Reverend Greene because he was close by and seemed as good a person as any to give a lashing to for the sake of unleashing that sadness. Now, Ned wouldn't need to pack it up and take it home and store it with the house full of grief he already kept.

"Sorry? You don't know from sorry. We'll see how sorry you are when you see how your congregation has fallen apart, how they've set on each other like starving wolves. You've neglected your people, you've turned your back, you've put a blind eye to grievances and sadness, to those who hate their children and hit their wives, to children who steal and adults who cheat and lie and hurt one another and themselves, and you offer no solace because your refuge you've built only for yourself. You hide in your church. You're a coward."

Reverend Greene knew in his heart that Ned was trying to hand his sadness to someone else to carry, and Reverend Greene knew that even if he wanted to he couldn't take it away, and that eventually Ned would go home and bury his dog and sleep in an empty house and the sadness would be there with him. But he also knew that Ned was telling him the right things, that he was not attentive enough, that his was a monastic relationship with God, this connection he made through birds that was like a channel that always calmed his conscience, but had also made him selfish and he had forgotten to share the wisdom of the birds with others. Reverend Greene did not get angry, as anger was never his way, but he did say, "You might be right, Ned," and the two men carried Holly to the bed of the truck and put Reverend Greene's bicycle in there, too. They drove in silence to Ned's house and by the light of Ned's porch light the two men dug a hole in the yard and put Holly in the ground near where Lila had planted daffodils that would come up in the spring. Then like men are able to do, they went inside and Reverend Greene had a little sherry and Ned had a beer, and they didn't need to apologize for what they'd said or even discuss it. The air between them was clean and fresh, so Ned decided to talk to Reverend Greene about what happened that night at the prayer social. Reverend Greene decided it was probably just about time to make some visits around the valley and check in on the parishioners who had languished while his rose garden flourished.

On a hot summer's day at the end of a peach harvest, staring down the beginning of autumn, Alden was living in a state that could be called "deep green," the color one sees in the late summer when the trees become their deepest shade of green, so deep it is one breath away from slipping into brown, the shade that remembers autumn is coming, that indicates one last pulse of color before the coming of change.

Alden felt this deep green. It came the night a contrite Bob Johnson returned to the farm leading Reginald by the hand. He helped Alden put him to bed and followed her into the kitchen where she poured lemonade and switched on the radio. Bach.

When Alden had come back to the house earlier that evening after watering and feeding the chickens and sheep, the house was empty. Reginald was gone. She looked through the entire house and then the yard. She called his name, her voice so loud and so unusual it brought Ronan and Nick out of the labor house where they were laying on their bunks, weary and hot and not speaking, because there was nothing for two people with nothing in common but being far from home to say to each other. It was Ronan who told her Reginald left with Bob Johnson and the other men, that when Reginald came to the front door and wanted to know where the men were going, and Bob said "to church," Reginald wanted to go because he thought there might be nuns there. He was so excited Bob didn't know what else to tell him but that it was okay for him to go with them, and so they left. Being clearly on the side of the Pope, though not practicing it, Ronan stayed behind, disinterested in Protestant affairs. Being clearly on the side of Alden, Nick stayed behind, too, sharing Alden's lukewarm association with religious affairs. But when Alden went about her evening chores and didn't linger on the porch or stop at the labor house and invite him to come to the house, Nick felt the press of her hands pushing him away across the distance between house and work house.

Now Bob had brought Reginald home.

"I didn't mean to get him so excited, Alden. I didn't know he would want to go so bad. You know how he gets. I couldn't even take time to find you and tell you. You know how he gets now."

Alden sighed. This was her season of sighing. It was not something she'd done in the past and if you asked her why she'd started now she would have been unaware that she was doing it, but there she was, sighing, joining the legions of humanity that reach a point between exasperation and desperation and sadness that is best released one mouthful at a time.

"I'm not angry, Bob. Ronan told me. I'm not mad. I just wish it was all different."

Bob sipped his lemonade, shuffled his feet, laced his hands in front of him on the table, unlaced them, placed them on his knees, cleared his throat, and drank more lemonade.

"There's something else, Alden. Something that happened tonight at that revivalist meeting."

Sigh.

"Well, I'm still gettin' to the bottom of all of it, but all you need to know is that things were said about you that weren't too kind. Things about sin."

Bob let the word hang there, hoping Alden would catch it out of the air and carry it away knowingly. However, not being one to understand sin much less her role in it, she didn't offer him any help, just looked at him quizzically, and he did something he did not do much at all, which was turn very red.

"There were people saying that you take up with men in a way that Godly people might not look too kindly on."

People had been talking about the heat needing to break, like waiting for a fever to break. Instead just like that, Alden's love season broke. It cracked surely as an egg on the kitchen table, and she and Bob stared there at the wood grain at the gooey mucus of Alden's personal life, undercooked and exposed. Alden denied nothing.

"That's my business. Who'd be talking like that about me?"

"It don't matter who. I'm gonna take care of that for you. But you should be careful. That preacher—I think he has it in for you."

"But why? He doesn't even know me."

In that ordinary, dark green moment, Alden became all that she was: a parentless child, befuddled by the ways of the world. And the question Bob knew she was going to ask when he told her all this, the question of why, was the question he'd been afraid he wouldn't know how to answer. But in that moment, he did.

"Because you're different, and to people like that, different is a scary thing."

Although there hadn't been a year on the farm that Alden didn't remember Bob being there for the harvest and although Bob still remembered Alden as a child slipping like a quiet shift of sunlight in and out of the orchard, they did not have the kind of friendship where they would exchange confidences. They weren't the kind of people who talked about secrets and love and sorrow and joy. Alden swallowed the knowledge that a piece of her was exposed with her lemonade. It was the piece of her that had kept her whole and balanced and fed each year of her adult life since she'd discovered the rejuvenating power of love. And she was sad, but not because she felt shame. She'd never been purposeful in keeping her lovers secret, it was just always that way, living apart from people on the farm. No, she felt only sadness because she knew the cycle of her life was forever changed, that the monotony of winter to spring to summer to fall would once again stretch as an unimpeded line toward the horizon of age.

These thoughts were with her and Bob in the kitchen as heavy thoughts always are, as present as the shadows of lost Forths who shifted in and out of rooms. But as there was nothing to say to these shadowy houseguests, there was nothing to be said of these heavy thoughts, and so Alden and Bob discussed what they both knew and understood and loved: the harvesting of peaches.

"It will storm soon," said Alden.

"Yep. Everyone's talking about it. Any minute now."

"Tomorrow we'll push to bring them all in, however long it takes. I want to pack them up and get them to town before the rain."

Bob nodded agreement. It was time for him and the other men to move on. There was only one problem.

"Alden, there's some trouble with that boy, Will, the scrawny one. You want me to take care of it?"

Alden sighed another deep soothing breath.

"We need his hands. If his problem isn't with working, let him stay. Just make sure you take him with you when you go."

Bob nodded and they drank lemonade and the quiet of the room filled with the high pitched mating songs of cicadas outside and the crackling voices from a news program on the radio.

In the workhouse, Will Field sat on his bunk staring at his hands. His options were slim. He knew Bob Johnson was talking to Alden, that she would fire him once she knew what he had said about her. And while Bob might have been old, he was still a big man. Will did not want to take his chances in a fight with Bob Johnson. He needed his wages, though. If he hit the road tonight with no ride and no money, where would he go? Reverend Beale would turn him away, that much was certain. He had gotten from Will what he required.

A shadow fell across his hands and when he looked up, Nick was standing over him, tension in his face making deep hollows and rigid lines of his angular features. He looked for a moment like he was cut from stone.

"What the hell do you want, foreigner?"

"I want you to leave. And never return."

The words, in perfect English, stumped Will. Nick had barely spoken a word to anyone all summer except Alden and no one knew how she could understand a thing he said. Will looked back at him, perplexed.

"What are you saying? How do you…What's goin' on here?"

"I just told you. Get out."

Will Field, a boy without options, was beginning to feel the pressure of people and circumstances forcing his hand. He had nothing left but youthful pride, and he was not going to let a foreigner tell him what to do.

"Go to hell. I ain't been paid yet so I ain't goin' nowhere."

It happened so swiftly, if asked to recall the event later Will would only say it was a blur. Nick swept Will up off the bunk and threw the boy against the wall. As he regained his wits, Will sized up the distance to the door – he could make a run for it. Then he looked at Nick, at the strangeness of his angled face, his aloof foreignness that felt like a snub, and though he knew Nick was stronger and stockier, though he felt the slimness of his own body, Will scrabbled to his feet and shook the stars from his eyes.

"So it's you been sleeping with the mistress," he said before lunging at Nick's midsection where he got his arms around his waist and tried to wrestle him to the ground. Nick's fist came up into Will's chest and the boy released his grasp, arching involuntarily up and away just as Nick's fist contacted his face, wrenching Will's head to the side and filing his ears with the sound of teeth cracking.

He crumpled to the floor. Nick did not move, simply stood, a stone sentinel. Will held one hand over his bleeding mouth and pushed himself back on his buttocks toward his bunk, eyes still on Nick. He pulled himself up to his bunk, pulled off his sleep sack and shoved his few belongings into it. On his feet now, he wiped his face and spit blood onto the workhouse floor as he walked to the door.

"I feel sorry for you, foreigner. They say she don't love anyone but herself. She don't believe in love. You're gonna hurt worse than me when you leave here."

The workhouse door slammed behind him. Nick lay down on his bunk and resumed his normal pastime of staring at the ceiling. John Gray, who had been sitting on his bunk smoking cigarettes and watching the excitement, got out his rolling papers and began stuffing another smoke.

XXI

Even in the blue light just before the sunrise, the air in the orchard was still and heavy. White mist clung to the trees and hovered above the grass; with no air to move it, it would hang there until the sun rose and burned it away. Alden and the men moved between the trees and up and down the ladders with automatic movements. Everyone knew they'd all passed the same night, lying on top of their blankets, limbs spread akimbo, listlessly trying to find a cool spot on the bed and the relief of a few restless moments of sleep. Everyone awoke groggy and ill-tempered. By seven in the morning, the men were shirtless. At the base of her bun, Alden's hair clung in wet ringlets to the nape of her neck.

In the afternoon, Alden went back to the farmhouse to prepare a large, late lunch. She stopped at the water pump near the barn, took down her hair and stuck her head beneath the cool stream of water. Her wet mane soaked the back of her shirt, already damp with sweat, and she felt a moment of relief. She looked in on the chickens, also listless in the heat. For a week now they'd hardly laid any eggs. Alden had broken the necks of two and roasted them the night before. They were waiting now to be served for lunch.

Inside the house the air was close. Humidity had crept into

every bit of the house so that it felt like it, too, was sweating. Upstairs, Alden unbolted Reginald's door and cracked it open. His drapes were only slightly ajar and the room was stifling. Enough sunlight filtered in that Alden could see Reginald napping in his chair, his chest moving rhythmically and the occasional snore letting her know he was well. She left the door open to allow some air to move into the closed space and went down to the kitchen. She carved the cold roast chicken onto a tray with thickly sliced tomatoes from the garden and a loaf of bread. She put leftover roasted potatoes into a bowl and tossed them with salt and vinegar. Outside, she put the food onto the table next to the laborer's cabin where a few flies, the only creatures that had much energy, quickly alighted. The workers came without being called, trudging out of the orchard to line up at the pump and run water over the heads, faces, and hands. They walked silently to the table where they heaped food on their plates.

"Where's the boy Will?" she asked Bob.

"Took off last night. No surprise."

"Too bad," she said. Alden made her plate and sat among them, but she had no appetite. "On the road with no money. He'll only get up to trouble now."

She watched the others at the table. They all ate heartily and slowly, enjoying the few moments of rest. Bob returned to his potatoes and John pulled out a toothpick and wheedled a tooth. Ronan kept his head down low, shoveling food slowly and mechanically into his mouth. Only Nick was watching her, though his eyes betrayed nothing of what he saw.

Alden knew enough to know that the silence at the table wasn't just about the heat and the fatigue and the hard work. She was weary. The summer began off balance and never righted itself, and now she was tired and ready to be rid of these men, and even of the peaches. She wanted autumn to sweep away what had grown here in the summer, for cool nights to bring Reginald more peace of mind and more eggs in the hen house. She wanted to be left alone with the radio and to plan for lambing season.

"Can we finish today, Bob?"

Even her soft voice startled them out of their stupor. Bob had finished his lunch and was letting his eyes droop a bit. He shook his head to remove the temptation of sleep.

"Don't know. We could use another set of hands."

"I want to finish today. You all get back to it. I'll go talk to the Powells."

She got up and strode across the yard and heard the men getting up from the table and stacking their plates; she knew without looking that Nick was watching her because the feel of his gaze was as familiar to her as his touch. She would not turn around because a balance had been disturbed and needed to be restored, and the only way to set things right was to move forward.

By the time Alden walked up and down the hillside that connected the Forth property to the Powells and was climbing the stairs to the front porch, she was drenched with sweat. Maggie Powell had seen her coming down the hillside and was waiting for her at the door.

"You better come sit down, girl, before you fall down."

Alden followed her inside and back to the kitchen table. Maggie poured her a glass of water.

"You ate anything, hon? You look like death."

It was true that Alden did not look as robust as was her usual way. She'd crossed a number of fragile thresholds — from thin to gaunt, pale to wan.

"I can't eat. It's too hot. This heat's making me sick."

Maggie made an indecipherable sound that was not agreement or disagreement, but just registering information in the way women sometimes do. She pulled something out of the ice box and set it in a bowl in front of Alden who ate it automatically, without knowing she was doing it and suddenly realized she was quite hungry and felt a little better.

"Rice pudding. Sometimes a woman needs something mild in her stomach."

It was as if Alden didn't hear her, though she nodded her head and Maggie made the undecipherable sound again, registering information, putting it away in her head where she would put it all together later and make sense of it when the time was right.

"Your peaches coming in okay?"

"Almost finished. Actually, that's why I came, to see if Bruce could come help today. We're almost done and I'd like to finish today. Before the rain comes."

Maggie Powell hadn't set one foot in Reverend Beale's tent church and she wanted to keep it that way from what she'd heard through the grapevine. Among what she'd heard was that Alden had a heap of trouble on her, not least of all Reginald's illness, of which the women never spoke directly. And Maggie had her own suppositions based on woman's intuition that more problems were coming Alden's way. She had no doubt the girl wanted to clean house and maybe, maybe, that was the best way. But she also knew her boy, and while he'd never said a thing, not one word on the subject his whole life, there are things a mother never needs to hear to know they're true. She knew how much Bruce loved Alden, and how much that love hurt him. He'd only go back to that farm now if his mother told him to go, which is just what she intended to do. If there was one thing Maggie knew intimately it was that life had to carry on.

"You get on back home, Alden. I'll send him along. He and his daddy still haven't come in yet for their lunch. I'll feed him and send him straight over."

"Thanks. And thanks for the pudding. I'll get that recipe from you."

"I'll send that up, too." Maggie followed Alden to the porch.

"You sleepin' okay, Alden? You look tired."

"Okay I guess, for the heat. But I've been tired lately. Dog tired. I guess age is catching up to me," she laughed.

Maggie just made that funny noise of hers and let the screen door close behind her.

Bruce did come. Maggie was not a mother to send her son on needless errands or to ask him to leave his own work on his father's farm unless it was for very good reason, so when she told him he was needed at the Forth farm and he better get on up and over the hillside, he couldn't say no. And what would there have been to say? If he'd made a scene about not going, it would have put it out in the world that he was in love with a woman who would never love him in return, though it seemed, according to gossip, that she'd seen fit to love just about anyone else. He no longer wanted to feel a fool. He wanted to be free.

This is how it happened that a middle-aged farmer, looking to redeem his broken heart, bumped into Reverend Greene on his bicycle, on his way to redeem himself with his neglected parishioners. The two men walked together the short space of road between the Powells driveway and the Forths.

In the orchard, Alden was not in a position to discuss the finer points of parish life.

"If you're looking for peaches, Reverend, you can help yourself out of any of these buckets. It's best if you take the bruised ones."

"Actually, Bruce tells me you might need some help. Thought I'd try to be useful."

Alden cocked her head, wondering at the odd occurrences of clerical traffic in the orchard that season and whether it might be a good sign or a bad sign or perhaps completely meaningless. But the complexities of spirituality were pushed aside by the reality of work. She saw Harold Greene as just another man, one in old trousers and a shirt patched with sweat, sleeves rolled up revealing pale, domestic wrists. Alden waved Bob over from under a tree.

"Bob will get you started."

"Thank you for letting me help." Reverend Greene was caught between his usual twitter and a self-deprecating chuckle. "I won't get in the way."

Alden reached out and grasped a pink wrist, felt its delicate softness. "It really is good of you to come."

She let the wrist go, felt it slip from her hand like lukewarm water.

"Watch out for bees."

The afternoon progressed slowly, methodically, as each man and one woman stretched out over the acres with their hearts and minds full of many things, and happy to have the monotony of relentless labor to keep them from sullen musings.

Despite the heat, Alden knew the season was ripe for change. She saw, as Ned had, that evening fell faster and earlier that day as they brought in the last peaches. When dusk encroached, the cicadas' screeching cry grew louder and more insistent. She wondered if they knew they were running out of time, that if they didn't find a mate soon the cold air would wipe out their line forever. The peach trees were littered with the creature's discarded exoskeletons, slit in a perfect line along the spine where the animal had set itself free. Funny, Alden thought, how life could look so much like death.

Everyone was tired, and the silence that had fallen over the entire company lasted into evening. Reverend Greene was deemed too slow to pick, but moved the crates to and from the wagon quick enough, and with Bruce helping in the trees and no one in a jocular mood, the work went by quickly. The setting sun filled the space between the trees with coppery light and a warm haze as Alden walked up and down the rows, deciding if the work was finished. She touched one of the limbs, still beautiful and green but fruitless, and she felt a pang of longing, a deep and terrible need to restart the summer and do everything differently. She knew in that moment that unlike any of the lovers who came before, she would miss Nick when he was gone. After a lifetime of being told what it was like to lose the people one loved, she would now know it intimately. She remembered her grandfather, and soothed herself thinking that she was saving him by sending Nick away, but still she thought of the fruitless tree and in it she couldn't help but see herself.

The orchard had been so quiet for so many hours that

when Alden heard the chattering of raised male voices it shocked her. The orchard was alive with calling. She heard several people shouting her name and, below that din, her grandfather calling for Francine. These sounds came to her across a wide space and touched a primal part of her that said, "run!" and she thought of sprinting over the hill and into the woods where she could shape shift into the slanting green light. But she ran to the voices, to something she did not understand but knew at once to be inevitable.

She might have thought they were dancing. She saw Bob, Nick, John, Bruce and Reverend Greene all in a circle waving their hands and jostling around something, like they were corralling a loose, wild horse.

"I owe you an apology, Alden. I never imagined he would become so agitated."

Reverend Beale was at her side. Beads of sweat were gathering momentum on his large forehead and running into the crevices of his knit brow. She realized distractedly that he was wringing his hands, noticed it and dismissed it like one sees the color of a bug just as you flick it off your arm. She stared at him, not understanding, trying to put together this strange and frantic scene. Then the dancers saw her and parted a moment to reveal her grandfather, red-faced and sweaty, stooped over yet determined, cradling his pistol against his chest. There was a moment of stillness when Alden thought how changed her grandfather was, how frail his chest looked against the heavy metal of the gun. Then everyone was shouting again.

"I know one of you dishonored my wife. Who was it? Damn you cowards, who took my Francine?"

Reginald's body was failing him as quickly as his mind and he stumbled as he whirled on first one man then another.

"You're crazy, old man," said John Gray. Perhaps thinking of the futility of the situation and not wanting to be a part of it, he tried to leave the little circle of frantic men but Reginald fired the gun off over his head. Everyone ducked instinctively and Alden, in the far reaches of her vision, thought she saw

Reverend Beale dive into a particularly tall patch of neglected field grass.

"Damn you, coward, no one leaves until I have answers!"

Alden was aware of mortality, for death had always been with her. It had swept before her, taking away her parents like a wind denuding the family tree, and it was a constant fact of life on the farm. Death was more a companion to her than something to think about and fear, as one might think about and fear a thing that is hidden or kept at a far off distance. And even in the grips of the illness of which no one spoke, Alden knew her grandfather would not harm her, would not take aim and pick off the last green shoot grasping the Forth family tree. She parted the workers and stepped by them. For an instant she felt Nick's familiar fingers graze her upper arm and the skin reacted with excitement even as her heart felt heavy with sadness. In a state of joyful sorrow, she stood opposite her grandfather and asked him to put down the gun.

What looked back at her was a stranger.

"Whore!"

She stepped back from him as if his words had slapped her.

"How could you do it, Franny? After all we went through to be together? All you gave up? What I built for you? How could you whore around with someone behind my back?"

As Reginald stumbled forward on uncertain feet, Alden stepped backwards. She could feel the phalanx of men moving with them, a school of fish moving as one.

"I'm Alden, Pop. I'm your granddaughter. Francine doesn't live here anymore. Remember?"

"Of course I remember! Don't you? Don't you remember when you lived here with me, when we started a family? Then you left me for another man. The church fellow, he told me. He told the whole town! You've shamed us all. Well, now we're going to make it right. You're going to tell me who he is and then I'm going to end this once and for all."

It was true that Reverend Beale was rather uncomfortable but, for the moment, safe in a patch of tall grass. There was absolutely nothing dignified about his current position and he was certain that a large insect was making its way up his pant leg, but he had no intention of moving one muscle and ending up on the wrong side of a madman. He thought back to his first visit with Reginald and the small, surreptitious ones that followed. He remembered the little gems of gossip Reginald shared about his neighbors. He knew that the man was not in his right mind when he spoke; he knew there were times when Reginald thought he was speaking to his dead son, but was it wrong to take that information and use it to bring about a greater good in the valley? And wasn't it a way of compensating the old man, Reverend Beale thought, to tell him how in danger his beloved granddaughter was of falling into a terrible oblivion? But then, the only thing Reverend Beale knew about Reginald's ailment of the mind was that for him, it had been a gift. That evening, when Reginald got out the gun, when he asked Reverend Beale to take him to the man who had stolen his wife Francine, he knew that what he'd thought was God giving him a gift was the devil in disguise and that once again, everything he'd touched in this valley had gone terribly awry.

As he watched the men corralling Reginald from between the blades of grass, Reverend Beale felt the presence of something uncontrollable in the air and he was aware of the press of the earth below his belly and the stretch of sky above him and the vastness of it all was terrifying; this thing he'd released might have no bounds. Reginald tottered in a graceless arch, the gun, growing heavy for him now, cradled against his chest.

"I'll kill each and every one of you if no one will step up and tell me, like a man."

"It was me, Reginald."

Bob Johnson stepped toward Reginald and reclaimed the last brilliant gold of the fading sun as the others melted into the undergrowth around the peach trees, drawn on imaginary strings. While Bob was no longer a young man, standing straight and barrel-chested he cast a shadow over Reginald and stepping between Reginald and Alden, who'd become as still and rooted as one of the trees, he completely obscured the woman from view. In the deeper gold of Bob's shadow, Reginald faltered.

"Bob?"

"I'm real sorry, but yes, Reginald, it was me. I was young and stupid and I took Francine with me that summer. I've been trying to make it up to you ever since. I come back here every year to set it right with you, but there's just no way I can do it. I don't think I ever could."

"Can you bring Franny back to me?" Reginald's voice was desperate now, a child on the verge of tears.

"I wish I could, but I can't. She only stayed with me a little while. She left me before Christmas that year and I ain't never heard about her since."

Alden stepped out from behind Bob and tried to put her hand on her grandfather's slim shoulder, but he shook it off. She knew he was lost to her now, that after the great confusion his mind had retreated deep into itself and it might be days before he returned to her, but she wanted to reach out to him anyway, to try.

"This is still your orchard, Pop. You belong here. With me. I'm still here and I love you."

He stared down as his feet; the gun still cradled against his chest like a child would hold a stuffed animal.

"Love destroyed everything."

Alden didn't know if he was talking about him and Francine or the whole Forth family or the whole world, but the place on her arm where Nick had touched her skin felt suddenly cold. She was reminded again of the corrosive power of coveting and the need to restore balance. She knew she needed to let all the men go, let everything go, if she was to bring everything back together again.

Reginald pushed past her, not aggressively, not quickly, but slow and defeated, harmless. The men were out of the shadows now, bolder, understanding that the fire had gone out in Reginald and he was entering a period of darkness. Bruce tried to stop Reginald, to help him back to the house, but the old man shrugged his shoulders and stumbled into the trees. The trees closed around him and the men kicked the grass with their feet, uncertain what to do next. Alden remained rooted to the ground, just watching the trees where Reginald had disappeared—or at least someone who looked like Reginald but was not him, not him in the least. She wondered then if she wasn't too late, if there was nothing left she could give up that would ever erase the smear of bad luck that stretched as far back as any Forth could see.

These are odd moments, when something large has happened and yet nothing really at all has happened, and no one quite knows what they're supposed to do until something comes along and kicks life back into linear motion again. And so it was that a few minutes passed in that transitory, waiting way, and then, the gun fired, and the men jumped, and Alden remained completely still.

A deep silence hung for a moment in the orchard. Alden stared fixedly at the exact place where her grandfather's retreating back had been only a moment ago, and she knew that somewhere written in her story this was always going to happen, that all the Forths were destined to leave her. It was her fate to take her turn with grief, to pick up the mantle of loneliness and to carry it until she too left the earth, the last of her kind. And then the Forths' bad luck would finally be at an end.

Everyone in the orchard found themselves in a rather awkward situation in that a great drama had just ensued, and everyone was of the assumption that an even greater tragedy had occurred, but no one seemed forthright in volunteering to break the stillness. Everyone knew that when one man moved, so must another and the spell that held them all suspended in time between what they thought had happened and what was true would be pushed unequivocally one way or the other.

The Reverend Harold Greene, who on account of his slowness with the peaches and his general reticence with most things could easily have been forgotten in the orchard scene, was the one who cracked this spellbound state. He walked to the break in the orchard through which Reginald had slipped and in he went, too. For despite all his shortcomings, Reverend Greene was also a companion to death, and knew the most merciful thing he could do in that moment was to protect Alden from what was held within the trees as he was never protected by his own mother, but was protected by a tiny bird. He came back a moment later and in his twittering voice, so completely out of keeping with the solemnity of his speech, he ordered Bob Johnson and Bruce Powell into the place where Reginald's body lay in an awkward heap on the grass, to take it to the Forth house and to wait with it there until he, Reverend Greene, could bring some of the women together to unpack the old rituals of preparing the dead. Surveying the remaining men around him, he alighted on Nick and noted the pained sadness in his face.

"Take Alden to the Powell house. You know the way?"

Nick nodded and Alden let herself be led away, her body now numb even to the feeling of Nick's arm across her back.

Bob Johnson and Bruce Powell, men who had known Reginald for many years, both before the ailment that had no name and after, found a stranger when they met Reginald's body. There was, of course, the newness of the fatal wound and the garish halo of blood and gore spread in the grass. But it was not these things that were strange to them, but the realization that Reginald had diminished so that it would only require one of them to carry him back to the house. His hands, once the thick paws of a farmer, had become skeletal, and his muscles deteriorated to loose folds of useless skin. As there had been a Reginald before the ailment and a Reginald after, here was Reginald at the end, a man so changed that he was a stranger to his friends, as he had become a stranger to himself. Thus, despite all the talk that summer of sin and punishment, despite the picture Bruce and Bob made, one man carrying a body and the other a pistol in a tellingly macabre parade, despite the obviousness of the sin they'd all been so close to they were nearly witnesses, as Bruce walked over the grass with Reginald's frail, fractured body cradled in his arms, the lightness of the burden felt less like sin and more like mercy.

XXII

The women left and Alden returned home late that night as far as the porch, where she sat with Bob Johnson. He felt her grief in the pulsing heat. Bob was a man perfectly happy with companionable silence and knew Alden well enough to know that her quiet didn't mean anything more than that she had nothing to say. But there were things that needed to be said between them, or things he wanted to have said, and so he broke that silence even though the sound of his voice seemed an ungracious intrusion on her naked grief.

"It was a good harvest."

"Yes," said Alden in near a whisper. "We'll… I'll be in good shape going into winter."

Her face was inscrutable in the darkness. Bob let his gaze rest on the yard as well. The lightning bugs, so prolific only weeks before, had already begun to disappear. It was time to move on.

"I imagine we'll shove off soon. More work to be had further north."

There was silence again. Bats shot back and forth across the yard.

"No one has ever been so dedicated about coming here," said Alden. "I don't remember a time, even when I was little, that you weren't here for the picking. You were like a favorite uncle, always turning up at just the right time. I never thought what made you do it. I just figured you liked the work."

"I needed to be here. I don't think I could have gone anywhere else."

"I can't imagine guilt like that. It makes you a slave to a place."

"You've got it all wrong, girl. I always felt badly about your granddaddy, that's for sure. He is—was—a good man. What I did to him, well, it wasn't right. Though if it hadn't been me it would've been someone else. Your grandmother was...a free spirit. So yeah, I came back to pay back your granddaddy with my sweat, but I didn't have to. I figure I rested my mind with that long ago."

The moon hung low on the horizon, yellow and wan and ringed with vapor. A dark mist rose up in the yard as the cooler evening air met the warm summer ground. Alden remained silent, knowing that if Bob had something he wanted to say he would say it, but it wasn't her way to go asking questions she had no right to ask. Bob knew she wouldn't pry any further, wouldn't make him say anything more than exactly what he wanted to say. He watched the mist move and thought of the many ghosts he'd known, and the ones he carried with him even now, and how perhaps it was time to let some of them go.

"When I'm here, I can be close to her, all over again. It happens when I least expect it, but there is always a day when I can feel her standing right behind me, or sense her hand hovering just by my face waiting to touch my cheek, or the grass will move and I can hear her small feet moving near me."

Alden had known plenty of death but hadn't ever seen a ghost, but there was something in what Bob was saying that made her feel that if she believed him, it meant that the people who had left her were not really gone. The idea of not being alone in her world was a comfort. She wanted to believe Bob Johnson could feel her grandmother's touch in the orchard as much as he did.

"I know it sounds crazy, but I fell in love with her here, right in that orchard. Your grandmother was like," he stopped, realizing he couldn't articulate how wildly he had once loved her. It was so many years ago he couldn't remember how it happened, hadn't even understood it then. And now, it was so ingrained in who he was that he couldn't tell Alden how he'd fallen in love with Francine any more than he could tell her how he learned to breathe.

"It was like a spell."

"Maybe I should cut down the orchard. Maybe that's the curse. Maybe Pop brought it on the peach pits and carried here in his pockets. He planted it here and that curse has just touched everyone who's touched those trees."

"You've got it wrong, Alden. That orchard is your birthright. The orchard's your story."

"Such a sad story. Who'd want it?"

Bob Johnson then did something he never did with just about anyone: he put his hand over Alden's hand and she felt the warm roughness, the clamminess buried in the palm.

"There's magic there, too. Your granddaddy knew it when he brought those trees with him, and I think you know it, too."

Then he let her hand go with a pat and strode off the porch. Alden understood then that Bob Johnson knew her most important secrets and had known them all along. In his own way, he shared in them and understood them more than anyone else could know, even her grandfather. She felt a sudden closeness with this man who she'd seen her entire life but never really known, and in knowing him she felt a terrible realization that now, unburdened, he might never return to the orchard again.

She called into the misty darkness: "Bob, wait!"

Even in the half-light she could sense his presence, knew that he had stopped, turned to her and watched her. She felt his eyes on her.

"Will you come back next year?"

Her soft voice fell at Bob's feet and he kicked the misty grass. Under the yellow porch light, he couldn't see Alden's face clearly but he could sense her desperation. At his back he thought he heard a familiar murmur that made his heart leap a little with excitement. He knew then that he could never stop, he could never keep away. Not so long as he breathed.

"Next year. I'll be back."

That was all he had to say. He strode into the orchard because he knew he was leaving tomorrow and he wanted to spend his last night with the ghosts that lived in his memory and with his past that lived in the trees; and if Reginald happened to intrude upon his private interlude that was fine, too, because Bob had made these ghosts and they in turn had made him. Now, he and the peaches and the grass and the remembrance of things long done were inextricable.

In the end, it was David who called Anna. She intended to call him, but after the great falling apart at Reverend Beale's Friday evening prayer social, the phone rang the next day in the Great Hall. The maid came into Anna's bedroom where she was fanning herself; she'd hit a stupid dog the night before and couldn't sleep well for fretting over the dent in the bumper. She was busy ignoring her breakfast when the maid told her that her husband was on the phone. Anna slipped on her lightweight dressing gown and went down into the hall to pick up the receiver.

She wanted to speak first, to tell him about her plans for Manhattan in autumn and Chicago in the snowy winter, but he spoke first and there was no more talk of travel once he began.

"I've been hearing things, Anna. Concerning things."

"Oh David, you can't listen to talk. You know how small this place is."

"Yes, a small town -- too small for so much talk of you. What is all this about revivals and our children running around like circus animals with a bunch of farmers?"

"It's lonely here, David. I'm just having a bit of fun."

"I received a call this morning from Chester French saying our credit is no longer good at the store. A call at the office.

On a weekend. Is that a bit of fun, too?"

"Chester's sore about something. I'll smooth it over with him. I'll give him a check for whatever we owe him."

There was a deep sigh on the other end of the line.

"It must end, Anna."

Anna Scott was not accustomed to commands except from her father, and those never went over very well. From David, it was downright appalling. Shocking. She registered her displeasure by seething silence down the phone line. David filled the quiet.

"I'm going to have the children spend some time with my mother in the city. She feels she never sees them, and I think it would be good for them to have some time away from the country, to learn some urban manners while they're young."

Anna had no interest in mothering and was certainly more than happy to pack Beryl and John off to her mother-in-law's townhouse in the city, but it was what would leave with them that she felt most acutely. The children gave her some power and he was taking them away.

David, knowing his wife far better than she credited him, anticipated her protest.

"It's already done. I've arranged it with the governess and the other staff. They'll pack the children this weekend and take the car into the city on Monday."

"The car! David, not my car."

He softened.

"The car will come back. The car is yours. It was a gift. I enjoy giving you gifts. You are, after all, my wife."

Anna felt the sensation of being shoved across the checkerboard, of becoming an instrument in someone else's game, of the balance moving from her hands. She fell back on an old friend of the Scott family in times like this, whether dealing with children or animals or business matters. She returned to rage.

"David, you are treating me like a child and I will not tolerate it. I am a grown woman and you cannot whisk the children away on a whim and shut me up in the house like you would put a naughty girl in her room. I will not have it!"

When faced with rage, David fell back on an old family trait that came out at times like this, whether dealing with children or animals or business matters. He returned to calm. It was David's unerring calm that would make him exceedingly rich in the years to come, richer than even Anna would be able to spend.

"But Anna, my dear, you *have* been a naughty girl."

If ever Anna had anger to spew down a receiver and into a phone line, she certainly did so then and, had the phone been a lesser instrument, the bile she spewed forth would have ejected itself onto David's face and burned like acid, so nasty and vile were her words. But the phone did as it was intended to do and worked over a long distance, so that when Anna's words fell into David's ear he heard them for what they were: the pleading of a beaten foe.

"Anna, if you wish to be treated like a grown woman, you can act like one. You can find a source of independence and divorce me and have your life back to run as you wish."

"Don't be stupid. What would you have me do, go be a washerwoman somewhere? A governess? It's not seemly for a woman like me to work."

"You could always ask your father for an allowance, or move back in with him."

It was an absurd suggestion and they both knew it, but what David also knew was that after all the other men, Anna chose him. Now it was his turn to truly possess her as she had possessed men in the past. That was a realization that just came to light in the far reaches of Anna's brain, and the light moved closer to the forefront until she could not diminish it, even with the strength of her will.

He had won. He possessed her. She had no options. She would not leave him. She would not return to her father's house. She would stay there in the valley and pick boarding schools for the children, and ride horses, and bark at the staff, and take up flower arranging or charity work, and take the children on trips abroad to visit their grandmother and improve their French. She and David would both have discreet affairs. There would be big parties at Christmas; parties people would remember for years after, and a wedding carefully crafted for Beryl, and the right college chosen for John. Through it all, she would keep her good looks until the very end because she had nothing else that belonged to her to hold onto, and so she would work at them, her good looks, like a job, like another woman would work at a tedious chore.

She hung up the phone and stared, enchanted by the artistic quality of her own slim fingers resting on the receiver, at the perfect deep blue of the sapphire ring against her porcelain skin. It was something a painter should capture, that moment in time when Anna Scott knew for certain that the ring was a shackle that tethered her to this life, this future she could see so clearly. But the ring was still brilliant, and she had chosen it, and her hand was still beautiful.

XXIII

The morning after Reginald's death Alden woke before dawn as was her way. She awoke with the feeling she had dreamed something terrible just before sleep slipped off her, but she could not quite remember what the dream entailed. All that remained was a terrible fatigue that gripped her, like the dream she could not recall would not let her go, and it pulled her down, down, down into sleep to force her to remember. When next she woke, it was to the sound of murmuring, so close she thought it was there with her in the room, or perhaps there with her in her mind, in her dream, whispering to her to remember.

As the sun pried open her consciousness, she realized the voices were on the lawn, sweeping up into her room through the open window. The distant rhythm of talk was so soothing she rolled over and allowed it to ease her back into sleep. It was Maggie Powell who woke her one last time.

"Alden, it's midmorning, you need to get up now."

Her voice was soft, gentle, and Alden thought in her semi-somnolent state, of the lost pleasure of being awoken by a mother. She lolled on the bed, but realized with a resigned detachment that she was unable to rise.

"I'm so tired, Maggie. I just can't get out of bed."

Maggie was no hard-hearted woman, but she was of a breed of person who delivered her babies and made breakfast the next morning, a woman who washed and dressed her own people when they passed, and laid them out in the living room for viewing, and made the luncheon besides. While making Alden get out of that bed might have seemed like the cruelest thing in the world, Maggie knew that if she did not get her up that morning she might not get up the next or the next, and women in their position did not live that way, or they wouldn't live at all.

"I know you are dog-tired, but you need to get up and get those boys out there their final wages, and you need to take your peaches to town. Mr. Powell thinks there's a storm brewing and the heat's going to break today."

Alden had almost forgotten the heat. The damp sheets, the faint moldy smell in the house, the permanent beads of sweat on her neck—they'd become like a part of her, a piece of the summer made physical within her. And then there was the realization of grief. Like a disease that sits hidden inside for many years, blooming without any outward symptoms. So, too, was Alden consumed with sadness, a feeling so intense and foreign to her she would never have been able to pinpoint that it was this that was devouring her. As a flame diminishes a candle, the reality of death and loneliness was slipping through and over Alden, washing away all memory. She'd forgotten the men and that they were finished with the peaches and were anxious to move farther north. She'd even forgotten Nick and that he would leave with them today. Remembering, she opened her grief more.

Maggie brushed tears off Alden's face that Alden didn't know were there.

"I'll go do the cooking. Those boys will need feeding before they go."

It's a funny thing how straightforward life can be, even in light of a significant change of circumstance. It was the morning after Reginald killed himself, and yet, it was a morning like all others. From the kitchen, Maggie produced plates of bacon and hardboiled eggs and biscuits. The men ate their breakfast, drank coffee, and threw the remnants at the bottom of the mug into the yard. John Grey rolled and smoked a cigarette. Everything was subdued, perhaps, but really, nothing had changed. Alden wondered at the relentlessness of life, its ceaseless need to move forward, and for the first time had a moment of fear as to how she would carry on when everyone left that day and she was truly alone.

Their wages paid, the men began to pile their few things into John Grey's truck, all but Ronan, who took his earnings and started walking into town. Ned Pfeiff had offered for him to stay on and work for him through the winter. Ronan had left Ireland to escape the incessant rain and to find a little peace in the world, but now he wondered if there was peace at all anywhere, or if life would always just be messy and loud. If that were the case, better to live that life here in the valley than anywhere else because at least here, there was still the hope for something more and not just the inevitability of rain.

Alden sat on the porch watching Bob and John smoking by the truck. She knew they were waiting, stalling. Nick came out of the work house with his bag. He paused and looked at Alden, who was impassive. He continued to the truck and hurled the bag in the back in an effortless arc. To her surprise, Alden's heart followed its trajectory and fell with a deep, painful thump in her chest. He came to her on the porch, his hand shoveling the blonde hair out of his eyes. Bob and John turned their backs, lit another cigarette, and faded away into the acreage.

In a relationship built on understanding silences, Alden and Nick did not know how to say goodbye.

"You will not ask me to stay?" he finally said.

"No one ever stays."

"That's all the past. You can start over now. Let your grandfather's beliefs go with him."

Alden knew he was right, that when Reginald did the unspeakable deed, which everyone knew of but no one would ever mention again, he set her free. Just as she knew the curse was broken, that she was free to love and begin again. She also knew she was not ready for this freedom. It was forced on her and it was yet another ill-fitting hand-me-down from the Forth family, one she needed to grow into, to understand and shape for herself.

"I won't ask you to stay."

Nick kicked the grass. She sat down on the porch and he stood in the yard and the space between them was taut, the impassable tension between opposing magnets.

"I won't ask you to stay," she repeated. "But I'll ask you to come back."

Nick had spent a long time moving away from places, through places, never staying and never ever going back. Now he knew there was nothing that could keep him from retracing his steps back to the farm, that he would walk on as was his way, and Alden would return to her solitude as was her way and, when enough time had passed, he would come back to her and they would create something entirely new.

More comfortable in the silence now, he stepped onto the porch. He stood over her and touched her hair and she touched his hand, pressed the back of it to her lips so she could feel the softness of the fine blonde hairs on his skin and breath in the scent of him as she would a ripe peach. Then Bob and John were in the truck and the engine turned over and Nick was off the porch and in the back of the truck. When the men left they did not wave; they moved on down the road to what was next for each, all knowing they'd be back again, some perhaps sooner than others.

The heat finally broke the afternoon of the leaving. Even Bruce was gone, bumping over the rutted road in the Forths' truck to sell the last of Alden's peaches in the city. After the great commotion of the morning, Alden was left alone on the porch to watch the weather move in across the field. Low, quick clouds darted like mercury before massive thunderheads and the wind flipped the leaves of the trees like so many old-fashioned ladies waving white handkerchiefs. Unstructured lightning filled the very atmosphere and wrapped menacingly around the porch. Still Alden waited, feeling the power of it, the great exertion of nature as it pushed away the oppressive heat. Finally, the rain fell, and it was gentler than Alden had anticipated. It was so soft and steady that she could smell the change in the earth as it opened its pores to welcome refreshment, as the trees laid down their hankies and went slack under the longed-for shower. Great booms of thunder shook the porch and Alden wept tears of grief, and also tears of joy and relief and anticipation. Grief is rarely just one thing, but usually a coming together of many emotions; the only thing to do is to weep them away.

It's hard to say how long Alden sat there on the porch and wept in the rain. Time takes on its own proportions during times of sadness and during epic summer storms. Alden had no need for time anymore. The peaches were gone, the laborers were gone, Reginald was gone. She now kept company with the rain, knowing that when this passed she would begin her life.

The sun set dramatically after the storm, stretching a vibrant pink archipelago across a roiling sea of gray and gold. Thunder still rumbled low in the distance, but the doily–headed Queen Anne's lace and stalwart corn flowers felt confident to reassert themselves in the hedgerow. The crickets dried their bent legs and commenced bowing. The air was rinsed clean and was cool, though Alden knew enough about late August in the valley to expect the heat to return before it retreated with finality. Still, there was something new, something that felt of fading away and of moving ahead, and she said out loud, "It smells like autumn," and she knew her grandfather was with her.

In the days that followed Reginald's dramatic departure from this earth, Reverend Greene continued his review of his shattered flock with subtle tenacity. More importantly, he pedaled his bicycle away from the parish house and down quiet country roads to the encampment of Reverend Arnold Beale, where he found the man wrestling his tent down to the ground, so involved in his task he didn't hear the faint creak and rattle of Reverend Greene's aging conveyance. Reverend Beale also had no reason to be expecting visitors and he was uncharacteristically askew, with shirt sleeves rolled up to reveal thick arms covered in salt-and-pepper hair. Reverend Greene dismounted and let his bicycle fall into the grass, a clattering that made Reverend Beale raise his head and drop the disordered lumps of canvas in his hands.

The two men regarded each other in momentary silence before Reverend Beale spoke.

"What, Greene, couldn't you raise more of the villagers to run me out of town?"

Reverend Greene's voice was as high and twittering as ever, but calm and gentle in its own way.

"Sarcasm does not suit men like us, Reverend Beale."

Reverend Beale resumed his struggle with the canvas tent.

"Well, certainly you aren't here to make a pleasure call."

"No. I came to see if I could help you. The summer is ending and I thought you might be moving on."

"Moving on? Moving on! What a laugh," Reverend Beale threw down the tent in disgust and walked over to his camp chair lying in the grass. He set it up vehemently and sat down. "You really are a deluded old fool if you think I'm just passing out of this place like so many others before. Never before have I seen things go so far astray. Never before have I seen people so committed to their way of life they refuse to see reason even when it's spelled out for them."

He put his head in his hands.

"And the sadness. All I wanted was to lift them up and instead, I've sown so much anger and grief."

He looked up at Reverend Greene.

"You must believe me. I never wanted it this way."

"I believe you."

They stayed liked that, quietly musing. Reverend Greene swatted a mosquito and Reverend Beale stretched his short, aching legs. When Reverend Greene felt enough pause had passed between them for their emotions to have quieted, he brought up mundane matters, the reminders of normalcy that help with introductions, awkward conversations, and difficult goodbyes.

"Where will you go next?"

Reverend Greene picked up an edge of the canvas tent and dragged it out flat. Reverend Beale got out of his seat and pulled the opposite edge. Eventually they had the thing straight and flat and could pick up the corners and walk them toward each other.

"I have personal affairs in Pittsburgh I've neglected for too long. I will go back and settle my father's estate. Then I think I might join some old companions preaching in the city. The country air…it doesn't agree with me anymore. Or I might join a mission. Leave this country entirely. Sell these things."

He waved his hand over the tent, now perfectly neat and folded. He collapsed the camp chair.

"You have no family left in Pittsburgh?"

"My father was the last to go, but we were estranged. My mother," for a moment, Reverend Beale felt the need to tell this fellow man of the cloth something of his own past, to experience the cathartic transformation of sharing the story of his naked mother in front of the mirror, that image that always haunted his dreams. The years of painful remuneration he endured. But old propriety was stalwart, and he stopped himself.

"Of course, I understand how complicated family life can be," said Reverend Greene. "My own mother – well, yes it is often complicated."

"But it isn't our fault, of course, what our parents did. Don't you believe that, Reverend Greene? It's not my fault."

"I believe we inherit things from our parents, good and bad, and things good and bad are bred into us by them as well. But our decisions are always our own."

"The triumph of free will," said Reverend Beale, "over determinism."

"Many believe free will is a gift from God," said Reverend Greene. "It is the foundation of your preaching, is it not, that man can change through the exercise of free will?"

"I suppose, yes."

"Then I hope never to be a slave to where I came from or what has happened in the past. We will all continue to move forward, making our little daily decisions, living through our little victories and defeats. Really, when you think about it, it's a small locomotive that propels most of us through this life. But it means something, even though it looks insignificant."

This was a moment when the two reverends could easily have slipped into their own memories and catalogued all the old wounds from their childhoods, so similar in their sadness and yet so different, too: Reverend Beale's marked by violent neglect, Reverend Greene's by merciless gloom. But they were aging men now, on a path to making peace with old ghosts or simply reaching that age when the specters of childhood dissipate into distant memory, and the present takes on the immediacy known to those who are aware of their closeness to their later years. Instead, they worked together to pack the tent into the car and tie the last of Reverend Beale's belongings onto the roof of the aging sedan. They shook hands and Reverend Beale got in the car and left the field and pulled onto the road.

When the car was no longer visible, Reverend Greene got back on his bicycle and pedaled toward his parish house. He passed the long driveways of the old guard, the wealthy families who had established themselves in the valley and built big houses to impress their prosperity upon the land. He passed the tenant houses and farmsteads, some so shoddy their very grasp on their foundations looked likely to come loose. And there was everything in between. Reverend Greene knew there were secrets and lies and joy and violence and pleasure down every driveway and inside each door, that the ancient feuds bubbled below the surface and that new ones would likely rise, that people would die and be born and move away. Whatever the season of life, it was his job to keep open the church doors in all weather.

He whistled a made-up tune as he pedaled, thinking of nothing more in particular.

XXIV

The Forths were renowned for their peaches but they kept three apple trees, too, practical trees that had grown large from benign neglect. At the moment that Reginald's life came to its abrupt end, these apple trees had already begun to drop fruit, small, hard, worm-holed golden and blush apples that attracted a constant cloud of bees. Time moved relentlessly forward, heedless of death. An aggressive cold snap appeared in early October and just like that, summer was gone and fall was upon Alden. It was in the chill of autumn that Alden went apple gathering, her fingers sticky as she hauled two large baskets full of over-ripe fruit back through her orchard.

The bees were gone, but other creatures were busy preparing for the coming winter. At dusk the deer would come through the orchard to eat the windfall apples Alden had left behind. In the evenings she would sweep black wolf spiders out of the corners of the kitchen and mice were leaving droppings in the pantry. As she made her way across the yard, two squirrels scampered up a tree chittering back and forth. In the nearby pasture there was the occasional, guttural bah of her sheep. Alden noted that the wooly caterpillars, frequently found wiggling their fat spiny way across the porch, were more black than brown these recent weeks; Reginald would say it meant a long, cold winter to come.

Alden, too, was preparing for the winter. The radio in the kitchen welcomed her with Brahms. She now left the radio on most days, to stave off the quiet. She brought a huge pot out of the pantry and set it on the stove, then began to peel and cut the apples to make into sauce. In the evening, she would sanitize jars and put the applesauce up in the pantry alongside the canned peaches and tomatoes, the bread and butter pickles, and the raspberry and strawberry preserves -- the jewel-toned remembrances of the season past that would sustain her through the season ahead.

As a woman in tune with the seasons, who relished the waxing and waning of moons, the depletion of one season and the abundance of the next, Alden knew early that she was pregnant. Were she a woman more prone to reflect on the past, she would have admitted that she'd known before the laborers left, that she'd known when she told Nick to leave. Though she was not a pensive person, she knew now, in this moment, that she would do it all again, that she was not ready for him to stay, that she needed to move into a season of her own before he returned. This was the season of remembering.

After the laborers left, Alden went through the ritual of burying Reginald in the ground. There was no luncheon at the Forth farm as was the generally accepted way, but most of the people of the valley resumed their earlier thinking that Alden was just never going to follow the generally accepted way. After the accusations at Reverend Beale's revival there were those who called for repercussions, those who said they would not buy the Forth's fruit, they would not let Alden buy their hay or their gasoline. But then word spread of Reginald's end and the only thing bigger than shame is death. Death quells all things, even gossip. For a time. The residents of the valley picked up their old ways of church going and working and petty squabbles and tiny joys and respected Alden's privacy and let her return to her farm, which she now seemed intent on running alone. In the end, they had their own lives.

Watching the summer die away to make room for autumn,

Alden realized the need for some things to end for something new and wonderful to begin. She also realized that the time in between, the time of the dying, the time between the warm long days and the short but brilliantly colored crisp fall days, were the hardest for her to bear. Too much now was going away, more than her fair share, and she became weepy and nostalgic and taken with a need to remember. But her memories of Reginald, of her entire family life, were limited not in quantity but in variety. There were no trips away, no special gifts, no landmark ceremonies. There were only memories of waking early, working on the farm, sleeping in a warm comfortable bed, memories of companionable silence over dinners or Reginald spinning stories, of reading aloud to each other in the wintertime, of listening to radio programs, and watching the stars from the porch with a cool drink. The memories, when she gathered them, were shockingly simple and, in their simplicity, they were a comfort to Alden.

As there had been a way of living in the Forth household before Reginald's ailment and a way after, as autumn took its true hold on the valley, Alden set about understanding what her life would be like without any family at all. It was into this musing that she recognized she was going to have a baby. At first, she wondered what she was going to do, but then she realized she'd spent her entire life preparing for just this moment, that everything about the farm had taught her to be healthy and self-reliant and, above all, pragmatic in all things. She did nothing more than what she knew to do: clean and close the labor house, clean out the chicken coop and lay down fresh bedding, move the sheep to their winter pasture, can what food she could from summer's harvest.

There was no one to give the occasion any fanfare, but Alden marked her time by making the house, so full of the memories of people she hardly knew, into her own home. She cleared the closets and sewed new slipcovers for the chairs. She ordered fabric and sewed herself some dresses that would be comfortable as the baby grew. She edited the bookshelves. The ghosts of Forths long past were with her, looking on with approbation. It was time for these old things to be laid to rest and only the precious things kept. The house breathed out its old, musty breath and inhaled the fresh promise of new life.

One fall evening, Bruce Powell came to visit as he sometimes did when he'd finished work on his own farm. His father was getting older. One day, soon, the farm would belong to Bruce. He'd begun to think about the future, about having sons of his own to help him run the place, and who could take over when he was old. But then he knew that he would never marry, not outside his dreams. For some people, loving once is enough.

Bruce no longer came to visit Alden with any expectation of changing her mind about marriage. And he knew, as everyone eventually knew, that Alden was going to be a mother. Someday soon, his mother would pay a visit to Alden and they would discuss this thing that was far too delicate a female matter for Bruce to bring up. So he ignored Alden's visible bump, but looked after her in his own way.

"Will you need help with the lambing season this spring? I'm thinking of hiring a man. Maybe I could negotiate some hours for you. We could work it out."

Alden had now left her season of remembrance and was fully invested in thoughts of the future, a new and exciting place for her mind to dally. Before, her life was an endless cycle spinning away to the horizon; now, her life was going to go in a new and unfathomable direction. She thought of early spring with expectation and no short measure of common sense. As is the way with some women in their pregnancy, Alden ran a hand carelessly over her small belly.

"You're right. I'll need to get some help around here."

Alden put a piece of pie in front of Bruce and set one for herself, and they ate and discussed their farms and nothing more until Bruce had the courage to say what he never thought he would be able to utter, but seeing his friend's progressing condition made him bold.

"Do you expect Nick will ever come back this way?"

"We didn't make any promises, but he'll be back. I'm sure

of it."

Bruce ate his pie in thoughtful silence and Alden, from years of deep friendship with Bruce, knew that he wasn't sure whether to believe her, knew that he would fret over her in his own way until Nick came back. Seeing Alden with another man would be painful for him, but Bruce's love for her was so deep and selfless it would only be satiated by her own happiness.

Alden ate her pie and felt, not for the first time, the pull of Nick, felt how weary his feet were from walking, how ready he was to come home to her. Just as each season before a new lover had emerged for her like a vision, she knew instinctively that Nick was making his way back to her. And if he got lost on the way or never arrived, this too was as it should be. In this new season of her life Alden was never alone, and she was never without love.

ABOUT THE AUTHOR

Christianna McCausland is an independent writer based in Maryland. She is a graduate of Emory University and attended Johns Hopkins University's Masters in Writing program. Her nonfiction articles have appeared in publications including *The Christian Science Monitor, Better Homes & Gardens*, *House Beautiful*, *The Washington Post*, *People*, and at CNN.com. She is the author of the nonfiction book *Maryland Steeplechasing.* Ms. McCausland's nonfiction work was acknowledged with an Excellence in Journalism award from The American College of Emergency Physicians and an Excellence in Journalism award from the Society of Professional Journalists. This is her first novel.

CPSIA information can be obtained
at www.ICGtesting.com
Printed in the USA
LVHW041529280619
622667LV00002B/360